Dolmarehn

Book Two of the
Otherworld Trilogy

by

Jenna Elizabeth Johnson

Copyrighted Material

This is a work of fiction. Names, characters and incidents are a product of the author's imagination. All material in connection with Celtic myth has been borrowed and interpreted for use in the plot of the story only. Cover image is the sole property of the author. The Faelorehn font on the cover image and interior of this book was created by P.A. Vannucci (www.alphabetype.it) to be used for the Otherworld Trilogy. Any resemblance to actual persons is entirely coincidental.

Dolmarehn

For Stacy and Jen

May this story conjure up memories of the hours we spent in cafés, poring over the tales of a land rife with myths and legends.

Contents

Dolmarehn

One

Absence

Fifty-one days. Fifty-one days ago Cade MacRoich walked out of my life like a ghost passing into the hereafter. And no, I've not been obsessive enough to keep track of the hours and minutes, or even the seconds, but I've noticed every single one of them. I probably wouldn't have been so fixated on his absence if he hadn't up and left the way he did. Of course, at the time I'd been too distracted by my recent trauma to truly grasp what was going on.

Nearly a year ago, I was certain I was just a slightly abnormal teen. Sure, I'm tall and gangly and insecure like everybody else my age, but now I know exactly *how* different I am. One day this gorgeous boy shows up, out of nowhere, with a simple explanation for all of my eccentricities: my changeable eyes, my tendency to hear voices and notice odd things, and the fact that I'd been found parentless as a toddler, roaming the streets of Los Angeles like a young girl who'd been separated from her mother in the women's clothing section of a super mall . . . He had come to tell me that I'm Faelorehn, immortal, from the Otherworld.

Shaking my head, I got back to work. Of course, watering Mrs. Dollard's plants didn't require much brain power. I had considered getting a part-time job in town this past summer, but when the old lady had come over to ask if I might feed her cats and keep her yard alive while she toured Europe, I accepted right away. She was loaded and she always over-paid me. Besides, working in a café or at a local clothing store meant dealing with the public. I didn't do well with the public.

The sharp caw of a crow made me hit the ground like a soldier avoiding gunfire. If acting like an idiot wasn't bad enough, the hose got loose and soaked me. I glanced up and released a sigh of relief. Only a normal crow. I climbed to my feet and tackled the errant hose before shutting it off. Yes, freaking out at the sound of a crow would be considered weird for any normal person, but when you've spent the last several months dodging a Celtic goddess in raven form, well, any large black bird would give you the heebie-jeebies.

The garden was watered, Mrs. Dollard's five cats were sleeping off a food coma, and the afternoon sun dipped low in the sky. The giant wet spot on my t-shirt was making me cold, and it was time I headed home. Didn't want to get caught outside after sunset. That's when the faelah are the most active.

A short bark greeted me as I made my way around the house. I smiled. A great white wolfhound with rusty colored ears sat patiently, panting and grinning.

"Hello Fergus. When's your master coming back?"

I placed a hand on his head and gave him a good scratch. He didn't answer my question, but I hadn't expected him to.

Absence

Mrs. Dollard's was only a few houses down from my own, but before I stepped inside, I kept on walking to the end of the street, bypassing the *Dead End* sign. I'd developed the habit of checking the knothole in the oak tree every day, hoping Cade had left me a new note.

I frowned in disappointment when the knothole proved empty, but it didn't surprise me. Cade's absence was understandable. A few months ago I crossed into the Otherworld, bent on saving him from some cruel fate. Turns out the Morrigan, one of the most powerful of all the Otherworldly deities, merely wanted me where she could conveniently kill me. Still being rather ignorant of my roots, I believed her when she told me Cade needed my help. Hey, she'd been pretty convincing, and well, I kind of had a huge crush on the guy, still do. As a matter of fact, I can admit that it's turned into something far more severe than a simple crush.

Pushing the hair out of my face, I climbed back up the slope and headed towards my bedroom on the basement floor of our house. I didn't like how much time I spent thinking about Cade; it couldn't be healthy, but he *had* saved my life after all. And he'd been the one to tell me the truth about where I'd come from.

My room greeted me with its usual chaos: various items of clothing spread all over the floor and furniture, computer screen saver glowing blue and green, comforter and sheets wadded up into an unintelligible mess.

"Meghan!"

I jumped, then grumbled. "What Logan?"

My younger brother, oldest of the five, stuck his head through the trap door leading up into the main part of the house. His blond hair fell to the side. I grinned. He looked like some miniature version of a pro surfer.

Logan's eyes found me and he piped, "Dinner! Oh, and we're going to the beach for my birthday party tomorrow, remember?"

I cringed. Ah, yes. Forgot about that one. Logan had turned eleven a week ago, but he hadn't had his party because most of his friends were still on their summer vacations.

"Alright," I said, "be up in a minute."

Logan disappeared and I shot a glance back through my sliding glass door. Fergus was gone, but I merely shrugged. He tended to vanish like that a lot. I had no idea if other people were able to see him or not (I didn't know if he could be seen by mortals), but maybe he didn't want to take the chance.

After quickly changing into a dry t-shirt and a pair of old sweat pants, I made my way up the spiral staircase and out into the circus that was the Elam family.

Mom darted about the kitchen, getting the last minute dinner items ready, Dad sat in his recliner, as usual, reading the paper, and all five of my brothers, Logan, Bradley, Aiden and even the twins, Jack and Joey, stared at the TV, thoroughly engrossed in some science special. I rolled my eyes. It was one of those 'deadliest insects' things and it included a detailed description of what sinister attribute made them so dangerous. My stomach churned when they started describing internal parasites.

"Boys, could you turn that off? We're about to eat dinner!"

Thank goodness for Mom.

Absence

We all sat down and tried to commence as a normal family would at mealtime. Too bad we weren't normal. One of us was a Faelorehn from the Otherworld. Of course, none of them were aware of my true identity. Like the adoption agency who found me those many years ago, they thought I was just another abandoned human child. I knew if I told my mom and dad what I'd learned over the past year, they wouldn't be able to accept it. Or they would drag me off to a new psychologist who would only prescribe mind-numbing medication. No thanks. I'd like to have all my wits about me when the Morrigan decided to attack again, thank you very much.

"Meg, you are coming with us tomorrow, correct?"

Dad's voice snapped me out of my train of thought. I grimaced. Honestly, I didn't want to go. Not that I had anything against Logan or birthday parties or even the beach, it's just that ever since my ordeal at the end of spring, I'd been extra wary about wandering too far from home. This is what made Mrs. Dollard's offer so appealing. Only four houses down the road, piece of cake . . .

"Sure," I shrugged and stabbed at some green beans.

"*Sure?*" Mom gave me one of her looks. "Meg, you've been practically cooped up in this house all summer. You only ever leave to take care of Matilda Dollard's cats, take those walks down into the swamp, or to visit Tully."

Okay, I had good reason not to wander far, reasons having nothing to do with my fear of the faelah creatures creeping out of the dolmarehn hidden deep in the woods. Up until a few weeks ago I had been in a leg cast, and that really limited my mobility. She couldn't count visiting Tully, my best friend, as 'never going out'. Tully lived all the way at the head of our street. A good fifteen or so houses down. And my walks in the swamp had the potential to be rather exciting. An Otherworldly creature might show up at any minute and cause quite a stir. And if that Otherworldly creature happened to be Cade . . .

I swallowed and put him as far out of my mind as possible. No need to get all dreamy-eyed at the dinner table. Regardless of what my parents thought, my walks were productive. If Mom knew I practiced with my longbow and arrows during my walks, maybe she would change her mind. Of course, I only went down there alone because Fergus always accompanied me. Should Cade's spirit guide suddenly disappear, I'd gladly admit defeat and take on the guise of a recluse.

"You have to go Meg!" Logan whined.

I glanced over at him, his blue eyes shining with unshed tears. My heartstrings tightened. How could I deny my little brother anything?

I released a sigh. "What beach again?"

"Avila," Dad said. "We're going to have a bonfire and everything, so be sure to bring your warm clothes. It'll get cold after dark."

I gritted my teeth despite my smile. *After dark* . . . I had been lucky the past few months. I'd only seen a handful of faelah wandering around in the swamp; small, demented rodents that often met their end in the jaws of a certain white wolfhound. My own intuition assured me Fergus would not be accompanying me to the beach. Time to face the truth: it had been too long since anything of noticeable significance had happened. I was well overdue for a good haunting.

Absence

❂ ❂ ❂

The sunny weather in Avila made me forget about my troubles for a while. I helped my parents drag our gear down to the sand and we propped the fold-out chairs, extra towels, bags of food and various water boards and toys against the picnic table closest to the creek fanning out across the shore. Almost immediately, my brothers went tearing off into the wide mouth of the stream, kicking up brackish surf as they screamed and splashed one another.

I looked at my parents and they nodded before they started setting up. We shared a silent agreement between the three of us. Since Aiden, my youngest brother besides the twins, had autism and had a tendency to pay less attention to his surroundings than the others, I made it a point to keep an extra eye on him. Jack and Joey, despite having turned three over winter break, were actually quite self-sufficient. Besides, my other two brothers stuck to them like glue.

Aiden, well, Aiden was different. We're not sure what caused his autism, but Mom and Dad always suspected it had something to do with the stress he was under during his birth. It had been a difficult delivery, and they had been terrified he wouldn't make it. He had to stay in the intensive care unit for a few months before we were allowed to bring him home. Perhaps he'd missed out on some vital element and was now trying to compensate. None of that mattered, though. I still loved him dearly; we all did.

I set my own bag down and headed after my brothers. They had all crossed over to the other side of the creek, climbing on the pylons of the road bridge stretching overhead.

I chose to cross closer to the shore. I wasn't a germ freak or anything, but semi-stagnant water just gave me the willies.

"Meg!" Bradley complained from the rock he perched upon. "I want to go check out the tide pools, but Logan's being a turd!"

"Hey! I said I'd go, I just wanted to wait for Meg!"

A shoving contest ensued as I reached down and scooped Aiden up, grunting a little at his weight. I couldn't believe how big he was getting. Soon I wouldn't be able to pick him up at all.

"Bradley, you do know it's Logan's birthday party, right? Shouldn't he choose what to do? His friends will start showing up at any minute, so we should get back to the picnic table and wait for them."

Through some miracle of older-sisterhood, I managed to round them all up and bring them back. Logan's friends arrived ten minutes later and soon we were all roasting hotdogs and eating cake.

About an hour before sunset, Logan insisted on going back to the tide pools on the other side of the creek. I shaded my eyes and squinted up at the sky.

"I'm not sure, Logan. By the time we get there we won't be able to do much exploring."

Well, if we left before the sun set. The walk didn't take long, but I wanted to be close to the fire once darkness started settling in. I had encountered the faelah in daylight before, but they preferred the darkness, and the worst attack I ever suffered on this side of Eilé had come right after sunset.

"Go on Meg, you have plenty of time before the sun goes down," Mom insisted.

Absence

I think she wanted the kids to play somewhere else so she and Dad could relax before we started roasting marshmallows.

I squirmed, torn between pleasing my brother and my own, semi-paranoid fear. Eventually I caved. I mean, what were the chances of faelah showing up at the beach anyway? Cade had never mentioned any dolmarehn around the Avila area, and I'm sure he would have if there had been any.

"Alright, but you and Bradley have to help me with Aiden and the twins."

The small herd of pre-teen boys all cheered in obnoxious unison. Oh boy, this was going to be *so* fun . . .

The rocky shelf that featured the tidal pools teemed with other beach-goers. I held Aiden's hand the entire time, pointing out star fish and sea anemones as we carefully walked across the slippery rocks, the deep sloshing sound of the ocean drowning out most of our words. Logan, Bradley, the twins and all of Logan's friends started hunting for crabs and after a handful of minutes, I allowed myself to relax a little. This was actually pretty nice. Spending quality time with my brothers like a normal, human teenager. Of course, the delusion didn't last.

"Seal," Aiden said, pointing towards the water rushing into the giant fissure between the rocks.

I twisted around and looked down, almost slipping on some seaweed in shock. It was a seal, sort-of. A dark head turned to gaze at me, but instead of seeing the cute, whiskered face and big brown eyes of a spotted seal, I caught a glimpse of the deep ocean-blue eyes of a young woman. I blinked several times, but the vision didn't fade. It was as if someone had skinned a harbor seal and now floated around beneath the tide pools, wearing the skin as some sort of gruesome robe.

Apparently, I wasn't the only one to be surprised. The seal woman's dark eyes grew wide and she pulled the seal skin over her face. I had to blink again. No human likeness remained, but in her place floated an actual seal. Wait, what had just happened?

"Perty," Aiden whispered.

I looked at him. He liked animals, and I'm sure he only noticed a seal. Cade had once told me about Otherworldly glamour and from past experience, I knew not all the faelah made their presence known.

"Yes Aiden, very pretty," I murmured.

The sun fell beyond the horizon and no more Otherworldly beasts surprised us. On our walk back, I contemplated what I'd seen. I mentally went through the various Irish myths I had read in one of my books. I knew the seal had seemed familiar, but why? A faded memory suddenly came back to me. The Silkies; Irish seal-people. Had the creature been a Silkie?

Now that I'd decided what she was, I wracked my brain for more details. When Silkies removed their seal skin, they became human, and if another human being got a hold of the seal skin, they could control the Silkie. I grimaced, hoping my obvious recognition would encourage the Silkie to find a much less populated beach to visit. Glamour or not, that was too high a price to pay if someone managed to steal her skin.

"Ah, there you are!" my dad crooned as we came traipsing back to the picnic table.

Absence

Delight coursed through me when I caught sight of the fire, for we were all soaked from the waist down.

"Who's ready for some marshmallows?"

I pulled up a lawn chair and jabbed a marshmallow on the end of my stick as I let the warmth of the fire pour over me. The boys started sharing ghost stories, but I blocked them out and instead focused on the sound of the waves crashing against the shore. I remembered Cade telling me once how the ocean soothed him. On a normal day, I would have been of the same opinion. The only problem was, he wasn't here at the moment, and that fact alone dashed away any hopes of feeling truly content.

Two

Reunion

A week after Logan's birthday party, the school year started. Normally, I would have dreaded the day, for I wasn't the most popular kid in school, but at least I'd get a chance to escape my room. Mom had been right; I had become a recluse. And for some reason, I entertained the idea that the Morrigan and her ilk would avoid harassing me at school. I hoped I was still right.

Thomas picked Tully and me up at the end of our street in his family's gold van. He had already been to Will's house. I smiled at my friends as I climbed in.

"So, ready for our senior year?" Hey, might as well act cheerful, right?

"Yeah, sure, a whole year stressing about filling out college applications and waiting to hear back. *So* exciting."

I brushed aside Will's negativity. He was under a lot of pressure to get into a good college. He had spent most of his summer researching one university after another. At least he'd been productive. What had I done? Oh yeah, I'd wasted my summer by hiding in my room and avoiding the outdoors as often as possible. But I had gone into the swamp to practice archery, something I thought I might be improving on. Finally.

"I'm ready for all the perks that come with being a senior," Thomas added, answering my question.

I wouldn't call exclusive lunch rights to the front lawn or the chance to take study hall for one of our class periods perks, but I shrugged anyway.

Thomas reached forward and changed the station before pulling out onto the next road.

We met Robyn in the parking lot, her usual Goth-inspired attire flawless. The teal streak in her hair had faded and appeared to be a little longer than the last time I'd seen her. I hadn't spent much time with Robyn over the summer, only seeing her twice at Tully's in the first few weeks after school let out. Despite her hair, she was just the same as always.

"Hey people! Ready to wreak havoc and cause mayhem? We're seniors!"

I would have laughed, but Robyn *would* wreak havoc and cause mayhem, given the chance. I had enough chaos in my life without even trying, so I merely shook my head, giving her what I hoped was an impish grin.

A few minutes later the bell rang and our talk of the long-lost summer and what our big plans were for the year came to an end. Shrugging my backpack further up my shoulder, I headed down the hallway to find my first class.

I spotted Adam Peders, Josh Turner and Michaela West along the way. They all glared at me. I gritted my teeth, then paused. These were the people who had tormented me since middle school, but hadn't I already been through a lot worse than what they'd ever been able to dish out? Hadn't I survived an attack from the Morrigan, a powerful Otherworldly being? Hadn't I recently learned I was Faelorehn, immortal, and potentially capable of unfathomable power?

I laughed out loud, startling the three lemmings that used to be the bane of my existence. Key word there; *used* to be. I lifted my chin, adopted the haughtiest look I could muster, and strolled right past them as if they were nothing more than snails on a wall. Michaela's gasp of outrage was particularly enjoyable.

Oh yes Robyn, I thought, *I am definitely ready to wreak havoc and cause mayhem.*

@ @ @

That first week flew by and I found myself facing a weekend of homework. Okay, maybe being a senior wasn't going to be that glorious after all. I spent a good portion of my Friday night getting my math done and working on an essay for my literature class. By ten, my eyes felt like they were caked with glue. I piled my books onto my desk and headed for bed. Sighing, I stared at my ceiling and did what I'd been trying to do since before the start of summer break: not think about Cade MacRoich.

Eventually I did get to sleep, but woke with a start several hours later. I blinked away the bleariness in my eyes. Had I been having another nightmare? I couldn't tell. I rotated my head to look at my alarm clock. Four fifty-one, in bright red, glowing letters, glared back at me. I groaned. Really? Why couldn't my stupid dreams let me sleep until at least seven?

I tried to go back to sleep, but I just tossed and turned until it started to get light outside. Finally, I got up. In a haze, I walked into my bathroom and turned on the shower. Perhaps it would lift my spirits.

Once done with my morning routine, I threw on a comfortable pair of sweatpants and an old t-shirt (a favorite ensemble of mine) and returned to my desk. Time to get some more homework done or waste a good hour or two on the internet.

A scratch at the sliding glass door drew my attention. I leaned back in my chair and glanced over. Ah, Fergus. He'd been a common sight at my door all summer, so I blew out a breath and hit the button to turn on my computer. When the scratching continued, followed by a whine then a sharp bark, I got up to go find out what the spirit guide wanted. He never seemed to want attention from me before, but there was always a first for that.

I unlocked the door and slid it open. "What's up Fergus?"

He backed away from me, panting and doing a little dance. Weird . . . Only when he turned to head down the horse trail, pausing long enough to glance back at me with his big brown eyes, did I realize he wanted me to follow him. My heart jumped into my throat. Was Cade back?

I threw on a jacket and stepped into some shoes. The morning was chilly, but I knew by noon it would be hotter. Not that I needed it to be any warmer at the moment. My heart raced and I dashed after the wolfhound, my mind abuzz with a million thoughts. Could Cade truly be waiting down the trail for me? Would he be glad to see me? Would he be recovered from the encounter with the Morrigan? Would he leave right away after talking to me? Would he have news from the Otherworld? Would he kiss me again?

I shivered at my last thought. Although I had convinced myself the memory of Cade kissing me had simply been imagined due to the trauma of coming darn near close to death, I couldn't help but wish it had been real. Almost every night, the scene replayed in my mind and I tried hard to remember the satisfaction of being held in his arms; the gentle touch of his lips pressed against mine, but the recollection of those sensations would not surface and I forced myself to accept them as semi-forgotten dreams.

I turned the corner and passed through the willow trees covering the land bridge over the swamp. A few more steps brought me through to the other side. And then I spotted him, standing dead center in a wide clearing, Fergus sitting and panting contentedly by his side. Cade MacRoich.

My knees buckled, bringing me to a dead stop. Stupid knees. He wore his trench coat, as usual, his arms crossed over his chest. As soon as he spotted me, however, he pulled down his hood and smiled. Oh, what that one action did to me . . . I took in his height, his posture, his face. He looked well, much better than the walking zombie he'd been when we last parted ways. His dark red hair almost glowed in the sunlight and his beautiful face no longer resembled a gaunt, white mask. But the light in his eyes proved he had finally recovered; dark green and sparking with life.

"Hello Meghan."

I forgot about my knees. I forgot about my thundering heart. I even forgot to keep that safe distance I always placed carefully between us. Apparently, I forgot to think as well.

Letting out a small squeak of joy, I bolted from where I stood and threw my arms around him, trapping him in a full-body embrace. I was so glad to see him. Unfortunately, my mind hadn't warned me about how foolish I appeared.

Fortunately, Cade hugged me back, making my imprudent behavior seem only a tiny bit ridiculous. Didn't stop me from flushing beet red, though.

I let go and stepped away, but Cade kept his hands on my shoulders, holding me only a few feet in front of him. I turned my head. I blushed far too often in his presence, and looking him in the eye would only make it worse.

"Are you unwell?"

His voice was gentle, betraying a smidgen of concern. My heart swelled.

"Um, I worried while you were away," I admitted.

Of course, I didn't need to go into detail about how my concern was more for him than myself.

"The faelah? You worried about them?" he asked.

I nodded. *Chicken.* Why was I so afraid to tell him how I felt? Like an idiot, I allowed myself to fall for him only to discover he had a goddess for a girlfriend (and then learning she *wasn't* his girlfriend after all), right before he left me hanging for the entire summer, wondering if I'd ever see him again . . . Ugh. I guess you could say my emotions had been banged up a bit.

He used his index finger to lift my chin so that I looked him in the eye. *Drat.* His had darkened even more. Mine, I couldn't say what color they took on at the moment, but if my nerves were any indication, I'd say they resembled a slide show gone berserk.

"Nothing attacked you, though, right?"

The hard tone of Cade's voice sent prickles down my spine. Why must he be so appealing?

"No," I finally managed.

He sighed and dropped his finger from my chin and released my other arm. He ran his hands through his hair and stepped away.

"Good," he said.

"I did run across a few things, over the summer, but only some more of those gnome creatures and they didn't bother me." I thought it best to make practical conversation as I recovered from being so close to him. "Oh, and a Silkie just last week."

Cade arched an eyebrow. "A Silkie?"

I nodded, wrapping my arms around my torso. A chill settled on my skin for some reason, as if leaving Cade's embrace also took away all my warmth.

"Logan had his birthday party at the beach, and when we went to the tide pools I noticed a woman in the water with a seal skin draped over her shoulders. She caught me staring, then pulled the skin tighter and transformed back into a seal."

Cade seemed to have stopped listening to me. He grew still and his face turned stony. "Logan?"

I blinked up at him, my mind blank. His height still astounded me. He stood a good eight or nine inches taller than me, and I was the tallest girl in my high school.

"Who is Logan?"

Uh . . . ? Had I never told him about my brothers? "My little brother."

Could I have been imagining things, or did that information cause him to relax substantially? Had he been worried? Jealous? A tingle of joy pulsed through me, but I squashed the stupid sensation and told myself I was being delusional again.

I cleared my throat. "So, how have things been in the Otherworld?"

I know it was a lame thing to say, but moving the conversation, even in the small talk direction, was better than silence.

Cade arched a brow and cast me a sidelong glance. Okay, was he *trying* to make me blush? Or was I just that pathetic?

He shrugged and glanced away. Thank goodness.

"I've managed to keep most of the faelah from trickling through the dolmarehn I'm responsible for, but if you're wondering if I've redeemed myself for breaking my geis, I'm afraid I have to disappoint you."

Oh. I hadn't been wondering, at least not until he brought it up.

"I'm sorry Cade," I confessed quietly, stepping even further away from him.

I couldn't imagine what being punished for saving someone's life felt like. Because of his actions on the day I almost got mauled to death in the Otherworld, he ended up breaking his geis, his taboo. Violating a geis came with a heavy price. True, I didn't know what his particular punishment was, but such a thing couldn't be pleasant.

Cade moved closer, following me. He spoke low, and curse it, his voice made me go weak in the knees again.

"Don't be sorry Meghan. I would make the same choice again in a heartbeat."

Oh, how I wanted those words to mean he liked me back. Perhaps they did, and perhaps he was about to say so, but unfortunately Fergus's bark interrupted any further conversation.

Cade tensed, and then forced himself to relax once more. "I've got to go Meghan."

I just managed to exercise a bit of restraint before wrapping myself around him again.

"When will you be back?" I wanted to know.

He smiled. "As soon as possible. In the meantime, keep up your archery practice and be sure to check the oak tree every once in a while."

I grinned back, despite my forlorn state of mind. I watched as he disappeared down the trail leading to the dolmarehn, the same dolmarehn that had thrown me into the Otherworld a scant few months ago. The memory of the ordeal made me shudder, but I focused on watching Cade for as long as I could. He was leaving, yet he promised to come back, and he had insinuated he would be dropping off messages in the oak tree. Love letters? I grinned in self-chastisement. *Silly Meghan! When are you going to stop daydreaming about him?* Unfortunately, my common sense told me the truth: *never.*

~Three~

Surprise

I spent the rest of the weekend in a fog of housekeeping and studying. I'd put off tidying my room for weeks and I had grown tired of wading through stray laundry to get to my bed. Besides, cleaning was the one activity I could actually accomplish while my mind was still caught up in the memory of seeing Cade.

By Sunday morning, however, I told myself to snap out of my weird funk and get some homework done. Moping around the house like some forlorn ghost would do me no good, and letting my grades suffer might have dire consequences. I turned on a classical music CD and got to work. To my delight, I only thought about Cade twice for the rest of the day. Maybe three times.

On Monday morning I woke up before the alarm clock, so I decided to get up earlier than usual. I showered, got dressed and headed upstairs for breakfast. My brothers nearly knocked me over as they ran circles around Mom. I grinned and managed to capture a bagel amidst all the chaos. I called a goodbye to my dad as I headed out the front door. I had every intention of walking down the street and catching a ride with Tully. As I angled down the driveway however, a sharp bark stopped me in my tracks.

Fergus stood by the old barbed wire fence denoting the road's stopping point and the beginning of the equestrian trail that led into the swamp. He wagged his tail and turned around, trotting into the woods. A goofy grin spread across my face and I took hold of my backpack straps and followed him. When he stopped at the oak tree, a small twang of disappointment snapped in my stomach. Oh, so he wasn't taking me to Cade.

Sighing and trying not to show my frustration too much, I stepped up onto a tree root and pulled the note out of the knothole on the other side. Fergus stared at me, panting as usual, as I unrolled the paper and began to read.

Meghan,

I hope your weekend went well. I'm very sorry I couldn't stay longer and catch up with you or even witness your progress with your bow, but I'm glad I was able to get away at all.

Unfortunately, I fear I'll be held up in Eilé for the next month or so, and will only be corresponding by letter. In order to make up for my rude neglect of you, do me a favor and take the back way to school this morning.

Sincerely,

C.M.

Despite my intense regret at learning Cade would be gone for a month, I smiled softly. He sounded truly remorseful that he wouldn't be able to visit me. I tucked the letter into a backpack pocket and made a mental note to set aside a shoebox for them before taking out my cell phone and texting Tully, telling her I was going to walk to school that morning. It was still early, so if I didn't dawdle I should make it before the bell.

Coastal fog curled along the trail and in the deepest recesses of the swamp. On a normal day, I'd be terrified to come down here on my own when it still wasn't fully light, but I had Fergus, trotting silently ahead of me. For the first time since the spirit guide had been left with me, I wondered if Cade was suffering because of it. I dashed that thought away before it culminated into a full blown, single-minded desire to go back to the Otherworld to check on him.

A small flash of color and a chirp that sounded similar to a cricket's stopped me dead in my tracks. I sensed myself going white. Were there faelah around? Why would Cade tell me to walk to school if he had somehow let faelah slip past him? Was the Morrigan trying to set me up again? But, wouldn't Fergus know if it was dangerous?

I turned to go back the way I had come, but Fergus blocked me. "No Fergus, perhaps this isn't such a good idea after all."

I started to text Tully again as I tried to get by him, but the wolfhound wouldn't budge. In the next breath, something the size of a swallowtail butterfly fluttered past my ear, making the soft chirping sound. I screamed and threw my arms up to protect my head, almost losing my cell phone.

Now I caught a glimpse of what had been creating the noise and my mouth dropped open. Was that a . . . fairy?! I shook my head and blinked my eyes clear. The creature's body, humanoid in shape, measured about the length my thumb and its brilliantly colored wings were somewhat translucent. I simply stood there, gaping and following the creature with my eyes. After floating in the air for a few minutes, the fairy landed among a thicket of ferns. Fergus pulled away from me then and trotted alongside the fronds, brushing them with his legs. What followed completely transfixed me. As he moved down the line of ferns, hundreds of the little fairy creatures took to the sky, chirping in agitation and flashing their multicolored wings. A living, breathing rainbow.

I was dumbstruck, and a sense of pure joy filled me as the fairies fluttered all around me. Wait, not fairies. In Irish lore fairies were more like humans, but with supernatural powers. The term 'fairy' might even apply to the Faelorehn. These charming faelah were most likely pixies.

Taking a deep breath, I tore myself away and started back down the trail, grinning like I'd received a dozen roses from a secret admirer.

Cade's gift probably meant I'd be late for school, but the delay had been worth it. Whether the delightful little creatures were pixies or some other form of faelah, I couldn't say. What I did know, however, was that Cade had more than made up for his so-called neglect.

The next several weeks passed with just a hint of bitter sweetness to them. Cade stayed away from the mortal world, like he promised, busy paying back the damage caused by his broken geis. He also kept his other promise and wrote to me at least twice a week.

Fergus was always diligent in letting me know if there was a letter waiting in the oak tree for me, but to be honest, I checked the knothole every day after school. Nothing thrilled me more than getting notes from Cade. He would start the letters by telling me how much he missed our archery lessons and how he was looking forward to showing me the Otherworld (without the Morrigan and her minions tagging along, of course). My heart would leap when I conjured up images of wandering those misty hills with him, to see him in his element. I also dreaded the possibility of my memories from that horrible night returning; when the Morrigan's demons nearly killed me. Despite everything, however, Cade would protect me, I hadn't a doubt.

As fall progressed, the days got shorter and my school work got more intense. Nothing I couldn't handle, though. I mean, what was an impending calculus test and a biology report compared to the anger of a Celtic goddess? Hah! A walk in the park! If only I could convince myself such thoughts were true.

A few days before my birthday and Halloween, I dreamed of my childhood again. I had almost forgotten about it, what with everything I'd learned in the last several months. But I shouldn't have been surprised. It came every year, and nothing had changed this year: the younger version of myself, wandering L.A.'s streets, clinging to a huge white hound.

When I woke up, however, I sensed the puzzle pieces of my mysterious past had finally fallen into place. Sure, they hadn't been pressed together yet, but I envisioned all of them clearly, lying on the glass coffee table in our living room, each one lined up and ready for my fingers to slip them into place. I had been taken through a dolmarehn at the age of two, I'd already determined that much, but who had brought me to the mortal world and why?

I grumbled under my breath and shut off my radio alarm, another old question floating up from the depths of my mind to mingle with my other thoughts. Exactly who *were* my parents? I still didn't know, and every time Cade had visited in the past, he managed to distract me with his essence, thus striking any other questions from my mind. Of course I loved my mom and dad, but some undetectable sense inside of me insisted on knowing who I had once belonged to.

Kicking off my bed sheets in frustration, I got up and decided to get ready for school. I would puzzle over my mysterious origins later. Time for me to think about something else. A few more school days remained before the weekend, until Halloween, the day I turned eighteen . . . What a daunting thought. I didn't feel any older, and I definitely didn't feel like an adult.

I cast my eyes around my room, wincing at its general, usual, untidiness. For Halloween this year, my friends and I had decided to have a stay-in party, hosted by myself. That meant cleaning my room. I glanced at my clock again and cursed. Housekeeping would have to wait until later. The shower beckoned and I needed to get going.

I spent the entire afternoon and the next working on making my room spic and span. Well, as spic and span as possible. I woke up early on Saturday to finish up, only to be delayed when my intrusive siblings dragged me upstairs to help them carve some last-minute pumpkins. Apparently, one for each of us didn't measure up to my brothers' high standards. I managed to escape in record time so that I could decorate before my friends showed up. I strung fake spider webs everywhere, the little arachnids belonging to them dangling from my spiral staircase. Tissue paper bats and ghosts added their own macabre presence, and bowls full of various, creepy foods sat on my desk, waiting to be consumed. I had also rented a few movies with a Halloween theme, one about vampires, the other a supernatural thriller.

I stood back and examined my work when I finished, grinning at the final result. I'd done a pretty good job. The clock next to my bed announced the time: four in the afternoon. I gasped and ran for the bathroom. My friends were due in an hour and I still had to get into my costume. While browsing through thrift stores two weeks ago, Tully, Robyn and I managed to find an old prom dress that fit me well. We all decided I should dress as some dead beauty queen. Normally, I wouldn't have gone for it, but they had been so insistent. Besides, I liked the color of the gown, a deep blue, faux satin, and I thought that particular shade went well with my eyes. Well, at least when they seemed more blue than any of the other colors.

Tully showed up while I was finishing my makeup. I hoped the pallid powder and fake blood did the trick. Tully's squeal of delight affirmed my suspicions. She had decided to mock Robyn by dressing as a Gothic witch. Robyn herself arrived next, toting Will and Thomas behind her. Robyn appeared to be a demonic fairy; Will a mad scientist and Thomas had adopted the garb of his favorite pop star.

"Nice blood Meg," Will commented as he took a seat on my old couch with Thomas and Tully.

"Don't mind if I take the bed, do you?" Robyn asked, plopping down on top of my comforter and depositing glitter everywhere. I shrugged and joined her. How pleasant to have a made bed for once.

The night progressed with us screaming and jumping at the movies I'd picked out. Every now and again I heard the doorbell ring followed by Mom's best interpretation of a witch cackling as she tried to frighten the trick-or-treaters. I snickered and thought about sneaking around the house in order to jump out and scare a few of them.

A glance towards my sliding glass door made me quickly change my mind. It also caused my heart to stop beating for a good three seconds. There was something out there. As all four of my friends yelled at the actress who was about to get mutilated in the movie, I merely stared in silent horror at the thing, no, *things*, crawling across my backyard. They were not much bigger than housecats, but they had the arms and legs of monkeys. Some of them touted leathery wings, others curved horns. Several of them had large ears and teeth protruding from their lower jaws. They crawled along like zombies freshly raised from a pet cemetery and I wouldn't be surprised if my theory proved true. Not a single patch of fur covered their wrinkled, mummy-like pelts, and all of their bones pushed out against their dark hides, creating a multitude of knobs and ridges. Their sudden appearance made my skin crawl.

"NO!" Robyn screamed right in my ear as our helpless heroine got cornered by a vampire.

I shouted as well, but more in response to Robyn's outburst. Everyone turned and eyed me as if I was crazy. Great. How would I explain this one?

Surprise

"Sorry," I grumbled, rubbing the back of my neck. "Thought I saw something in the backyard, and I got distracted for a moment."

Of course, everyone turned to look. I cringed, but cast a wary glance myself. I breathed a mental sigh of relief. The faelah were gone. Not that I was worried my friends would notice them. Only I saw the faelah.

"I don't see anything," Will proclaimed.

"I know, like I said. I *thought* I saw something."

To my immense relief, no more faelah came to pay my yard a visit for the rest of the evening. By ten, both movies were over and everyone decided to call it a night. I didn't mind. After all, I had creepy crawlers haunting me and I didn't need my friends around when they came back. I saw them out, and then returned to my room with the intention of washing off my makeup. The trick-or-treaters were gone and my brothers were slowly making their way to their own beds. Time to call it a night.

When I got to the bottom of the stairs, however, I found that I had a late night visitor. Fergus's white form sat patiently at my sliding glass door. I walked over to give him a pat goodnight and to ask him to chase away any freaky faelah that might still be lurking about. I slid the door open and before I could so much as smile in his direction, he bolted towards the oak tree. I groaned. I looked forward to Cade's letters more than anything else, but the last thing I wanted to do was go anywhere near the swamp on Halloween night, especially after seeing those strange creatures in the backyard just an hour or so before.

A sharp bark followed by a whine floated up from the equestrian trail. Gritting my teeth, I turned around and grabbed a flashlight out of my desk drawer. Feeling I needed more than light to defend myself, I picked up my umbrella as well. Yes, an umbrella proved a poor weapon compared to a bow and arrows, but I didn't want to cart those down to the tree. It was only a few dozen yards away, and I hoped the pointed tip of the umbrella would work just as well at thwarting goblins and such. Besides, Fergus had gone down before me and he'd attack anything overly dangerous. Still, my nerves weren't too happy with my decision.

I pulled on a sweater and stepped through my door. There wasn't much of a moon this Halloween, so I was glad I'd grabbed the flashlight. I climbed down the slope that dropped behind our backyard and aimed my light towards the tree. I spotted Fergus immediately, his tall shoulders resting against the tree as he wagged his tail slowly. Wait, not leaning against a tree, but . . .

"Cade?!" I breathed.

I forgot about my fear of wandering around in the dark and, hiking up the long skirts of my costume, I ran the last few meters to reach his side. This time I exhibited a little more self-control and didn't fling myself at him.

He stepped away from the tree and the dim light my flashlight provided showed me his grin.

"How are you Meghan?" he asked in that calm voice of his.

"Oh, you know," I offered in a nonchalant manner, waving my hand around. "The same as any senior in high school. Keeping busy with homework and avoiding faelah.

Thank you, by the way. For guiding me towards the, uh, pixies. They were beautif-"

I cut myself off when Cade grabbed my shoulders. He'd abruptly grown tense and for a moment my mind went blank. Was he trying to make me shut up? Was he going to shake me? Press me against the oak tree and kiss me . . . ? I waited in slight anticipation.

"What happened to your neck?"

His voice was cold and serious, and for several seconds I held as still as possible, speechless. My *neck*? My neck, my neck . . .

"And your face."

He lifted one of his hands and caressed my cheek. He no longer sounded dangerous, but concerned.

Uhhhhhh . . . I think that single touch might have fried my brain cells. But my brain managed to revive itself and I became aware of what he was talking about.

"Oh! No, it's nothing. Makeup for my Halloween costume! I decided to dress as a dead beauty queen this year."

I tried grinning, but boy, did I feel stupid.

"R-really," I stammered. "It's fake blood, and only pale makeup for my face. It's a stupid costume, really. Dead beauty queen . . ."

I trailed off and Cade took his time releasing me from the death grip.

"No, not a stupid costume," he murmured, his voice more relaxed. "Well, perhaps the *dead* part is inaccurate, but . . ."

I wished I hadn't dropped the flashlight, because I wanted so badly to study the look on his face right then. Had he just started to compliment me? A strong desire to clap my hands and jump up and down in glee took hold of me. To my unending relief, however, my common sense *was* awake tonight.

"So," I cleared my throat to break the discomfiting silence and equally awkward moment, "what brings you to this side of the dolmarehn on Halloween night? Have you fulfilled your penance for breaking your geis?" *Oh please say yes . . .*

A sigh from the darkness in front of me told me no. I tried to contain my disappointment, but what he said next made it even worse.

"I'll never be able to repay the debt I owe for breaking my geis."

And you're to blame for his broken geis . . . my conscience reminded me.

"Oh Cade, that is so unfair. Who placed the geis on you in the first place? Maybe we can talk with him?"

He flinched. Hard. "No Meghan. There is no reasoning with them, and I can't tell you who did this. You must believe I do not regret my decision in the least."

His words should have warmed me, but I hated that this was all because of me.

"Perhaps I can do something to help."

The strain keeping him so rigid gave me his answer before he spoke.

"No. Please Meghan, don't try to help me in this. Help me by continuing your longbow practice and getting ready to come to the Otherworld with me soon."

My knees nearly melted. Terror and elation rushed through me at the same time. Go to the Otherworld, *with Cade* . . .

Surprise

"You have been practicing, correct?"

"Uh," I managed, "yes, as often as I can."

I spoke the truth, but my definition of 'as often as possible' probably wasn't enough to satisfy Cade. I made a mental note to make more of an effort from here on out.

Cade shifted his weight, and although I couldn't see much in the dark, I sensed his head had turned towards the path disappearing further down into the swamp. I knew he had to leave soon. I so desperately wanted to hug him, to ask him if he had discovered anything more about my Faelorehn parents, to learn more about that night he had saved my life, when I thought he had kissed me . . .

"I must go Meghan, but before I leave, I want to give you something."

Joy coursed through me, then guilt. He had given me so many gifts; the bow and arrows, the books on Celtic myth, the mistletoe charm I wore all the time, and the beautiful torque tucked away in my desk drawer. I never felt comfortable with the idea of wearing something so obviously from the Otherworld (I had a nosy family and even nosier friends), but perhaps I should reconsider.

"Cade," I said quietly, lowering my head because I was sure he could see my face despite the darkness, "I can't accept any more gifts from you. You've been too generous already."

He shook his head and I thought I glimpsed the flash of his white teeth through the dark.

"Then let's call this a trade, since I'll be needing Fergus back soon. Though I'd rather like to call it your birthday gift."

He knew today was my birthday? And trade? For Fergus? Before I could consider it further, he climbed behind the tree and pulled out a wooden container about the size of a shoebox. As he moved back towards the front of the tree, he bent down and retrieved my fallen flashlight, placing it in my hand. Carefully, he opened the lid of the box and gestured for me to shine the light inside. What I observed totally confused me. The object inside looked like a fuzzy, white tennis ball nestled amongst a bunch of dried grass.

"What is it?" I whispered, trying not to sound disappointed. Honestly, you'd think I was expecting diamonds or something.

Cade chuckled. "She's a merlin."

I blinked. "Merlin? Like the wizard?"

Cade only smiled, his face eerily lit by the wayward flashlight beam.

"A merlin is a small bird of prey, like a kestrel or a falcon."

My cheeks began to burn. Oh, *duh*.

At that moment, the little merlin decided to wake up and make a fuss. It must have only been a chick because its wings were tiny and its eyes still closed. The minuscule bird opened its mouth and let out many demanding chirps.

I glanced up at Cade with a question in my eyes. Was he giving me this merlin? If so, why? How was I going to take care of something so small and helpless? What was I supposed to feed it?

"She isn't just any merlin, Meghan. Look closely behind her eyes."

I obeyed, having nothing better to do, and shone the flashlight back into the box. The poor thing, covered in fuzz and bald patches, looked like any baby bird. I examined the small beak, pallid eyelids and reddish-brown ear patches. Wait, reddish-brown? I shot my glance back up at Cade, my eyes wide and my mouth hanging open.

Eventually I spoke, "An Otherworldly spirit guide?"

Cade's smile almost lit up the night.

"For me?"

"She's all yours."

Surprise hit me like a glass of ice water, and I brilliantly asked, "How can you tell it's a she?"

"Spirit guides take on the gender of the master they bond with."

"Um, are you sure she'll bond with me?"

"Yes, of course, because she is just hatched and you'll be the one to raise her."

"What?"

My joy at his precious gift slowly turned to panic. I couldn't raise a baby bird. Where would I put her without anyone seeing her? I knew most faelah hid themselves from humans by using their glamour, but enough spirit guides had been seen by the ancient Celts for them to conclude Otherworldly creatures were white with red ears. I'd learned that much in my research and from talking with Cade. The chances of one of my brothers stumbling upon her at some point in the near future seemed highly likely, and should she not have enough glamour to render herself invisible. . . ?

"Spirit guides are different than other faelah," Cade continued. "They have much more power, even more so than many of the Faelorehn and they only reveal themselves to mortals when they wish to. They don't have to return to the

Otherworld in order to regain their glamour, and newborns are especially magical. No one will know she is here, except you."

Oh, good. What a relief. But I had other questions.

"What do I feed her?"

Cade grinned again, a feature hidden due to a lack of light, but I heard it in his voice. "Fergus will hunt for you. You can feed her whatever he brings back, but it will get messy."

I grimaced, even though I was no shrinking violet. Okay, maybe a little, but I was pretty sure handling raw meat fell within my range of abilities.

"Care for her well, and she will be a good friend to you. When she starts to fly you'll be able to detect her, in here."

He traced a gentle finger down my temple and I shivered, both at his touch and at the thought of having a bird messing with my head. Communicating telepathically might not be too bad, though. Cade didn't seem to be burdened by Fergus.

"Goodbye Meghan, for now. Fergus will stay with you until your spirit guide is old enough to protect you."

He began to depart, leaving me standing in the dark, in the stupid, blue prom dress with a wooden box in my hand.

"Cade, wait," I called out after him. Propriety be damned.

He paused and turned around to face me.

I strode up to him and threw my free arm around his shoulder and gave him a genuine hug. Not the psychotic, obsessive full-body tourniquet I'd been applying of late, but an honest-to-goodness hug.

"Thank you," I whispered in his ear.

Surprise

I released him and turned back up the path, casting him one last glance before I crossed my lawn. His shadow stood in the same place where I had left him, and if I didn't know any better, I would have sworn he was frozen in shock. I grinned. Might as well let that fantasy play out since no one was here to convince me otherwise, not even my annoying conscience.

Cade's shadow had vanished by the time I closed my sliding glass door, but for once I wasn't completely torn up about his abrupt departure. He had given me a great gift, a rare and special one if my instincts had anything to say about it. Someday I would ask him more about spirit guides, but for now, I wanted to tuck my little merlin away somewhere safe and warm and get some sleep before any other supernatural interruptions had a chance to stop me.

Four

Meridian

The next morning I woke to an annoying chirping sound. At first I entertained thoughts of my brothers playing a birthday prank on me. When the chirping continued and no one came flying onto my bed to force me awake, however, I concluded the noise had nothing to do with them.

I sat up, feeling groggy and slightly dazed. The racket was coming from my bathroom. Had Logan and Bradley planted some weird booby trap for me? Grumbling, I got up and shuffled over to investigate. I nearly screamed when I peered into the bathtub, and then everything that happened the night before came flooding back: Cade, the baby merlin, *my* spirit guide . . .

The little chick stopped chirping as soon as it, *she*, saw me. Her eyes had opened and they stared at me with doleful longing. Then the merlin opened her mouth impossibly wide. Oh. She was hungry.

"Um," I fumbled, looking around as if some form of sustenance would appear out of thin air. "Hold on a moment little bird."

What the heck was I supposed to feed the poor thing? I was already failing as a mother.

A scratch at my sliding glass door caught my attention. Fergus! I dashed over, almost tripping on all the empty bowls from last night, and yanked open the door. The wolfhound sat waiting in silence, something with red fur and a tail hanging from his mouth. He dropped the dead animal at my feet and I squealed, hopping out of range. *Gross!*

A few seconds later and I remembered what Cade had told me the night before. Oh, right, food for my spirit guide. Ugh, this was going to be all kinds of unpleasant. I took a closer, wary look at the furry thing. It resembled the demented squirrel I had seen chatting with the raven those many months ago. He had brought me something Otherworldly.

"Is it safe for her to eat? I mean, I saw it fraternizing with the Morrigan once."

Fergus flicked his ears forward and panted. Okay, I guess that was a 'yes' on the safety of its consumption. But I knew there was no way the little bird could eat this thing whole.

"Hang on a moment Fergus."

I walked over to my desk and flipped on my computer. As it booted up, I tried to ignore the hungry cries of the baby merlin. So she seemed invisible to people, but would they be able to hear her? The computer monitor was asking for a password and soon I was browsing the internet for information on feeding merlin chicks. Apparently the parents fed them meat, torn off in little bits from whatever prey they caught. My stomach churned. I had to cut the dead thing up? *Wonderful . . .*

Sighing, I pushed away from my desk, picked up a pair of scissors and my manicure tweezers, and walked back to my door where Fergus lay patiently waiting. *Okay Meghan, you can do this. The faelah's already dead, and you have a hungry baby in the bathroom . . . Just like dissecting a frog in biology . . .*

After fifteen minutes of snipping and tugging, three near-puking incidents and several muttered grievances, I managed to accumulate a small pile of meat strips for my bird. Placing them on a stack of several napkins, I carried the mess back into the bathroom and set it in the tub next to the box with the baby merlin. She must have smelled the blood, because she started cheeping more insistently. I'm glad I chose to keep her in the bathroom because the tub would be the easiest thing to bleach when feeding time was over.

I fed the merlin with the tweezers, dangling each strip of meat in front of her. The spirit guide was an enthusiastic eater, and despite my earlier disgust with regards to how to feed her, I smiled. She was rather cute.

"Good job little bird!" I whispered as she polished off the rest of the meat.

When she was finished, she gazed up at me with big, dark eyes and released a few cheeps. I interpreted them as sounds of satisfaction and became even more convinced when her eyelids drooped. She fell asleep with her head tucked next to one wing and I felt my heart melt. I was already in love with my little spirit guide.

"Sleep well, little merlin."

As I watched her snooze, a thought hit me. I couldn't keep calling her 'little bird' and 'little merlin'. She needed a name. I stood up and cleaned up the mess I'd made and left my tweezers and scissors to soak in bleach water. I moved my spirit guide out onto my desk while I took a shower and scrubbed the bathtub. When I was done, I put on my old bath robe and wrapped a towel around my head. Time to research some names . . .

I spent a good half hour browsing through websites featuring old Celtic names. I sighed. Many of them seemed really unique and fitting for an Otherworldly spirit guide, but for some reason they didn't quite fit. Giving up, I pulled out my Irish myths book and browsed through the glossary, looking at the names of the characters.

I snorted after reading the first few entries. For all I knew, some of these legendary heroes were still living in the Otherworld and I might be meeting them one day. It would be pretty awkward if I stumbled upon one of them and they learned I had named my bird after them. No, that wouldn't do.

"Meg!!"

Bradley's harsh voice startled me into dropping my book. Luckily, the noise didn't wake up the merlin.

"What?" I hissed back.

"You gonna come up and open your presents?"

Oh, yeah. It was my eighteenth birthday. How on earth had I forgotten that?

"Yeah, um, let me get dressed. I just got out of the shower."

I carefully carried my spirit guide back into the bathroom, placing her box in the bathtub. I gave her one last look and smiled. Her name would have to wait until later. I pulled on some jeans and a t-shirt and headed upstairs, anticipating some grand attack from my rambunctious brothers.

❦ ❦ ❦

I spent the afternoon getting some homework for next week out of the way. True, I could have taken my family up on the offer of all of us going out to catch a movie, but to be honest, I had had my big birthday surprise the night before. I told them that if they just made something special for dinner, I'd be happy. Of course, Mom being who she was, insisted on running to the grocery store to pick out all my favorites. She forced Bradley and Logan to go with her, and I couldn't help but grin. They would be good sports for my sake, but they hated shopping. Dad, being left with Aiden and the twins, decided to take them on a walk.

"I think we'll check out that swamp at the end of the road that you're so fond of Meggy," he told me as he lathered them up with sunscreen and mosquito repellent.

I froze for a second, suspended in fear. Would the faelah bother them? Would my family even notice them? The day remained bright and sunny, so I released a breath, telling myself that I needn't worry about Otherworldly monsters lurking in the swamp. Despite the fact that today was Samhain, the one time of year they preferred to sneak into our world, the sun would surely encourage them to stay in Eilé. I winced. Robyn had mentioned doing something for the Celtic New Year earlier in the week, but I'd been too distracted to pay attention. I thought about calling her later, but honestly, I'd experienced enough Otherworldliness for the time being.

After Dad and my three youngest brothers left, I returned to my room. I checked on the merlin chick right away and she blinked up at me, cheeping in hunger. I sighed. I should have cut up more meat to store for later. Though I didn't know where I could have stored it . . . If I put the faelah meat in a sealed container in the refrigerator, would it look like something else? Would someone eat it, not knowing what they consumed? I grimaced. Okay, so I couldn't save anything. I glanced over at my door, wondering if Fergus was around. A twinge of disappointment hit me, but then I caught sight of a small, red furry lump on the concrete right outside the glass. I walked over and grinned, despite the gory scene. The hind leg of the faelah I had cut up earlier, if I was judging correctly.

Okay Meg, time to feed your baby . . .

Cutting up the raw meat wasn't so bad this time. Perhaps I was getting used to the gore or maybe I knew my baby needed this sacrifice from me. I carried the bloody strips in on a paper plate I'd filched from our pantry. As I fed my little bird, I kept thinking about a name.

"What am I going to call you little one?"

Of course she didn't answer, only snapped at the strips of meat and swallowed them whole.

Eventually, I ran out of food. I took the plate to our trash bin outside and scrubbed my hands and set the tweezers and scissors to soak in bleach again. I made sure to clean my merlin too, using a wet paper towel to wipe off the blood. Not wanting to go outside again, I flushed it down the toilet.

Finally, I picked up the box that acted as a temporary nest for my chick, admiring the design and wondering who had carved the wood. I placed the box on my bed and grabbed my world history book. Time to study for a test.

The baby bird examined me for several minutes before she let out a tiny cheep. I peeked at her, but she didn't open her mouth, begging for food. Shrugging, I got back to studying the old Atlantic trade routes and the list of goods shipped along them. Cotton, sugar, tobacco . . .

Another cheep interrupted me. I peered down at the white fuzz ball. She continued staring at me again. Out of curiosity, I lowered my hand and gave her a little pet on the head with my index finger. Immediately, she started chittering enthusiastically, trying to cuddle up against my palm. Oh. She wanted attention.

Smiling, I carefully lifted her up and set her in my lap. She cheeped some more and scuttled around in a circle, making herself comfortable. I returned to my book when she stopped moving. She made a pleasant warm spot up against my stomach, and every now and then she let out a tiny cheep of satisfaction. As she dozed, I read. At one point I turned the page in my history book and glanced at a world map denoting the different routes early explorers took. I studied it for a while, marking the equator and the Prime Meridian.

Something in my mind shifted into place. *The Prime Meridian.* I knew about the Prime Meridian, the invisible line that ran from pole to pole. Why did that particular name stand out to me? I lowered my gaze only to find my merlin chick focusing on me with alert eyes.

Almost against my will, I said, "Prime Meridian. Meridian?"

The merlin cheeped once and lowered her head, going back to sleep.

Meridian, huh? I tried it out a couple of times and grinned foolishly. *Meridian it is then.* I caught a glimpse of my little merlin, full grown and flying through the sky, pure white except for her rusty colored ear patches. Yes, Meridian was a wonderful name for such a creature.

⊚ ⊚ ⊚

The next morning I woke up to find another dead animal lying just outside my bedroom door. This time the creature might have been a normal earth mouse, but I couldn't say for sure. I fed Meridian, smiling every time she cheeped in happiness. Of course, I only assumed it was happiness. After tending to her, I set the merlin on my desk and took a shower, emerging twenty minutes later, wrapped in a towel and humming some ridiculous song I'd listened to on my radio alarm only an hour before.

"What's in the fancy box?"

I screamed and almost dropped my towel. One of these days I really was going to kill my brothers.

"Bradley!" I hissed in irritation, "What are you doing down here?!"

I scowled at him, but he was unperturbed. Every now and again my irksome siblings managed to sneak into my room, but they normally had the decency to leave me alone while I was taking a shower.

Bradley shrugged. "Aiden kept waking me up, so I went into the kitchen to get something to eat and I heard you were up."

Like that was a legitimate excuse . . . He could have put on his favorite cartoon instead.

"So, what's in the box?"

He stared at the wide-open box with a rather curious Meridian gazing right back at him. To my immense relief, she remained as silent and still as a statue. So, he couldn't see her. Good, but I prodded him anyway.

"Why do you want to know what's inside?"

"Well, I tried checking myself, but the lid wouldn't come off."

A mixture of relief and annoyance coursed through me. Clutching my towel and grabbing Bradley's arm, I herded him back to the staircase.

"It's my box and my business. How'd you like it if I snuck into your room and started going through your stuff?"

He shrugged. "I have nothing to hide."

I winced inwardly. Oh, I had plenty to hide . . .

"Look, girls have certain things they don't want their brothers poking their noses in, so please stay out of my room."

There, that should appease his curiosity.

"What could you have to hide?"

I groaned. He wasn't going to give this up. So I distracted him with a question.

"How did Aiden wake you up anyway?"

Bradley rolled his shoulders once more. "Nightmare I guess. He started acting funny after our walk in the swamp. I think he said something to Dad about seeing monsters or something. Meg, you okay?"

I stopped dead in my tracks and tightened the grip on his arm. My face paled and I sensed my eyes shifting color.

"Yeah, fine," I recovered, "just don't like the idea of Aiden having nightmares. He's never had them before."

I managed to get Bradley out of my room, and once he'd disappeared up the stairs I leaned against the wall, still clutching the towel around myself. My head wouldn't stop spinning. Had Aiden seen a faelah? *Impossible!* They used glamour to hide themselves from mortals. Then again, enough of the ancient Celts had to have noticed at least a handful of Otherworldly creatures in order to build their mythology around them.

I finished drying off and got dressed quickly, returning Meridian to her spot in the bathroom with a few more pets and words of affection. Next, I plopped down on my bed and contemplated writing a note to Cade. I still had half an hour before I should leave for Tully's, so I had plenty of time. After considering it for a minute, however, I decided to wait. Aiden probably hadn't seen anything. If the nightmares continued or if he said anything to me about seeing monsters, I would send a message to Cade right away.

Shaking off the weird sensation that had almost taken root, I gathered my things and headed upstairs. Thick fog hung heavy in the air and as I made my way down the street, I caught a glimpse of Fergus, disappearing down the equestrian trail. I loved having him around, but soon I wouldn't need his guardianship any longer. I was saddened by that thought, for he had become like a pet to me, but Cade needed him in the Otherworld.

A deep breath helped ease my mind. I continued on towards Tully's, forcing myself to focus on the school week ahead. I had two tests, a paper due and Tully and Robyn had talked me into going to our homecoming football game with them. I flat-out refused to go to the dance (there was only one person I wanted to dance with and I was too chicken to ask him and he was stuck in Eilé making up for his geis violation), so in order to appease them I'd agreed on the game. I didn't mind football. In fact, I watched a pro game on TV with Dad every now and again. High school football was another thing entirely.

I sighed, my breath tingeing the air white and joining in with the fog. I doubted we'd be paying much attention to the game. Besides, our reasons for going had everything to do with showing our support for Will and Thomas. I didn't know if cheering for the band was socially inacceptable at a football game, but I didn't care. It's not like I could get any weirder, and unlike last year, the popular kids didn't intimidate me anymore.

~Five~

Danger

By Wednesday, I welcomed the approach of the weekend. My essay was turned in, one test was out of the way, and Meridian found some sick joy in keeping me up half the night with her chattering. Somehow I managed to stay awake during class, but lunchtime was a whole other story.

Tully, Robyn and I reclined beneath the shade of a tree perched beside the track. Will and Thomas had lunchtime band practice, what with the game coming up and all, so the three of us decided to eat away from the crowd. Not that I worried about being pestered by the lemmings. At least not anymore. Adam Peders hadn't bothered me since the day Cade picked me up in his Trans Am. I grinned to myself at the recollection as I nodded off.

A sharp snap just in front of my face jerked me back awake. Robyn eyed me like a ruthless hawk; a look that made her appear quite fearsome. The black eyeliner only added to the effect.

"What's with the Sleeping Beauty act?"

I scowled at her.

"Haven't been able to sleep much."

"Guy problems?"

My scowl hardened and my face warmed. Ever since 'admitting' to being interested in a guy outside of our high school last year, Robyn had been interrogating me like some caffeine-injected detective. Only one problem there: the guy *wasn't* imaginary.

At least for now I allowed myself to tell the truth. "No, not guy problems." *Bird problems.* Yeah, that would be fun to explain.

"Well, what then?" Tully asked as she balled up her paper lunch sack.

"I just haven't been able to sleep. Restless, I guess."

I had considered telling my friends who, *what*, I was at some point in the future, but that consideration only lasted for a few ridiculous seconds. True, it would make my life a whole lot easier if they knew of my Faelorehn ancestry, but they would never believe me. And I'd no idea what the repercussions might be for flat out telling mortals about the Otherworld. Finding out on their own was one thing, laying it all out in front of them was quite another. Besides, I didn't want that to be another tool the Morrigan could use against me.

A brisk wind rustled through the eucalyptus trees and forced a few of the remaining leaves on a sycamore to break free from their branches. I tilted my head back and shut my eyes again. My friends were free to form their own ideas, as twisted and inaccurate as they might be. At least it would keep them safe for the time being.

Danger

The bell sounded in the distance and I groaned. I just needed to survive the next few days of school and the game, and then I could sleep all day Saturday. Well, as long as Meridian did the same.

⛉ ⛉ ⛉

Friday night held a crisp chill, typical early November weather on the Central Coast. Robyn picked Tully and me up that evening, all three of us wearing long jeans, a jacket and our warm shoes. We had made some effort to wear our school colors, pale turquoise and black, but on the whole, we valued comfort over style. Definitely not the most school-spirited lot, my friends and I. That sort of enthusiasm belonged to the jocks and popular crowd.

The parking lot was jam-packed so we parked a block away from campus. Robyn grumbled the entire five minutes it took to walk from where we'd left the car to the stadium. Tully and I only hid our grins. Perhaps complaining made Robyn warmer.

The stands brimmed with people, the Black Lake High fans on one side, our opponents, dressed in red and silver, on the other. The fact that I didn't even know the identity of our team's rival should have been a good clue as to how much I wanted to be at the game. *You're here for Thomas and Will,* I told myself. Robyn's aptitude for tardiness brought us in just as the floats drifted by.

Michaela West, wearing a tiara and what appeared to be a red robe some long dead king might wear, stepped down from a convertible, grinning like an idiot and waving to the crowd. I snorted. Homecoming queen. Big surprise. I paid little attention as she shed her royal attire and joined the cheerleading squad moments before the whistle blew for the kickoff.

"How about the top?" Tully asked, jerking her thumb towards an empty section on the far end.

I nodded. Not only would we be furthest away from the spirit section, but we would also be a bit closer to the band. I grinned and waved at Thomas and Will as we climbed the steps. Finally we were settled and the game started. I tried to pay attention for the first half, following the plays and giving my own, subdued cheers whenever our team earned a first down or stopped the other team's offense.

By halftime neither team had scored, so we found ourselves staring blandly at a basic routine from our own cheerleading squad. We shouted the loudest, however, when the band spread out on the field.

The third quarter rolled around and I went back to watching the game and trading remarks about the lemmings with Tully and Robyn. What we would usually do on any weekend, except tonight we happened to be sitting out in the cold with stadium lights glaring in our eyes and hundreds of other high school students cheering and taking part in some form of drama all around us. I let my mind wander after the opposing team scored their third touchdown, although that fact made me smirk a little. Adam Peders may be the best track athlete we had, but his quarterback skills were definitely lacking.

Being in my self-directed haze, I didn't notice anything odd until I caught the edge of Robyn's horrified gasp. "What the hell?"

I blinked, temporarily blinded by the lights, and gazed in the direction her finger indicated. I almost fell off my bench.

Danger

"Are those *bats*?!" Tully gasped in disbelief. "But, bats wouldn't do that, would they?"

No. Certainly not bats. They were easily the length of my forearm, and no bat I'd ever heard of purposely swooped down on people, especially not in huge numbers. I understood why Tully thought they were bats, though. They did have leathery wings, but when they passed in front of a stadium light I caught a glimpse of red, a shade that conjured up thoughts of dried blood. No, I didn't know what they were, but I knew one thing for sure: they were Otherworldly.

Either their glamour was minimal, or they hadn't spent enough time recharging in the Otherworld. The screams and shouts of confusion around me suggested other people could see them, but apparently everyone believed they were bats. *Perhaps they're merely disguising themselves by using the image of an earthly animal,* I thought. Regardless, they made my skin crawl and my mouth dry up.

One of the faelah swooped down near us and we screamed, lurching back into the people sitting behind us. This time I got a better glimpse as it swiped long, needle-sharp claws at me. The face was cruel, not cute like a bat's, and four curved horns protruded from its ugly head.

As the demon-bat dove at us again, raking its claws for a second time, I covered my head to protect my face. A sharp sting, followed by a burning sensation, blistered across my exposed hand. I gasped and pulled my hand close. A long, nasty cut ran from my pinky to my thumb. The edges of the incision looked burned.

I bit my lip and risked a look. There seemed to be more creatures, but they weren't really attacking anybody, just diving at them and sending them scrambling from their seats. As one crossed in front of the lights again, I noted a long tail ending in a barb. Was that what had cut me? Far below, the game continued on, the players and refs un-harassed. To my great relief, the opponents on the other side of the field seemed safe from this attack as well. Oh, of course. The faelah were after me.

"Come on," I hissed to Tully and Robyn, "let's get to a lower level. Maybe there are a lot of bugs up here or something."

They nodded and, using our jackets as some sort of cover, we climbed down the stadium steps and made our way to the understructure. The last thing I wanted was for my friends to get hurt because I happened to be sitting next to them.

I felt safer under the stadium seats, but the screams of the spectators chased after us as the faelah dove at them, trying to get to me. They must have been programmed to hunt Faelorehn, or me in particular, because between the spaces in the seats and other peoples' legs, I spotted the demon bats, trying to sniff me out. Maybe being under the stadiums wasn't such a good idea after all.

"Gross!" Robyn hissed as she avoided a wad of gum. "This place is like a dump!"

I couldn't help but agree as we kicked aside old soda cans, water bottles and empty food wrappers.

The whistle blew on the field above us, announcing another touchdown for the opposing team.

"I say we get out of here," Tully mumbled.

"Good idea," I agreed, grateful I didn't have to come up with some other excuse.

Danger

We'd seen Thomas and Will, and the faelah didn't seem to be going away. I didn't even want to think about what might happen once we reached the parking lot.

We picked our way towards the edge of the stands, Robyn cursing when she almost got hit with a wad of something being spit out from above.

"Cretins!" she hissed.

Once we were out in the open my anxiety took over and I started noticing the cut on my hand. I stole a glance at it, using the orange street lights to get a good look. I grimaced. The gash was worse than before.

"What did you do to your hand?" Tully asked, concern etched in her voice.

"Nothing," I mumbled, trying to hide my fist in my jacket pocked.

"Lemme see." She pulled my arm free and I winced as she turned my palm over to assess the damage.

"Meghan! How did you do this?"

"Um . . ." *One of those demented faelah bat things scratched me with their talons . . .* "I cut it on a piece of metal under the stadiums."

"You'd better get a tetanus shot then," Robyn said, not breaking her stride as we drew closer to the street where she'd parked.

A sharp screech made me flinch and pull my hand free of Tully's examination.

"Watch out!" Robyn yelled as she broke into a run.

Apparently, the faelah had found me.

We ran the rest of the way back to the car, Tully and Robyn shrieking like a pair of helpless girls from some horror movie, me just praying we'd reach the car before those things attacked me again.

Robyn whipped out her key and got her car unlocked in record time. We all piled in and I managed to slam the door shut right before one of the faelah dove for me, its grotesque form slamming into the window instead.

"What the frick!?" Robyn exclaimed, breathing hard as she gripped the steering wheel. "First that stupid crow before summer, and now these bats. What have you done to piss off the wildlife, Meghan?"

I blinked at her, my face draining of color. I'd hoped they'd forgotten the incident with the raven . . . I took a deep breath. *Things could be worse, Meghan; at least they aren't seeing these creatures for what they truly are.*

I merely shrugged and said, "I have no idea, but let's get home before anything else weird happens."

"Yeah, really," Robyn muttered as she turned the key in the ignition. "What next? Goblins and werewolves?"

I'm not sure if I covered my flinch well or not. *Stick with me long enough and you might get your wish.*

🌀 🌀 🌀

The next morning I woke to an intense pain in my hand. I groggily climbed out of bed and cradled my right arm against me. I shuffled into the bathroom only to be greeted by a hungry Meridian peeking up over her box.

"I'll feed you in a little while," I groaned, my eyes still half closed. As much as I dreaded what I would find, I had to examine my injured hand.

I fumbled for the switch and squinted as the light glared on. Eventually, my eyes adjusted and I stole a peek at my right hand. I almost sobbed in shock. The cut from the night before appeared to be in much worse shape. My hand was swollen and pussy and I could barely move my fingers. If only I hadn't broken my geis last spring, I wouldn't be suffering from the nasty side-effects of a faelah attack. Oh well, too late now. And even worse: there was no way I was going to be able to hide this from my parents.

Soap and water made the wound sting. Peroxide made it sting even more. Gritting my teeth, I dabbed on some ointment and wrapped it up in gauze, but it didn't do much good. The pain lingered and my entire hand felt hot.

Fergus was at my door when I emerged from the bathroom. To my vast relief, he had captured something small. Meridian had grown much faster than I had thought possible, and she was able to strip off her own meat as long as whatever I gave her wasn't bigger than she was.

I picked up the animal's reedy tail with a paper towel and marched back towards the bathtub. My spirit guide let out a screech of impatience and pounced eagerly when I dropped the Otherworldly rodent in her box. When I stepped back out into my room, relief flooded me as I caught sight of the white wolfhound. I cleared my throat and moved forward.

"Fergus," I said, feeling ridiculous, "I need you to take a note to Cade."

I grabbed some paper and a pen from my desk and quickly wrote a message describing what had attacked me and how the cut had become terribly infected overnight.

Carefully, so that I didn't agitate the wound, I folded the note and tied it to Fergus' collar.

"Take that to Cade as fast as you can," I whispered, patting his head with my good hand.

He whined softly and turned away, jogging back down into the swamp. I hoped he had understood.

I stood up and got dressed, careful not to bump my hand. As I had predicted, Mom threw a fit when she spotted the cut.

"What on earth did you do to your hand?!" she demanded.

I wanted to chuckle. *Well, nothing on earth did this...*

Instead, I stuck to the story I told Tully. "Cut it on a sharp piece of metal on the stadium seats last night."

Mom grabbed her keys and purse. "Peter, watch the boys. Meghan, we're going to the emergency room right now to get you a tetanus shot."

I groaned. I hated shots, but there was no way to get out of this one. Although I knew a vaccine probably wouldn't do any good, I suffered the visit to the health clinic and came home with a polka-dot band-aid on my arm. The doctor had also insisted on cleaning the cut, which hurt ten times as much as the shot. I tried not to grimace too badly when she washed it and re-bandaged it, but I'm sure I acted like a wuss.

"I'm going to go take a nap," I muttered once we got home.

"Good idea," Mom said, "let that nasty cut heal."

Meridian greeted me with her usual chatter as I entered my room, so I took her box out and placed it on the table beside the bed. I was amazed at how big she'd grown. She had most of her feathers too, and only a few patches of fuzz remained. I'd never heard of a baby bird getting all its feathers in only a week or so after hatching, but perhaps spirit guides were different.

Yawning, I pulled on a pair of boxer shorts and an old t-shirt before snuggling into bed. To my relief, sleep came almost instantly.

@ @ @

I must have slept much longer than expected, because the next time I woke it was to the sound of something tapping on my sliding glass door. I groaned and tried to open my eyes, but a searing headache made that feat impossible. I shifted under my comforter and gasped. My whole body ached and I felt clammy, but from the way my hand throbbed I imagined some flesh-eating virus was wreaking havoc on my skin.

Fighting the tears of pain that were gathering in my eyes, I curled up into a ball and took slow, deep breaths.

This couldn't be good. The tapping at the door grew more urgent, but I ignored it. Whoever wanted in could just go away. Couldn't they see I was sick?

When the annoying noise didn't stop, I turned my head on my pillow to glare at them. I could barely make out a human-shaped figure against the dark night sky, but I had no trouble recognizing the ghostly white dog beside him.

Crying out in joy and exhaustion, I used my uninjured hand to push myself up. I think I fell out of bed, but I managed to crawl across my floor, stretching my good arm upwards. With a final burst of energy I switched the lock so Cade could get in. The swish of the door sliding open and a breath of frosty air greeted me as I collapsed to the floor.

"Meghan!"

Strong, gentle arms lifted me and carried me back to my bed. I turned my head, not caring about how needy I appeared, and pressed my face into Cade's shoulder. His scent filled my nostrils and immediately my headache eased off. I found comfort in the smell of the wild winds and deep forests of the Otherworld. I smiled and allowed myself to doze off.

"No Meghan," Cade murmured.

His voice sounded deeper than usual, raw even. I would have wondered why if my mind hadn't been so fuzzy.

"Drink this," he said, pressing a flask to my lips.

I obeyed without hesitation. The liquid cooled my throat and reminded me of mint and raspberries. I took one more sip, then another.

"Good girl. Now you can rest."

Nothing more than a whisper. Before I drifted off, something soft and warm pressed against my forehead. Cade's lips, I realized. I wanted to giggle. Why did he only kiss me when I was about to die? But I felt nothing beyond that and soon I succumbed to darkness.

@ @ @

"Meghan."

I was having the most wonderful dream. An old castle with a hidden waterfall loomed behind me, and a garden full of colors spread far past my vision. A light summer breeze fingered my hair, and the air smelled of wildflowers.

"Meghan."

I stood on the stone roof overlooking a small river snaking through green fields resting below tall, forested hills. My heart filled with warmth and a wave of bliss lifted me. Someone called my name. I turned to answer them, but before

I could glimpse their face, someone drew me away from the enchanted place.

"Meghan, you need to wake up now."

I blinked in irritation. Who kept bugging me and why would they take me from this wonderful world? Whoever it was put their arms around my shoulders and started lifting me up. I swatted at them.

"No," I mumbled.

"Meghan, look at me."

The voice again, stronger this time. I opened my eyes.

"Cade?" My voice crackled silently. "What are you doing here?"

I turned my head to make sure I was still in my room. Yep. I'd recognize that messy desk anywhere. The sudden realization that Cade held me close, in my own bed, made the grogginess vanish with a flash. I tried to push myself up, but cried out when I put weight on my right hand.

"Easy now," Cade murmured.

He loosened his grip and eased himself away from me, letting me lean back against my pillows.

Embarrassed, I smiled sheepishly and instantly became aware of the mild throbbing of my hand. That is when everything from the weekend flooded my mind. The football game. The flying faelah, their sharp claws raking at my skin. The sickness I experienced afterwards. And then last night . . . I shook my head and winced at the remains of the pounding headache. I'd been terribly sick, but Cade had come.

Taking another deep breath and pushing aside my humiliation at how awful I must've looked, I glanced back up at

Cade. He stood only a few feet away from my bed, his hands relaxed at his sides, his gaze focused on me.

I bit my cheek. "I'm sorry."

Cade's sigh sounded overly relieved. Was he afraid I'd be mad at him? Of course he was. I had just acted as if he'd been a stranger barging into my room to take advantage of me.

Putting on a face of bravado, I reached out my good hand and sought his. He stiffened, but took it gently, his fingers warm and dry. Mine were still clammy.

"Really, I'm sorry Cade. I didn't mean to act so crazy just now, I-"

"That is why you are apologizing? Meghan, you should have contacted me the second the faelah hurt you!"

His aggressive interruption shocked me. He had moved in close once more, and before I could so much as apologize, *again*, he scooped me up into a tight hug. My nerve ends caught on fire. No, he wasn't kissing me, but something about this one action felt suspiciously intimate. I returned his embrace with the same intensity, being careful of my hand.

"You might have died."

His raw voice suggested withheld emotion and I wondered, with a thrill, if he would kiss me after all. Oh, wouldn't it be nice to be conscious this time?

But when he pulled away he only held me at arm's length and gazed at me with dark eyes.

"Promise you'll not let this happen again. If something of the Otherworld harms you, you let me know as soon as possible. Send Fergus or your own spirit guide. Promise me."

His words came off as more of a demand than a question, but I shook my head, my emotions still going haywire.

Danger

The unmistakable sound of my brothers clambering out of their bunk beds upstairs caused me to jump slightly.

Cade grimaced. "I must go."

He stood and walked away. I gritted my teeth as severe disappointment slammed into the pit of my stomach. No kiss after all.

When he reached the door, Cade gazed back over his shoulder. "Can you meet me in the swamp next Saturday morning? At sunrise?"

I put aside my disappointment and peered up at him, my mouth curved in a grin. "Of course."

"Good," he said, "bring your bow and arrows."

And with one last glance, he slipped from my room and disappeared into the early morning fog, Fergus trotting silently behind him.

I sighed and fell back into the pillows. For the first time that morning I glanced at my hand. I blinked in surprise. Cade had bandaged it. Carefully, I pulled away some of the gauze, afraid to find a horrible mess beneath. To my astonishment, the wound seemed to be much better, not the red, festering gash from yesterday afternoon.

Giving up on trying to sleep, I got up, brushed my teeth and put on my Sunday clothes: sweatpants and a t-shirt. Hey, if homework has to be done, I might as well be comfortable.

Meridian greeted me when I stepped into the bathroom. I gathered her up with my good hand and walked over to the perch I'd made for her in the corner, placing her on the highest branch.

Once I finished taking care of my morning routine, I plopped myself in front of my computer, cleared off a spot on my desk and opened my math book. Time to be a normal, teenage girl. Sighing with boredom, I glued my eyes to the book and did my best to tackle calculus, but it was very hard to focus when I had some new memories of Cade to fill my mind.

Six

Visit

The following week dragged by at a snail's pace. Early Saturday morning I woke to a gray sky and Fergus standing outside my door. He hadn't been hanging around as much, now that Meridian was almost full grown, so his presence only meant Cade lingered nearby. I cursed silently when I glanced at the clock. The glowing digits read eight in the morning.

I threw on some warm clothes and headed for the door. Fergus' whine reminded me to go back and grab my bow and arrows, and to release Meridian for the day. I grinned when I shot her a glance, asleep on her corner perch. She would have insisted on being let out already if she'd been awake. Last Tuesday I'd crawled out of bed only to find her flying around the room like a crazed bat. Okay, maybe a bat was not the right comparison, not after what happened at the football game.

I freaked out at first, before realizing the creature was Meridian. So she'd finally learned how to fly and probably wanted outside. If my own intuition hadn't told me as much, the strange tingling on the edge of my mind, followed by a sharp, internal voice crying *OUT!* would have been a pretty significant clue.

The mind link startled me at first, but then I remembered what Cade had said to me about communicating with my spirit guide. I wondered if I could speak back to her, so that afternoon I stood on the small patio outside my door, closed my eyes and concentrated. I tried to summon the weird itchy sensation I'd noticed when she first spoke to me.

Meridian!

Nothing.

Meridian! I tried again.

Just when I started feeling really foolish, she'd returned with a single thought. *Up!*

I turned my eyes skyward, grinning after finding her perched in one of the eucalyptus trees at the edge of our yard, tearing at some small animal she'd caught for lunch.

That had been four days ago, and now as I crossed the room to open the door, she shook her feathers out and flew from her perch, gliding across the room to land on my shoulder.

Morning, she sent to me.

Yes, I returned with a smile, *lovely. Like Meridian.*

She nibbled affectionately at my cheek as we stepped onto the equestrian trail. I practically ran into the swamp, tripping over the exposed root of a tree along the way. I barely missed impaling myself with one of my arrows. Meridian left my shoulder in a flurry of feathers and soft chirps for the safety of the sky.

Visit

By the time I reached the small meadow where Cade always waited for me, I was out of breath and in a bad mood. He stood there, patiently of course, with an amused look on his face.

"Tough morning?" he asked.

I grimaced at him and mumbled some answer about sleeping through my alarm clock. He insisted on examining my hand, which showed signs of healing. Ten minutes later we stood side by side, plunking arrows into the targets he'd set up before I arrived. Several weeks had gone by since my last practice, but, to my great relief, I hadn't lost too much of the skill I'd gained over the summer.

After about an hour of me doing my best to hit the center of the target and Cade's gentle coaxing, I was ready for a break. Cade nodded his agreement and set his bow aside, walking over to a fallen tree to rest against. I sat down beside him on the log, leaned my bow against its side, and proceeded to peel off my archery glove.

Finally, Cade glanced up and caught my eyes with his. There was something there, something more than what he normally revealed, but I couldn't quite grasp it. My heart sped up. Stupid organ. If it wasn't such an important necessity to life, I'd try to find some way to get rid of it. Hearts caused far more trouble than what they were worth.

"I want you to come with me to the Otherworld, to Eilé, for a visit."

Oh. From such an intense gaze I expected something much more daunting, or revealing. My heartbeat slowed, but my skin prickled with goose bumps. *He's only asking you to go with him to the Otherworld. It's not like he's asking you out on a date!*

"Go with you to Eilé?" I asked as I rubbed at my arms in an attempt to make the goose pimples vanish and to force my conscience to shut up. "Sure, I mean, I guess I'd like to go to Eilé, again. As long as I don't have to go by myself. Because, well, if those faelah decide to show up . . ."

I was babbling. I shrugged and grinned, trying to lighten the mood. When had everything grown so serious? We had been laughing only a half an hour ago. Heck, I was even hitting the bull's eye two times out of . . . twenty.

Before I could consider his proposition any further, Meridian swooped down out of the canopy, screeching her delight as she came to rest in a small oak growing only a few feet away. I glanced at her, grinning when I saw the tiny dead faelah hanging from her beak. It was the size of a mouse but had long, ugly, reptilian feet, and black, hairless skin.

"Good girl," I murmured.

She chittered and got to her meal. *Tasty*, she sent.

I chuckled and turned my eyes back on Cade. He gave me a small grin and I caught my breath. He looked so relaxed now, sitting in the sun, leaning over with his elbows resting on his knees. His dark auburn hair was slightly disheveled and for the time being his eyes shone with a pale hazel green.

I released a tiny sigh and looked away. Would there ever come a time when he didn't have such a distracting effect on me?

"About going to the Otherworld," Cade continued after a few more moments of silence. He gestured in the general direction of the dolmarehn lying hidden up the gully several hundred yards away.

"The reason I want you to go is so I can test your magic potential."

Huh? "Test my magic potential? What do you mean?"

He took a deep breath and sat up a little straighter.

"Do you remember Meghan, when I told you about the Faelorehn and their glamour? How it is connected to Eilé itself and how yours isn't strong because you've been in the mortal world all this time?"

I nodded. I remembered. I also remembered that if Cade or any of the faelah stayed in this world too long their natural magic would drain and they'd need to go back to the Otherworld to recharge.

"I guess what I'm saying is, I want to see what you are like, fully charged, or at least more so than you are now."

"Okay," I replied, still a bit confused.

He acted as if he planned on asking me to make some impossible sacrifice or suffer through uncomfortable pain.

"In order for that to happen," Cade continued carefully, "you'll need to stay in the Otherworld. For more than a single day."

"Okay."

I still didn't fully understand what he meant. What was the big deal? Why did he appear so wary? I could brave the Otherworld for a few days, as long as Cade stayed with me and . . . *Oh*. Stay more than one day in Eilé. Got it.

I brushed back my hair nervously, turning my eyes towards Meridian. She had managed to gut the creature she'd killed, but witnessing her gory snacking skills felt safer than looking at Cade.

Apparently my brain was on standby mode because it sure wasn't working very well today. If I wanted to 'recharge' enough to display any power, I would have to stay in Eilé for more than twenty-four hours. Which meant I would be alone with Cade for over twenty-four hours. Alone with Cade, *overnight*. Now I realized the problem. Funny thing was, the longer I thought about it, the more appealing it seemed. Unfortunately, my parents wouldn't think so. And this explained Cade's aloofness. Made perfect sense now.

"Meghan, I would never take advantage of you, or such a situation-"

"No, I know," I said, cutting him off. *Though sometimes I wish you would . . .*

I glanced up and smiled, despite the flush creeping along my skin. He still seemed a little guarded, but he relaxed when he realized he hadn't offended me.

"Your parents will agree to this?" he asked softly, lacing his fingers together and leaning back over his knees.

No. They wouldn't. Not even if I introduced them to Cade and we both signed a document in our own blood swearing we would keep our hands off of each other. I couldn't tell them the truth, not yet. One day, far away from now, I would confess everything. But I was still not a hundred percent sure as to what *exactly* I was. And I really had no idea how to tell them either. I needed to go to Eilé, like Cade suggested, to figure everything out.

"They won't agree Cade, no matter what we tell them. I'll have to come up with another way."

He nodded somberly. I expected him to argue; to insist my parents be informed of our plans, but I think some part of him knew the same thing I did: they would assume I was suffering from another psychotic episode and that would get us nowhere.

"I'll ask one of my friends to cover for me," I said.

He nodded again. "It will only be overnight and a few hours into the morning, this time."

I swallowed. *This* time?

Putting on a grin that showed more backbone than I had at the moment, I said, "Don't worry. I'll figure something out."

Maybe.

◎ ◎ ◎

The entire next week I fretted about asking one of my friends to lie for me. Perhaps I could talk Tully into having a sleepover. Her parents usually went out late on Saturday and came home to sleep half of Sunday away. She could just tell them I planned to come over later and stay the night. They would never know the truth. But I dismissed those thoughts almost as soon as they came to me. I wouldn't ask Tully this favor. If I did she would insist on learning every detail before forbidding it outright. She would tell me that if I had to sneak off with a boy my parents didn't know about, then he meant to cause trouble and I should cut him loose. Oh, if only I *could* tell her the truth. Yes, Cade was trouble, but not in the sense she would think.

No, she would refuse to help me and when I wouldn't see things her way, she'd threaten to bring it up with my parents and that was too much of a risk.

Robyn on the other hand . . .

At the end of the day on Thursday I managed to pull Robyn aside after school.

She gave me one of her questioning looks and I told her what I had to say was top secret. Her dark eyebrows lifted with interest. She pulled a soda can out of her backpack and popped it open, taking a sip as she eyed me expectantly.

Taking a deep breath, I delved into the story I had invented. I needed her to cover for me at some future date; to say I planned to spend the night on the weekend.

"Not that I'm agreeing," she said in a casual tone as she examined a dark red fingernail, "but my parents are going to a church convention this weekend. They're leaving Friday and coming back Sunday."

My heart skipped a beat.

"Oh Robyn, could you please pretend I'm staying the night Saturday? There is something I have to do and I can't tell my parents, and it will take longer than a day."

I should have known better than to lay all this out before her and not expect to make some payment in return. This was Robyn, after all.

"Okay, I'll cover for you," she eventually conceded, her voice cool and in control. "But you have to tell me what is so important that you've got to lie to your parents and stay out all night."

I grimaced. I knew this was coming, and whatever I told her next had to be scandalous enough to garner her support.

I took a deep breath and said, "I'm meeting a guy."

Robyn nearly choked on her soda. She coughed a few times, but once her breathing returned to normal she shot me a pointed glance. "Are you freaking serious!?"

"You can't tell anyone, okay!"

Visit

I looked away and scowled. Why hadn't I come up with a better story before pitching this to her?

"Way to go Meg! Oh, you *have* to tell me about him. What's his name? Is he cute? Does he go to our school?"

I blinked, stunned. She was actually smiling.

"I'm going to give my mom and dad your cell phone number," I continued. "I'll tell them your parents don't ever answer the phone unless they recognize who is calling. So if they call you, say I'm in the shower or the bathroom or something."

"Wow Meghan," Robyn said with a mischievous grin, "must be some guy."

"It's not what you think," I mumbled back.

Well, at least I was pretty certain it wasn't what she thought.

"Uh huh, sure it isn't."

"Thanks Robyn, I owe you one."

"I want all the juicy details when you get back. And I hope we get to meet this mystery man some day."

"Okay."

I waved a hand over my back as I started off across the track, seeking the path leading off into the swamp. When I reached the oak tree closest to my house, I pulled off my backpack and ripped a piece of binder paper out of a folder and dug around for a pen. I quickly wrote a note to Cade, telling him I was free this weekend to go to Eilé with him. I rolled the letter up and placed the small tube in the knothole.

Once inside, I found the house dark and empty. Thirty minutes later, Mom arrived with the boys. I told her about my plans for the weekend; how I was staying over at Robyn's.

"That's nice honey. It will be good for you to get out of the house for a while. Just be sure to leave their number."

I grinned to cover my grimace, trying not to feel guilty about my double lie. Not only would Mom and Dad be appalled at my intention to spend the night with a boy, but they would never let me stay over at a friend's house if their parents were gone.

Shaking off the pall of guilt, I descended into my room, turned on some music and tackled a pile of waiting homework.

The next morning I checked the oak tree and found a reply.

Meghan,

I'll meet you tomorrow morning in your backyard before sunup. Be sure to set two alarms this time.

-Cade

I sighed, my breath forming a cloud in the early December air, and folded the note up, placing it in my pocket.

As I walked to Tully's to catch my ride to school, the anticipation which had begun as a small kernel started expanding in my stomach. I was going to the Otherworld with Cade, to stay overnight. I tried to hide my smile, but Tully noticed.

"Have a good dream last night or something?" she asked as we climbed into her car.

My grin widened. "You could say that."

@ @ @

An annoying buzzing sound woke me way earlier than was considered decent by most people. I groaned and cracked open an eye. Four in the morning. Why on earth had I set my alarm clock for that early? Then my mind cleared. I shot up in bed. Cade! The Otherworld! I tossed my sheets back and started getting ready. I had a small backpack loaded with what I'd need: a change of clothes, a few snacks, necessary toiletries . . .

I scribbled a note to my parents, explaining that I decided to go over to Robyn's early and I'd be back on Sunday. It was a Saturday morning. They wouldn't be up until at least nine, so hopefully they'd think I had left around eight, not five. I crept upstairs and left the note on the island in the kitchen where it would be found.

I did one last check after returning to my room, then stepped towards my desk and coaxed Meridian awake.

Danger? she sent.

No, journey, I returned with a bit of joy.

She fluffed her feathers and grumbled in her avian way, but didn't protest as I shifted her onto my shoulder.

The morning was cold when I finally escaped the house. Darkness shrouded the sky, but eventually my sight adjusted and I spotted Cade and Fergus standing at the edge of my backyard. I moved quickly over to them.

Cade had his hood up and I couldn't see his face, but I heard the humor in his voice when he said, "Right on time."

He shifted and in the dim light I could barely make out a hand reaching in my direction. I stepped back in surprise.

"My power is stronger than yours at the moment Meghan. Let me guide you in the darkness."

Laughing nervously and shaking off my unease, I took his hand and the reassuring grip warmed me.

When we reached the mouth of the small cave that would take us to the Otherworld, the black sky had lightened to deep blue. Cade dropped my hand as we started making our way in the dark once again. I was nervous and my heartbeat increased as we moved forward. Images and memories from the last time I'd experienced this flashed through my head. For a moment I was convinced I wouldn't be able to go through with this after all, but the tightening of Meridian's claws on my shoulder and her soft, *Protect,* brushing my mind reassured me and gave me new courage.

After taking several steps into the cave, Cade stopped. He reached back and took my hand once more. He laced his fingers with mine and tightened his grasp.

"Do you trust me Meghan?"

His voice was soft, almost pleading. I swallowed and tried hard to discern his expression in the dark. The paltry amount of light reaching this far into the small cavern glinted off his eyes, giving him the appearance of a demon trying to tempt me into doing something evil.

"Yes," I answered, my own voice a mere whisper, "I trust you."

"Good."

He gave my hand a quick squeeze, and then I was pulled forward into the icy abyss that loomed before us.

Seven

Dolmarehn

The experience of passing into the Otherworld brought back unpleasant memories from several months ago. The ancient chill swirled around us, making me dizzy and breathless, but during the whole ordeal Cade held on tight to my hand.

Mist and a frosty air greeted us on the other side, and I had to exercise a great deal of self control to keep from bolting back through the dolmarehn. The familiar stones, like the lifeless bodies of some long forgotten beings, loomed in the fog, reminding me of my last visit here.

Cade must have sensed my unease, because he moved closer and pressed a hand to the small of my back. I almost leapt out of my skin.

"It's okay Meghan," he whispered, "the Morrigan isn't here."

Forcing myself to relax, I stepped forward. I knew she wasn't here, but the mere familiarity and memory of this place put me on edge.

Meridian flew from my shoulder to join Fergus, chattering with joy. I smiled. She must recognize her homeland.

Magic, she sighed contentedly against my mind.

I winced as fresh guilt for keeping her in the mortal world for so long washed over me.

We left the haunted hillside and the tension drained from my body. Cade found a path and we started to follow it, moving further and further away from the dolmarehn. For about thirty minutes we walked along a wooded ridgeline, but I never could see far enough past the mist and trees to get a better view of what lay ahead of us. We moved steadily uphill for quite some time before stopping for a break, and I wondered where we were going.

Before I got the chance to express my thoughts aloud, Fergus loped up, his long tongue lolling and a mischievous grin on his face. He came to rest beside Cade, leaning affectionately against his thigh and gazing up with longing.

Cade spoke a few words in the language of the Otherworld and gave his dog a scratch behind the ears.

Meridian found her favorite spot up against my neck and settled in for a snooze.

Good exploring? I sent to her mind.

Happy trees, she responded, *snacks.*

I smiled. Who would have ever thought I would be so pleased by the thoughts of a bird?

"So, uh, where are we heading exactly?" I said as we began walking once more.

Cade cast a glance over his shoulder and gave an impish grin.

"You'll see."

I snorted at that, slightly worried but also excited.

The scenery changed once we started heading downhill again. This time the trail wasn't surrounded by looming oaks, but was open and spacious. Enormous broken rocks littered the ground and the fog lifted enough to reveal the frost dusting the earth like powdered crystals. I sighed in appreciation, slowing my step in order to store the enchanted scene in my memory.

Unfortunately, the magic was broken when the trail curved around a massive tree and something dark appeared out of the corner of my eye. I gasped and pressed myself up against Cade's back. An animal about the size of a pig and close enough in resemblance to one was standing on the trail eating something. Only it wasn't a pig. At least not a live, normal one. The creature had the coloring and rotten look of one of the Morrigan's faelah. As soon as it spotted us, the Otherworldly boar let out a terrible squeal and took off.

"Fergus, go!" Cade shouted, his voice rumbling in his chest and reverberating against the cheek I had pressed against his back.

He twisted around to find his spirit guide trailing behind us. The hound released a single, sharp bark, then growled and bolted after the demon pig. Meridian screeched from above, darting after Fergus.

Help. Spot ahead, she sent me. I let her know her efforts were appreciated.

Cade had stopped moving the second I'd plastered myself against him. As we stood there waiting, I asked, "What was that?"

"Mucdiahb," he said, the cut of his mouth grim, "evil pig."

I fought the temptation to wrap my arms around him.

"How is it evil, exactly?"

"Other than the fact that a mucdiahb will attack and kill just for the fun of it," he replied as he took a tentative step forward, "it will readily do the bidding of the Morrigan. They generally stick to the woods, but on occasion they wander out into the open. They are a great nuisance to the Wildren of the Weald."

I allowed him to step away from me, but scanned the other boulders for more mucdiahb, just in case one was hiding and waiting to pounce on us.

In order to keep my nerves settled, I asked, "The Wildren of the Weald?"

He only smiled and returned his eyes to the path ahead, his step more confident than cautious now. We had started ascending back into the forest after crossing the creek running alongside the bottom of the open gully.

"The wild children of Eilé," Cade finally answered, giving me a hand-up through a rather steep part of the trail.

His face took on a dark, regretful pretense. "The unwanted children of this world."

I furrowed my brow and my mouth dropped open. *Un*wanted children? Were there no orphanages or foster homes in the Otherworld? I bit my lip. Of course there weren't. Wouldn't I have remained here if there had been some sort of child care system to take me in? Might I have ended up with these wild children had I not been sent to the mortal world?

I shook my head to banish the depressing thoughts. Instead, I focused on the other thing Cade had said. "What's a weald?"

"*The Weald*," Cade emphasized both words, "is what we call the massive forest growing several miles north of here. It begins on the western shore of our largest lake, Lake Ohll, and spreads far to the north and even further to the west. Legend claims that no one has ever traveled the entire length of it."

He sighed and looked back up, studying the trail ahead of us. "Many believe that the Weald never ends, that the wood goes on forever."

"And you said the, um, Wildren live there. The unwanted children?"

Cade drew another deep breath and gradually released it. His pace slowed as the path narrowed and the trees grew thicker and larger. I welcomed the darkness their interlaced branches created, even though they had lost their leaves for winter.

"Eilé isn't like the mortal world Meghan." Cade's voice took on a somber note. "Children are often born here, ones that are, I guess *unplanned* is the kindest term to give them. Sometimes acknowledging them can bring about severe repercussions, for both the parents and the children, so they are abandoned to the wilds."

My stomach twisted with pity. Sure, I had come to a similar conclusion earlier, but to hear someone admit such cruelty out loud, to tell me these terrible thoughts were actually true, was something else entirely.

"No one could be that cruel," I whispered harshly as the cold air grew colder.

Well, okay, maybe the Morrigan, but who else would do something so heartless?

Cade came to a stop on the trail and held up his free hand to keep me from saying anything more.

"It's how things are done here, Meghan. As appalling and unkind as the practice may seem, it is accepted. Don't fret too terribly, though. The other Wildren find them and adopt them into their family. In fact, the people of Eilé now know where they can leave their young ones so they may be well cared for. They make their home in the Weald and grow extraordinarily close to the land itself. They've become the greatest wielders of power in the Otherworld. Besides the gods and goddesses of course."

His slight grimace came right after a grin. Cade took a deep breath and started walking again. "The Morrigan has been trying to get to them for centuries now, but the trees won't let her in. As long as the wild children stay within the forest, she can't touch them. It's quite entertaining to watch her, actually, when she thinks she's finally slipped past the barrier of magic. Have you ever seen a grown woman throw a temper tantrum Meghan?"

I fought a chuckle, despite what I'd learned about kids being abandoned to face the wilderness on their own. The image of the Morrigan throwing a fit kept my mind occupied for the next several minutes.

We reached the top of the hill and the thick, ancient oaks opened up just enough to host a scattering of small meadows. A sharp bark from ahead of us caused both Cade and I to slow to a stop.

Fergus broke free of the underbrush, panting and giving us his usual grin. I smiled, glad to see him, then curled my lip in slight worry. Splotches of blood covered his face and neck.

Cade went still for a few moments, and I got the impression he was sharing information with his spirit guide.

Land?

I jumped at Meridian's sudden intrusion into my mind. I wondered if I'd ever get used to her silent words.

Yes, I answered back, and a minute later she swooped down from the canopy and alit on my shoulder. Relief prickled across my skin when I found no blood on her.

"Good boy," Cade said to Fergus, and we started walking once again.

"The mucdiahb has been taken care of," he offered grimly.

"Oh, wonderful."

I still felt a bit troubled by our last conversation, but I shook those thoughts off. I could do nothing to help at the moment and I didn't think anything I said would change the current situation. Besides, if Cade told the truth about the abandoned children having family with others like them, then I'd be content. At least for now.

We soon passed through a meadow carpeted with frost encrusted ferns, and a living cloud of pale blue moths with metallic gold spots on their wings fluttered up from their resting places. This time I didn't bother to hide my gasp.

"How beautiful!" I nearly tripped over my feet as I turned in a circle to get a better look.

"Careful," Cade chuckled as he wrapped his free arm around me, catching me before I lost my balance.

"Sorry," I mumbled, fixing my hair nervously as I planted my feet firmly on the ground. Good thing he hadn't been walking too far ahead of me or else I might just have face-planted into the ferns.

"Don't be," he answered, releasing me and turning back towards the trail. "These moths are rare and are hardly ever seen, even by those who live here year round. In fact, I'd say this was a good omen, especially considering how late it is in the season."

I turned around and blinked back at him. "Really? You're messing with me."

Cade held up his right hand as if to swear an oath. "Nope."

I narrowed my eyes at him. His vow seemed genuine enough, but there was humor in his ever-changing eyes.

Snorting, I followed after him, but kept an easy pace so I could still admire the beautiful insects. We passed through the meadow, leaving the moths and their good tidings behind, and traveled for another hour.

At one point I tried asking Cade where we were going again, but all he said was, "The best camping spot in this part of Eilé."

My heartbeat sped up and I drew in a sharp breath as I once again remembered why I had made this special trip to the Otherworld. To stay overnight. With Cade. Alone. Perhaps Meridian and Fergus could act as chaperones.

"Are you alright?"

Cade had stopped walking, his arms crossed over his chest, his head cocked to one side as he studied me.

"Um, yeah." I remembered to breathe. Eventually. "Just, uh, thinking about the moths again."

All Cade did was quirk an eyebrow in return.

I gritted my teeth, nervous all of a sudden. *Honestly Meghan, you knew you'd be spending the night with him!* The backpack I'd been carrying for the past two hours seemed to grow heavier.

Once we reached the end of the meadow where the trail started dipping downward again, Cade lifted a hand. "We're here."

"Is this where we're camping out?" I asked, sliding the backpack off my shoulder.

"Yes."

I glanced around the small hollow, more of a depression in the hillside surrounded by trees and lichen-encrusted rocks than what I'd call an ideal site to make camp. A small ring of blackened stones denoted a fire pit and the thick layers of moss covering the open space suggested that although the night might be cold, at least the ground would be soft. And then it occurred to me that I hadn't packed any camping supplies. No sleeping bag, no pillow, not even an emergency blanket. And since Cade hadn't brought anything at all, I figured he was in the same boat as me.

"Um, Cade?" I said, rubbing my elbow and searching the area for any form of cover. "If we are camping, uh, what are we going to use as sleeping bags?"

Of course, at that exact moment an image of Cade stretched out before the fire with me snuggled in his arms flared in my mind. A fierce blush crawled up my neck and warmed me up a bit. Okay, more than a bit.

"Don't worry," Cade shot over his shoulder as he squeezed into the narrow crevice of an oak tree, "I keep this place stocked for situations such as these."

Good. He hadn't seen my bright-red face.

"Uh, how do you mean?"

Cade maneuvered himself out of the tree hollow carrying a giant, weatherproof duffle bag. His grin helped ease my nervousness.

"I'm sorry I don't have a tent, but there are at least three separate sleeping bags in here and some extra blankets of course."

He dropped the bag and yanked back the zipper, pulling out what appeared to be the warmest sleeping bag before handing it over to me. Without even glancing in my direction, he pulled another sleeping bag out and quickly started unrolling it beside the duffle bag. Next, he took out a few more things: a sack of dried food, some bowls, spoons and a pot.

"I'll sleep over here, and you can have that side. The rocks create a natural barrier against the elements and you'll have the fire on this side to keep you warm enough."

I hid my grin and pushed my earlier thoughts out of my mind. He sounded just as nervous about our sleeping arrangements as I felt.

"Good idea," I agreed with a relieved breath.

Cade passed over some extra blankets and I piled them on top of my sleeping bag. They smelled slightly musty and stale, but they were clean and dry.

"I used to come up here often as a boy with my foster father," Cade said, sighing and lying back on his sleeping bag. "There is an old castle about three miles away from here, a place of ancient legend. As a child I loved exploring the abandoned halls and caves behind it."

I sat down and crossed my legs, listening to Cade's soothing voice and letting the embarrassing thoughts of earlier fade away as the sky began to turn gold and rose with the approach of sunset.

"Why is the castle legendary?" I asked.

Cade turned his head to look at me and a stray piece of his dark copper hair came loose to brush his forehead.

"Because the caves are full of dolmarehn, dolmarehn that can take you to all the corners of the mortal world and to the many realms beyond Eilé."

His voice was softer, revealing more awe than before.

I released a breath I'd been unconsciously holding and looked him in the eye. He was studying me once more, as if waiting for some answer to a puzzle he couldn't quite figure out to appear on my face. I blushed again.

I cleared my throat. "Do you still visit this castle?"

He grinned. "Sometimes."

"And, can I go with you one day? I mean, if you ever go back when I'm here in Eilé?"

The way he kept his eyes on me was just short of unnerving, but not in a negative sense. I glanced away, picking at some moss growing too close to one of the stones standing guard over me.

"Yes, you can come with me the next time I visit."

The tone of his voice sent shivers up my spine, and I made an effort not to shudder this time. I stole a glance at his face, but he no longer studied me. Instead, he stared into the leafless canopy above. I pursed my lips and considered him, for once not fixating entirely on his beauty.

"Your foster father?" I pressed after awhile, remembering what he had said at the start of this conversation. "Were you an orphan too?"

He inhaled deeply, still staring at the canopy when he answered, "It is customary for children to be fostered by someone other than their parents. My father died long ago, and my mother," he paused and took another breath, his eyes, once fixated on the treetops, became obscured and lost, receding somewhere far away.

I held my breath. Cade seemed bothered by something, and he undoubtedly had many things to trouble him, what with his responsibility of keeping the faelah in line and chasing them from the mortal world, yet I'd never given much thought to the other details of his life. Was he on good terms with his family? Did he have friends here in Eilé? I honestly had no idea.

His soft chuckle pulled me away from my meandering thoughts. Cade sat back up and ran a hand through his hair, which only added to the disarray.

"Let's just say she had more important things to do than fuss over a small boy."

A sharp pain jabbed at my heart and I absentmindedly reached out to him. Sure I'd been hurt when I learned that my Faelorehn parents had abandoned me, but I had my mom and dad in the mortal world who had loved me as their own for so many years. Did Cade have anyone who cared about him here?

Cade must've noticed some sign of concern on my face because he lifted a hand to ward me off.

"No Meghan, don't fret. It's something I've come to accept. Now, you were asking about my foster father?"

And just like that, he threw his vulnerability into a dark room within himself, slamming the door so I could no longer see it. My heart twisted with disappointment, but what had I expected? For him to pour out his soul to me?

I sighed and let my worry fade. If Cade could overcome his woes, then so must I. I put on a bright smile and said, "Yes, please tell me about your time here as a kid. Who is your foster father?"

Cade grinned with mischief. "The Dagda."

I furrowed my brow in confusion at first. The Dagda? The Dagda, the Dagda . . . The name sounded so familiar.

Cade shot me one of his looks, a look that informed me I should know who the Dagda was. I pressed my lips together in concentration and scoured my brain. After several seconds, a memory surfaced.

"Oh!" Now I remembered. "The Dagda? Really? Like, the one from the Second Battle of Maige Tuired? The god with the magic cauldron?"

Cade smiled, relaxing back against the stone on his side of the fire ring.

The Dagda, like the Morrigan, was a legend of Celtic lore. I recalled reading about him in one of Cade's books or during one of my internet hunts. He was said to be one of the few gods who excelled at many things, and he had a reputation for being . . . I guess saying he was friendly with women was a civilized way of putting it.

I snorted as I conjured up the image I had of him: an older, pudgier man with an unkempt beard and mustache. Now that I knew he existed, I wondered if the picture in my mind matched the reality.

"And yes, he does live up to his wild reputation," Cade said cheerily after a while.

My face must have given me away, so I covered it up with a blush.

"I wasn't thinking so badly of him," I insisted. "But what is he really like?"

Cade straightened up again and leaned forward, staring into the empty fire pit as if expecting the wood to burst into flame on its own. I scrutinized his face once again. He seemed to be thinking carefully, as if picking and choosing what he thought would be best to tell me. I stifled a laugh. The Dagda must be notorious indeed.

Finally, Cade spoke, "He has a rather overwhelming personality, there's no denying that, but he is a gracious soul and is willing to get to know a person before passing any kind of judgment. He will be the first to defend a companion if they are wronged, though, and I wouldn't get on his bad side if I were you. His forgiveness isn't easily earned. Oh, and he is famous throughout all of Eilé for throwing the most lively parties."

Cade smiled up at me and I had no choice but to return the gesture.

"Don't worry Meghan, I'm certain he'll love you."

"Wait, what? I'm going to be meeting him? The Dagda?"

I felt my face drain of color for a moment, but Cade's laughter helped ease my harried thoughts.

"He isn't nearly as terrifying as the legends make him out to be, I promise. And you won't be going alone when you meet him, so if he tries anything I'll be able to come to your rescue."

The expression I gave him conveyed my horror, but the glint in his eye sobered me almost immediately. Oh. He was teasing me.

I thought about that for awhile: meeting the Dagda. I'm sure the experience would be a bit intimidating. However, it would be a pleasant change to meet someone friendly. Well, at least someone who didn't consider my death their highest priority, like the Morrigan.

"So," I said, clearing my throat a little, "how did you come to be the foster son of one of the Celtic gods?"

"Luck."

A glimmer flashed in Cade's eye, but I knew he wasn't going to give away anything more.

He squinted up towards the sun again. "I think we had better gather some firewood before the sky grows too dark and the frost settles in."

I shook my head and made to stand up, but Cade, the quicker one to rise, reached down a hand to help me up.

I graciously took it, expecting him to lift me to my feet. Instead, he tugged hard enough to pull me up against him. My surprise kept me from pushing away immediately, so when I blinked up at him in astonishment, I found his face mere inches from mine.

I opened my mouth to say something, and nothing came out but a small squeak that got caught in the back of my throat. His eyes seemed to burn into mine and as I watched them, they

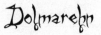

changed from pale silver to dark green. He leaned his head closer and . . .

A sharp bark followed by the annoyed chatter of a bird broke the strange enchantment.

"Whoa now," Cade murmured in a soft tone, wrapping one of his arms around my waist and pulling me away from the place I'd been standing.

Fergus went tearing by, his ears pinned back and his tongue lolling as Meridian chased after him, diving at his tail.

Cade said something in his native tongue, scolding the animals for playing so recklessly in such a small area, I assumed. I had trouble deciphering anything, especially since I was still flabbergasted about what had just happened. Wait, what *had* happened? One minute Cade was talking about his childhood, then he mentioned something about firewood, and in the next second he pulled me close in an almost embrace. No, I wasn't complaining. Only a bit confused.

Eventually, Cade realized he still held on to me.

"Sorry," he mumbled, releasing me before turning his head away. "Fergus forgets how big he is sometimes."

He offered a half-hearted grin and I decided, given the situation and the lack of a private, quiet corner where I might sit and untangle this latest mystery, that perhaps shrugging and raising my arms in a gesture I hoped stated, *silly spirit guides,* was the best thing to do for the moment.

"So, firewood." I clapped my hands together and looked around.

For the next thirty minutes we scoured the hilltop seeking out dead branches. Cade stayed further away from me than usual, and I was certain his distance had something to do with the earlier interruption from our spirit guides.

But, what *had* almost happened? Now would be a good time to rifle through those thoughts from before. If I didn't know any better, I would have sworn he was about to kiss me. The very thought of his lips brushing against mine caused me to tremble with delight, and I ended up dropping most of the kindling I'd gathered.

Cursing inwardly, I fought off my jumbled daydreams and snatched the branches back up. *Cade MacRoich did not drag you up to this hilltop to make out with you Meghan, so stop your fantasizing!*

Oh? Then why had he pulled you so close, hmm? Why had he bent his head just so? Admit it, if his dog hadn't almost trampled you, you two might still be lip-locked at this very moment.

I gritted my teeth and grabbed on to the closest log I could find. Sure, the heavy branch was way too big for me to lift, but I needed a distraction so my stupid conscience would shut up. I hated that it had multiple personalities.

On the third yank, I managed to free the half-buried log, only to scream when I saw what went skittering out from underneath it. That wasn't a snake, or a lizard. More like a salamander crossed with a centipede. Or a giant, elongated spider with slimy skin.

I dropped the log with a small screech and backpedaled, tripping over one of the many stones in the clearing. I went down cursing, but Cade was standing over me before I could so much as flip over and make a crawl for it.

"What happened?"

Cade sounded concerned and he leaned down to help me up. Oh no, no more of that. I didn't want my conscience to start up again.

"I'm fine," I insisted.

When Cade knelt down to get a closer look at me, I scooted back and held up an arm.

"Something startled me is all. Some creepy thing living under a log."

I pointed over my shoulder, hoping he might go investigate and leave me to recover on my own. I wasn't normally spooked by creepy-crawlers. You couldn't afford to be when you had a house full of brothers. But that thing was enormous. And I'm pretty sure it hissed at me.

"Ah," Cade merely said, "probably only a litter bug."

I shot him an incredulous look. "Are you making a joke?"

He grinned and shook his head. "Litter as in leaf litter. There are all different types of them, but we refer to all of them as 'litter bugs'. Most of them aren't dangerous, and they only bite if you try to grab them."

I cringed. Well, at least I knew the giant bug wouldn't hurt me, because there was no way in this world or the mortal one that I was going to touch it.

"We can stop gathering firewood now. I think I found plenty."

I glanced over at the pile Cade had made and grimaced. We'd have enough wood to last us a whole week. What did I have to show for myself? The two pieces of kindling I had managed to hang on to while being hunted down by the litter bug. Wonderful.

Cade didn't seem to notice, or comment, and in no time he had the fire lit as well. We ate the food from the bag he had stored: beef jerky, thick bread and a rather tasty soup he'd made with some dried supplies and water from a half-frozen spring a few dozen yards from our campsite.

After throwing more logs on the fire, Cade slipped into his bedroll, fully dressed, and sighed.

"Using and detecting your natural magic works best early in the morning, so we should probably both get to sleep as soon as possible."

I blinked in surprise. Oh yeah, the real reason for being here. To gauge and recharge my magic. I sighed and glanced up. Late twilight settled around us, but it couldn't be later than six o'clock. Meridian had long since fallen asleep and Fergus still roamed the woods.

When I turned my eyes towards Cade, I found his back facing me, his own breathing deeper.

Biting my lip and taking the blanket in my hand, I followed Cade's lead and snuggled in as best I could. I had told myself I didn't want Cade to try anything else with me, but of course that wasn't entirely true. Yet, his interest one minute and then his distance the next was rather jarring, and I wish he'd just make up his mind, one way or the other. Judging by his quiet demeanor during dinner and his terse goodnight, I'd say he planned to keep his hands to himself. I tried to ignore the tiny sting of disappointment.

The fire continued to crackle and an owl cried out in the distance. As I slowly fell asleep, I hoped to convince myself the ache in the pit of my stomach was fear for what might attack us in the night, and not a result of Cade's cold dismissal.

Eight

Power

The next morning I woke to the sharp tang of smoke and the sting of icy air on my face. For a moment I tried to figure out why my room would smell like a campfire and why I shivered. My eyes shot open when the thought of a fire flew through my mind, but in the next heartbeat the memories from the night before came flooding back.

Someone clearing their throat snagged my attention from my thoughts. I turned my head and caught sight of a cloaked figure standing against the pre-dawn light. At first I tensed up, but drew a calming breath when I realized the stranger was Cade.

"The fire went out last night and I thought a new one would be a good idea this morning."

He gestured towards the stone circle where a healthy crop of flames, and smoke, stirred.

Yawning and stretching my stiffness away, I curled out of the blankets, reluctant to leave their warmth behind and cringed as I heard the distinct crackle of frost. A film of white coated my sleeping bag.

I stretched again, teeth chattering at the cold, and wondered how scruffy I appeared, but a need to find somewhere to go to the bathroom quickly erased those thoughts. I peered over my shoulder at Cade and blushed, voicing my concerns.

He shook his head and glanced off to the side. "You'll have to find a patch of bushes or group of stones to your liking. I'm sorry. I don't often have a young woman with me when I'm sleeping outdoors."

Was it my imagination, or were his cheeks turning pink? Knowing Cade was capable of being embarrassed warmed me and helped dash away my own discomfiture.

While I was gone, I thanked my lucky stars I'd had enough sense to pack a toothbrush. I couldn't think of anything worse than bad breath, especially when you were alone with a guy. Not that anything was going to happen, but you never know. Of course, after yesterday evening I'd thoroughly convinced myself nothing ever *was* going to happen. Ugh, I needed to focus on the reason for my being here: to appraise my glamour, *not* to moon over Cade.

Magic Meghan, you are going to learn to use your magic! Isn't that more exciting than some guy? Too bad I wasn't ten and still under the delusion that boys had cooties. It would make my current predicament so much easier.

When I returned to our campsite, I discovered Cade had rummaged up something for us to eat. I sniffed at the pot over the fire and my stomach grumbled.

"What's for breakfast?"

"Oatmeal with walnuts and honey."

My stomach complained again.

We ate in silence as the dark sky turned pale gray, revealing a thick blanket of fog covering the forest and hilltop.

After cleaning up and gathering Fergus and Meridian, Cade led us through the trees once more, and once again I wondered where he was taking me, but I kept my questions to myself. Eventually, we came upon another clearing, this one littered with ancient, tall stones, similar to the ones scattered near the dolmarehn that connected Eilé to the mortal world.

"What is this place?" I whispered.

A secret sacredness seemed to cling to the air around us and I imagined that if I spoke too loudly, my voice would shatter this serenity and some fae spirit would come seeking revenge.

"This used to be one of the sacred henges, similar to the one near the dolmarehn leading to your home."

"You mean, like Stonehenge?" I asked, feeling a bit silly.

These stones, though rather large, were pebbles in comparison to the monoliths of Stonehenge.

Cade nodded and gave me a calculating look. "Stonehenge, in the mortal world, is the most famous example, but several exist. They help the Druids channel Eilé's natural power more efficiently."

I arched a brow at him.

He sighed, though not with impatience. "Try to picture the sun shining on a cloudy day. Although the light reaches the ground, it's even brighter where the clouds part. The sun's radiance is emitted everywhere, but is concentrated only in certain areas. The stone circles help concentrate the earth's magic because they are an extension of Eilé herself. Stone being of the earth, and placed in a circle to extend towards the sky, helps channel the magic from the ground and pulls it upwards. Before the glamour can escape and become part of the soil once again by falling in the form of rain, the person calling upon the magic stands in the center of the stone circle and absorbs the power into their body. It isn't the only way to absorb magic, but it is a quicker and more effective way to do so."

In a weird, science fiction sort of way, what he said made sense.

"So, like a gas station of sorts, for someone who uses magic."

Cade grinned and his green eyes flashed more towards brown. "Yes, that's also a good explanation."

I smiled, the usual response whenever I saw Cade do the same.

"Now, although the stones have been knocked down, we should still be able to channel some power. In fact, I'm glad most of them aren't standing. If the magic of the earth is prevailed upon and answers in full, the result can be rather, uh, overwhelming."

That sounded a bit daunting. Cade had said the purpose of my visit to Eilé was to soak up magic, but surely he didn't mean for me to recharge here in this fallen circle where I could potentially damage myself. I had no idea what I was doing, after all.

"So, you're just going to show me the process this first time, right?"

Cade's responding grin seemed almost wicked. I caught my breath. This expression proved even more disarming than his cheerful ones.

"No Meghan. We came here so you can learn what it *feels* like to channel your own power."

"What?"

Was he serious? He wanted me to step into the ring without first showing me? Was he crazy?

"Cade," I said, licking my lips nervously, "are you sure this is a good idea? I've never done this before, I don't even know if I really have any power, remember?"

"You do," Cade insisted, "trust me."

"Yeah, okay." I snorted softly and crossed my arms.

"Come on."

He reached out and took one of my hands, pulling me towards the center of the circle.

I was anxious, though I wasn't sure why.

He placed me in front of him, keeping his hands on my shoulders, my back to his chest.

"Now," he whispered right behind my ear, "we ask Eilé to recognize your power, and to feed your own glamour with her magic if it is hungry."

I quivered. Cade made it sound like I had some living creature inside of me. He confirmed as much when I asked him.

"Your power is a living thing, just like you and all the parts that make you Faelorehn. Your lungs need oxygen, your stomach craves food. Your heart desires love."

I drew in a breath at that.

"Now close your eyes, and let us both take from Eilé what she has to offer."

"Do we need to say anything special?" I blurted.

He shook his head. "No. Just let your senses become aware of the presence of the earth around you."

I did what I was told. I closed my eyes and let myself drift, soaking in the gentle, cool caress of the fog and the spongy softness of the moss below my feet. I let my nerves take in Cade's presence and my fingers and toes began to tingle. The forest was silent, until a soft chant, not terrifying or demanding, but celebratory, began floating through the air. The scent of old woods, wet stone and deep earth surrounded me, and when Cade sighed and gently pushed me away from his body, I almost fell on my face.

I looked back at him and blushed.

He smiled, his eyes so dark green they appeared black.

"Did you sense anything?" he asked, his voice a whisper.

"I, I think so," I croaked. "I noticed the presence of nature, but nothing else."

Cade's brow furrowed and his intensity seemed to lessen. He drew a deep breath and raked a hand through his hair, stepping closer to me.

"You would've known if you felt it."

"Felt what, exactly?" I wanted to know. Perhaps I did perceive it, whatever *it* was. Or maybe my glamour was a dud.

"Your own magic awakening, but don't worry. Sometimes a person's magic will stay hidden and safe within them until something profound happens. I hoped coming here would do the trick."

He shook his head and the corner of his mouth curled up.

"What?" I said, nervous.

"I might as well tell you what to expect, just in case your glamour decides to wake up when I'm not around to explain."

"Or perhaps I was right. About not having magic," I mumbled, disappointment hitting me like a load of bricks.

Again, Cade shook his head. How could he be so confident I carried any glamour when I couldn't even sense the magic myself?

"The sensation is like a warm blossom, opening up and sending fire through your blood. Not an unpleasant experience, but one that can be uncomfortable at first. One day you'll learn to welcome the flow of your magic, and to wish for it."

Okay, I'll bite. "And where exactly does this magic reside?"

He took another step towards me, that dangerous look gathering in his stance and flashing in his eyes again. I found the simple act of breathing difficult.

"Here is where you'll sense your power growing."

Cade placed his hand on my chest, right below my collar bone, slightly above and to the right of my heart and against the bare skin where my shirt collar had fallen open.

I tensed and my heartbeat sped up. I was almost certain the tingling of my nerves was due to Cade's touch and not the result of any power or magic awakening, but I'd stayed the night in the middle of the woods in the Otherworld. I must have been 'recharging' even before this early morning visit to the ruined henge. Surely I would have detected something by now.

Power

And then it started. A tiny itch that soon turned into something else, something sharper, clearer. The sensation began as a small pinprick and soon unfolded within my chest cavity, as if I were growing a second, more permeable heart.

The experience wasn't unpleasant, just different. I imagined I had a tiny sun lodged within my ribcage, keeping my heart company, and it had grown so large its brilliance began spreading throughout my whole body. I felt light on my feet, as if I could fly by simply spreading my arms and reaching towards the sky.

I met Cade's gaze, and noted the grin on his face.

"Now, here is something you can do with that power, should you wish to."

And before my very eyes, he dissolved into our surroundings. I gasped and started when his hand left my skin. I reached out, grasping nothing but thin air.

"Cade?" I whispered.

The mist in the trees had lifted a little, but the woods were still so ethereal; so Otherworldly, and the few stones that remained standing resembled sentinels watching my every move.

"Cade?" I asked again, louder this time.

Meridian chattered from her watch above us, breaking the relative silence. I stretched out a hand, trying again to touch an invisible Cade. I imagined I looked like a little kid at a party, blindfolded and wandering aimlessly as I tried to locate the piñata. I also felt foolish and a little annoyed. Why was Cade messing with me?

"Glamour has many wonderful uses," he said from somewhere behind me.

I turned around and began groping in that direction.

"Invisibility being one of those uses," he continued from a different location.

I growled and started heading the other way.

"Makes it easy to sneak up on people," he whispered next to my ear, his warm breath sending goose bumps down my neck.

I whipped around, partly in reaction to being startled, partly because I wanted to catch him. My hand brushed his . . . shoulder? His arm? Then he managed to slip away again.

I huffed a breath of frustration and just walked, full force, towards where I thought he might have headed.

Halfway across the stone ruin, someone grabbed my arm and spun me around.

Before I could voice my protest, a gentle hand came to rest on my shoulder, and then on my cheek. Something warm, soft and inviting pressed against my parted lips, and I realized Cade was kissing me. My eyes widened and I gasped, inadvertently deepening the kiss. Moments seemed to pass by and I barely recalled wrapping my arms around my indiscernible companion, returning the kiss with equal strength.

Cade pulled me closer and ran his fingers along the back of my neck and through my hair, as if he feared I would run away. I lost track of all sensations except for the touch of his skin, his unique scent and the glowing joy that was my very own Faelorehn power, now a pleasant warmth coursing through me.

Eventually, Cade broke the kiss and stepped away from me. I opened my eyes, not realizing they had been shut. I was too overwhelmed to speak or even think, but it didn't matter. Cade materialized before me, a slow, eerie process, and I found the expression on his face to be almost heart-breaking. He looked guilty, remorseful, regretful. Disappointed.

My own elated joy vanished in a heartbeat. What was wrong?

"Forgive me Meghan."

His voice was ragged and he ran his hands through his hair, keeping his eyes lowered. I should have been grateful, for my own were filling with tears.

"I got carried away with the moment. I'm sorry for my behavior."

I'm not! I wanted to scream, but clearly he believed he had made a mistake.

He held out his hand and smiled, but he still wouldn't meet my eyes. "Let me return you home before you are missed. I can teach you how to channel and use your glamour another day."

Fighting the tears of hurt and confusion, I stepped ahead of him and followed the trail out of the woods. Meridian swooped down to dart in and out of the oaks in front of me.

Sorrow? Her mind brushed against my own.

Yes, I returned, *but it will fade.* I hoped.

She released a mournful cry for my sake, but sped on ahead, keeping a lookout for hostile faelah while we made our silent, somber way back to the dolmarehn through the misty woods. Fergus came up from somewhere down the path and trotted past us, leaving Cade to trail behind. The hound seemed relaxed, his ears pressed back against his head. I wondered, as we moved further towards the stone gate that would take me home, what conversation he was sharing with his master.

Nine

Solstice

I was stuck in a bad mood all the following week, snapping at my friends or simply ignoring them when they asked me menial questions. It was stupid and selfish of me, but I couldn't stop thinking about Cade's kiss and why he had been so eager to disregard it. Had I disappointed him somehow? Would he completely forget me now and leave me to fend for myself?

Coming up with the 'juicy details' Robyn insisted on learning the moment she saw me on Monday morning had been even more trying on my nerves.

"I want to know everything!" she hissed in excitement as she pulled me off to the side so our other friends wouldn't hear.

I had to thank her for that much, at least. I wasn't ready for the boys or even Tully to know about Cade, especially since I sought out Robyn's help and not hers.

I shrugged, forcing the bitter disappointment to go away.

"Did you kiss him?"

I blushed so hard it sent Robyn into a fit of hysterics.

"Spill Meghan!"

"Spill what?" Will asked as the bell warned us to get to class.

"Nothing," I grumbled as I shuffled away from them. Robyn's giddy laughter chased me all the way back to class.

At lunch time she bullied me into giving her more details, so I made up some story about how, yes, we kissed, but the experience hadn't been all that exciting and rather disappointing. Well, it hadn't been disappointing on my end, but I wasn't about to tell Robyn that.

Robyn crossed her arms and scowled. "Well, if you spend the night with him again, I hope you get a whole lot more out of him than a kiss."

I gasped in shock, hitting her on the shoulder.

"Ro-*byn*!" I hissed.

She only grinned impishly as she rubbed the spot I had smacked. "What? Don't tell me you haven't thought about it."

Too irritated and embarrassed to respond, I hurried away to my next class, muttering under my breath about presumptuous friends. Let Robyn think what she wanted, especially since she had a point.

To my immense relief, Robyn didn't pester me any further that day and by Wednesday she'd dropped the subject completely. I guess my moodiness had finally worked its magic. Without Robyn breathing down my neck, I retreated back into my shell to spend the rest of the week festering in my own turbulent emotions.

The weekend helped recharge me, and although I still hadn't received word from Cade, I was feeling like a whole new person. So he kissed me and acted distant afterwards. So what? Happened all the time to other girls, how was I any different?

But by Monday morning I crashed back down into my old emotional abyss, and at lunch time I might as well have been eating alone. In a huff of frustration, I crunched my soda can up and tossed it towards the closest recycling bin, missing by a yard, of course.

"So anyways," I heard Robyn say.

Oh. I guess she had been telling us something.

"I wanted to have a bonfire, but my dad says there's been some strange activity going on down in the swamp. Maybe Meghan could tell us," she shot me a wary glance, "if she wanted to be part of the conversation."

I glanced up, my mind backtracking as I tried to remember what they'd been talking about. Um, when we first sat down Thomas had mentioned something about his family being gone for most of the winter break because they would be visiting relatives in Mexico . . . Will had said he should be available, Tully too . . . Oh, right! Robyn wanted to have a winter solstice party. Okay Meghan, you can do this. You can pine after your crush and be a good friend at the same time . . .

"Yeah, I think someone's been killing animals and mutilating them," I lied. "My parents won't let me go down there anymore."

Another lie, but honestly, ever since the events of last year, I thought keeping my friends away from the swamp and the dolmarehn hidden in the shallow canyon might be the best safeguard against the faelah.

"So, will you be free then Meghan?"

"Huh?"

Robyn rolled her eyes at me and sighed. "On the twenty first? For the solstice?"

I gritted my teeth. Sure, I hadn't been the greatest friend in the last week, but it didn't give Robyn an excuse to treat me like an imbecile. I pushed my annoyance aside and grinned. "Should be."

She clapped her hands and beamed. "Excellent! Now all we need is the ingredients to make soul cakes and some cider for wassail . . ."

I let Robyn's voice trail off as I got back to my lunch. A party would be a welcome distraction, but at the moment I needed a little more time to crawl out of my pit of self pity.

◎ ◎ ◎

School let out the next week for our winter break, and Robyn's solstice party fell on Saturday night. I wasn't in a festive mood, but I had to put on a good face or they would suspect something was up. They probably already did.

I borrowed my mom's car to drive into town since my parents and brothers planned on staying home that night to make cookies.

"Be back before eleven!" Mom shouted as I headed out the door.

"I know!" I said.

When I got to Robyn's I found everyone crowded in her small bedroom. I endured the suspicious glares of her mom and dad as I crossed their living room and walked down the long hallway. I smiled but received no warmth from them. Oh well. I'd grown used to their apathy. Robyn's parents had never liked me very much. I think their ultra-religious personalities detected my Faelorehn essence. A year or so ago, that would have terrified me. Now, having become aware of the truth and knowing I'd come from somewhere outside this realm, it didn't bother me as much. I was from Eilé, strange yes, but only in their eyes. Yet, how Robyn managed to continue her Wiccan tendencies in such a household was a mystery. Perhaps because no one, not even her own parents, could control her.

Smiling, I opened Robyn's bedroom door and stepped into a room buzzing with new age music and Robyn's voice droning out some solstice story she'd dug up from somewhere.

Tully and Will were already there and they turned to grin at me. "Hey Meg!" Tully said, patting a place next to her.

I smiled and sat down. I'd been terribly neglectful of my best friend lately and the guilt washed over me like a cold wave. Tully, however, didn't seem to notice. Sometimes I imagined she had a sixth sense and could discern when I needed to talk or when I needed to just be alone with my worries. She was nothing short of a blessing in my life.

Simply spending time with my friends suddenly made me cheerful and grateful. I enjoyed having something to think about, other than the mysteries invading my life, the biggest one being Cade, for once. The last few months had been trying; my existence split between two worlds, here and Eilé. How refreshing to only focus on one of those worlds tonight.

The party ended up being rather fun and for the first time in two weeks I didn't feel depressed about Cade. At a quarter to eleven I told everyone goodnight and headed out to the street where I had parked. The evening was cold and dark with a clear sky full of stars. For a moment I leaned my head back and exhaled, my breath misting above me.

Solstice

I fumbled in my purse for the keys to my mom's car, having some trouble in the dark. A street lamp glowed orange halfway down the street, but hardly offered much help.

As I searched, something in the bushes beside me rustled and growled. I froze, my entire body flushing with fear. I recognized that sound, and so did my magic as well.

A tiny pinprick of heat burst in my chest next to my heart. With my mouth becoming dry and my palms growing clammy, I turned to study the black clump of plants several feet away. The darkness hindered my sight, but there was no mistaking those glowing eyes.

Before I could so much as scream, the creature burst from the hedges and charged me. Crying in fear, I lurched to the side and the faelah slammed into my mom's car, snorting in outrage.

Without giving it much thought, I rolled under the car and willed my heart to slow down. That pinprick of magic throbbed and the odd sensation of Otherworldly glamour spread throughout my body. Crap. How much did I have and how the hell was I supposed to make use of it?

The creature snorted and bellowed in frustration as it tried to get to me. Like all the others, the faelah was grotesque, the sickly light from the distant street lamp displaying just enough features to send terror through my heart once again. If I had to describe the animal, I'd say someone had killed a wild boar and let it rot for a week before stretching it out to match the size of a large dog. The stench permeating the air only helped back up my theory. I was aware of only one person, no, *goddess*, who would do such a thing. The Morrigan. So, she still wasn't giving up. I wondered, as I lay on the cold, gritty, oily asphalt, watching the creature's sharp, cloven hooves scrape at me, if she knew of my recent visit to Eilé with Cade.

I shuddered. Just thinking about the Morrigan made me ill. Instead, I focused on getting out of my current situation. Wouldn't anybody hear the noise this thing was making? Oh, wait, faelah, duh. I'd probably be the only one to hear any of this. Perhaps the ugly creature would manage to kill me after all.

I gritted my teeth and tried to probe the well of magic living within my ribcage. That made the warm spot begin to sting, as if someone were driving a hot needle into my chest. I *really* needed to learn how to use this stuff.

I released a huff of breath and wiped away the tears running down my cheeks. To my surprise, I realized they were a result of my frustration, not my fear. I didn't know if I should be proud of myself or not; for managing to gain control over my terror of the faelah. Of course, it could just be a sign of my impending insanity.

I lay still for at least another ten minutes before a familiar screech filled the air. Meridian?

The scratching stopped and a blast of brilliant, bright white light slammed into the car and dissipated in the dark night. I blinked rapidly, trying to clear the spots from my eyes. By the time I recovered I noticed something black and charred lying beside the car. The faelah. Had Meridian used some spirit guide power to incinerate it?

The light flutter of wings and a friendly chitter forced my attention to the other side of the vehicle. Meridian sat on the sidewalk, eyeing me curiously.

Safe? she sent.

S

Yes, thanks to you, I replied with a heavy sigh of relief.

She chirruped as I crawled out from my hiding spot. I didn't even look at the creature, well, whatever remained of it. But I did catch a glimpse of the side of the car. I winced. That was one heck of a dent. The faelah might be able to make themselves invisible to human eyes, but there was still substance to them.

Taking a deep breath, I dug through my purse again, finally finding the keys. I got into the car, whistling for Meridian before I closed the door. She settled down on my shoulder and soon fell asleep.

Drained, she sent, her psychic voice sounding very weary.

I'll bet, I returned.

I had no idea a spirit guide could wield so much power, especially one as small as Meridian.

As I drove home, I formulated an explanation for my parents: a deer had leaped onto the road and managed to glance off the side of the car. Yes, that story would work perfectly.

All the lights were off when I got home, so I entered the house in silence and headed to my room, washing off the grit before collapsing onto my bed in exhaustion.

Before falling asleep, I thought about how I needed to be a little more vigilant. I should have known after the demon bat incident at the football game that the Morrigan hadn't forgotten about me. Now, with tonight's attack, I knew for sure she was back to her old tricks again.

@ @ @

I woke the next morning to the sound of my mom shrieking about the huge dent in her car. When I fed her the deer story, she went from livid to concerned in two point five seconds.

"Oh Megan! Were you hurt?"

She quickly started checking me for bruises and cuts and clucked when she found nothing worse than a small scratch from when I had crawled under the car.

"Um, got them last week at school."

Mom gave me one of those looks she used like tweezers to extract information. I wasn't about to budge.

"Well, do drive more slowly from now on, especially at night."

Sighing in relief, I returned to my room and glanced around, marveling at the lack of clutter. The long narrow object wrapped in a towel in the corner caught my eye. My longbow. After last night, I thought some practice couldn't hurt. I got dressed and threw on some shoes, grabbed my bow and arrows and shouted up the stairs that I was going for a walk.

"Come on Meridian," I called to the white ball of feathers in the corner, "I need you to keep me company while I practice."

Most of my winter break passed this way: working on my archery skills when I wasn't hanging out with my friends or being pestered by my brothers. I had almost forgotten about Cade and the awkward way we had parted, but during those last few days before school started again, Fergus showed up at my door right before dawn.

He led me to the oak tree and inside the knothole I found a note.

Meghan,

Solstice

I apologize for not contacting you for so long and once again for my inappropriate behavior in the Otherworld. I hope you'll forgive me. I was wondering if you would like to visit Eilé for a couple of days. There are two people I wish for you to meet.

-Cade

My heart fluttered and gave off a pang of hurt. So he still regretted kissing me. I must be terrible at it.

I slumped against the tree and squashed my disappointment. *Well Meghan, at least he still wants to be your friend.* Yeah, I could live with that. Maybe.

I called Robyn later in the day, hoping she would cover for me, again.

"Oh sure, but you know the price. Details my dear, details," she crooned over the phone, a hint of malicious glee in her voice.

"If there are any details to spare, then you will have them," I promised, well aware there would be nothing to tell this time.

I finished the call and wrote a return note to Cade, informing him I'd be available on Tuesday. In the mortal world we would be celebrating New Year's Eve, so I had a valid excuse to go over to Robyn's and spend the night.

The next morning I got a response. Cade would meet me at my door once again, before dawn.

On Monday night I had an awful time falling asleep, most likely because I was excited about going to the Otherworld again. Ever since returning from the last trip, a small part of me yearned to go back. Perhaps because my magic now knew where it belonged, or maybe I was nervous about seeing Cade again. Either way, I didn't drift off until after midnight.

Ten

Cauldron

C ade met me the next day in his usual, unobtrusive way. Before stepping through my bedroom door, I grabbed my overnight bag and whistled to Meridian. We made our way silently through the woods of the swamp, the dark morning adding to the general gloom.

Cade didn't speak to me until we reached the dolmarehn.

"Ready?" he murmured, holding out a gloved hand.

I laced my fingers with his, relishing the slight squeeze he gave my hand as he led me deeper into the small cavern. This time the passage into the Otherworld didn't make me so dizzy.

Once on the other side, we moved east instead of north like last time. The air was freezing and the ground covered in frost again. It didn't take too long to make our way out of the trees, and when we finally crested the top edge of the last hill, I stopped dead in my tracks. A breathtaking scene of rolling land and more forested hills spreading far ahead of us came into view.

"Wow," I whispered.

Far below us green pastures, frosted with ice, rested in the cold sunlight of a winter morning. Several ponds of various sizes gleamed like shiny black pebbles in the distance, the mist rising from their surfaces reminding me of Yellowstone's hot springs. A narrow river twined out of the hills opposite us and meandered past the ponds and on through the valley and eastward. I had never seen such a beautiful sight in my life. Even the views from the Mesa in Arroyo Grande didn't come close.

I sighed again and warmed a bit when Cade took my hand once more.

"We usually have at least a light dusting of snow by now," he murmured, his breath misting in the air to match the fog. "I hope the frost will suffice."

I glanced up at him, feeling like I'd just awakened from some fantastic dream and my senses were still somewhere far away.

He smiled and gestured with his other hand.

I turned my head to see what he pointed at. This time I think I made some sound of surprise. I hadn't noticed it before, what with the mist acting as a screen, but several miles away on the opposite side of the shallow valley and nestled against those other hills, was an old castle like the ones pictured on travel brochures from Scotland or Ireland. The stone fortress looked mostly intact, but I got the impression that the far side might be caved in, for the tower appeared damaged.

I studied the ancient structure and when I narrowed my eyes just enough, I spied some movement behind it . . . A waterfall.

Something tickled my memory but I couldn't quite grasp it.

"That," Cade said, his voice holding a great deal of reverence, "is the castle I told you about the last time you were here."

"Oh, I remember. The one with all the dolmarehn, right?"

Cade grinned and nodded. "Exactly."

Then his tone took on a more cautious pitch. "We need to get a few things from the castle before we start out."

I ignored the change in his voice and instead asked, "Start out?"

"We're going on a journey Meghan."

I stared at him. "You know I have to be home by tomorrow night, right?"

Cade grinned. "It won't take us more than half a day to get to where we are going, and we won't stay too long. We'll use the dolmarehn."

I breathed a mental sigh of relief. "So, where are we going?"

"A few places, but first we'll head east and pay a visit to my foster father."

I shot Cade a look of horror. "The Dagda? You're taking me to visit the Dagda?! Are you sure you want him to meet me? I mean, shouldn't I stay away from all the Celtic gods and goddesses until I at least know how to use my power?"

Cade's smile turned soft and he shook his head.

"Oh no, I very much want you to meet him. Him and someone else."

Meet the Dagda? I shivered, a reaction to my sudden apprehension, and glanced back at the castle. I judged the distance across the small valley to be at least five miles, and with all these hills and rocks scattered everywhere, getting there quickly would prove a challenge.

"Won't it take us forever just to reach the castle?" I wondered aloud.

Cade smirked impishly. "Don't worry, I've got it covered."

Shrugging, I followed Cade as he started out on a trail leading down into the valley. Within half an hour the land leveled out and we were starting to cross the fields.

A white flash and a cheerful bark announced Fergus' arrival. He came loping up, panting and wagging his tail.

"Ah, here we go," Cade said, his attention on something other than his spirit guide.

I jerked my head up and followed his gaze and gaped when I saw the horse standing about a hundred yards away. He was solid black and his coat shimmered and gleamed in the sun. When he spotted Cade he threw back his head and whinnied, pushing himself up onto his hind legs and coming back down like a battering ram, tearing up the earth with his hooves.

I gasped and darted behind Cade. I had been around horses before, but they were the docile and stodgy old mares that people rented out at the dunes for an easy ride to the beach. This horse was a stallion and judging by his appearance, he might not be friendly.

Cade's laughter in the next breath managed to keep my fingernails from digging into his shoulders. He broke away from me and I cried out, thinking he planned on abandoning me. As I watched him, my mouth hung open in surprise. He ran right at the animal, crouched down as if he were playing a game of hide-and-seek with a child.

"Cade!" I hissed. "He'll kill you!"

The horse stopped twitching and held perfectly still. He faced away from Cade, but his ears flicked to the side, as if listening for an ambush. Cade quietly walked up behind him and to my utter horror, shoved him hard on the rump and then went tearing off across the field.

The stallion reacted almost simultaneously, turning sharply and taking off after Cade.

I cried out again, torn between chasing after him and fleeing back towards the hills to make myself less of a target.

The black stallion caught up with Cade and just as I was sure he was going to kick out with his front legs and knock Cade to the ground, he jumped in front of him and pressed his forehead against Cade's chest.

I waited for him to fall over, to scream in pain from the blow, but all he did was laugh. I blinked in confusion, shaking my head as I stared at them again. The horse had stopped moving, and Cade had hooked one arm over his thick neck.

"You caught me boy! I think that's a new record, huh?"

If my eyes grew any wider, I'm sure they'd fall right out of my head. What the *hell* just happened? Cade had enticed that demon of a horse to chase him, and had been moments from being trampled to death. Now he was petting the stallion like some enormous puppy seeking attention.

Cade finally glanced in my direction, the carefree smile on his face fading to a warm grin as he turned to the black stallion to whisper something in his ear. The animal shook out his mane and blew out a huff of breath, but walked alongside Cade as he came towards me. My first instinct told me to bolt. Sure, the horse liked him, but what if he didn't like me?

Unfortunately, Cade caught my eyes with his and something about their color warned me not to run away. They came to stand right in front of me, and it took every ounce of energy I had to keep still. The horse was even bigger close up, his shoulder level with my head. He was all strong, lean muscles and high-strung tension. I wouldn't be surprised if he suddenly burst into flame and singed us both. *It must be the magic of this place that makes him seem so powerful,* I thought to myself.

"Meghan."

Cade's voice nearly made me jump. "I want you to meet Speirling, my horse."

Ah, *his* horse. Of course.

"Um, hello, uh, Speirling."

I kept my hands clasped behind my back and my shoulders slumped forward. I hoped my stance exuded the aura of a docile prey animal.

Speirling blew out a hot breath and leaned his nose into my hair. I squealed in surprise, but he only smelled me. When he started to nibble at a loose strand I forgot about acting like a weakling and stepped back.

"Hey!"

Cade's laughter split through the air and Speirling eyed me curiously. If I didn't know any better, I'd have sworn the horse showed hurt feelings in those dark brown eyes of his.

"He's quite harmless, I assure you. Besides, he likes you, and that's high praise indeed."

I allowed myself to relax. The huge horse still made me feel uneasy, but if Cade said he wasn't dangerous, then I would trust him.

A bark and a shrill screech announced the return of our spirit guides.

"Now that introductions are over, I think we should be on our way."

I nodded and waited for Cade's next instruction. He turned his back to me and, grabbing a hold of Speirling's mane, launched himself onto the horse's back with one quick, agile move.

I gaped again. I was doing far too much of that today. Did he expect me to walk?

Once settled, Cade reached down and offered a hand to me. I only stared. He wasn't suggesting what I thought he was suggesting, was he?

"We'll make better time if we ride."

"What?" My question came out as a croak.

"Come on Meghan, I'll help you up safely."

"There's no saddle!"

"We don't need one."

"What am I going to hold on to?!"

Cade grinned and pulled back his arm, lifting the tuft of mane he had gripped in his other hand. He inclined his head downward and nodded at his knees. Okay, so I needed to cling on to a wild stallion using only my hands and legs? A sudden, sick image of all those poor little kids who get talked into riding sheep at the rodeo flashed across my mind. At least with the sheep they had loads of wool to hang on to. I was doomed if I got on Cade's horse.

Cade reached out his hand again. I hesitated.

"Trust me." His voice was calm, quiet.

And because I had no other choice, but more so because I was beyond smitten and my common sense fled whenever Cade stepped into the picture, I gripped his fingers and let him guide me up to sit in front of him.

"Oh, I forgot one other thing," he whispered into my ear. "*I'll* hold on to you as well."

Before my brain had a chance to over-analyze what he meant, Cade's free arm wrapped itself around my waist and he urged his horse into an easy trot, forcing me to forget about everything except keeping myself from falling off.

Cade didn't slow Speirling until we were just outside the entrance of the castle. The ancient fortress nestled neatly into a narrow canyon, and the creek running from the base of the waterfall circled around it like a moat. An old drawbridge lay open and Speirling's hooves thudded against the old wood as we crossed over the stream.

Once within the spacious stone courtyard, Cade slid off and helped me down. Fergus and Meridian followed after us and I spun around in order to admire the architecture. I had been correct in assuming part of the building was damaged, but not to a degree where the tower might crumble to pieces any time soon.

"Stay here Meghan, I'll be right back."

Before I could protest, Cade took off up some stairs and through a massive door. I wanted so badly to explore, but I didn't want to get lost either. He returned within ten minutes, carrying a couple of bags designed to be draped over a horse's back.

"Ready?" he asked with a grin.

I let the soft rumble of the waterfall fill the silence for a few moments. "I guess so."

Cade furrowed his brow. "You sound disappointed."

I winced. I hadn't meant to sound dismayed. "Well, I hoped to see more of the castle."

He smiled. "I haven't forgotten the promise I made to you last time. Today we go to the Dagda's and this afternoon we'll come back here to spend the night."

My eyes grew wide. "Really?"

"I promise," Cade vowed.

Once the bags were on Speirling's back, Cade climbed atop him and then helped me up again. As we crossed back over the drawbridge, I caught sight of the sun pulling free of the hills in the east. We were making great time.

Cade kicked his horse into an easy trot, and we started meandering our way up the hills behind the castle. The land lay dormant now, since it was still the dead of winter, but the bare branches of trees and shrubs promised to display leaves and flowers in only a few short months.

I closed my eyes and tried to imagine this beautiful place in the springtime. Grinning, I leaned back into Cade's comfortable embrace, but bolted upright when he released a small sigh, his arm tightening a bit.

My cheeks started to burn. That had been stupid. The only reason he'd been holding me was so I wouldn't fall off his horse.

I cleared my throat, deciding a conversation would help ease the awkward moment. "So, um, when will I be able to use my magic?"

Cauldron

Cade tensed as I regaled to him the incident with the faelah the other night and how Meridian had come to my rescue. Only after I assured him I hadn't been hurt did Cade relax.

"It's different for different people, and those with less magic than others sometimes can't ever properly use their glamour. But if you truly are half Fomorian like I believe, you will have more power than you'll know what to do with, when it's ready to be wielded."

His response only encouraged me to ask another question, one that had been fluttering around in the recesses of my mind since the beginning of summer.

"Cade," I said warily, "you told me, after the Morrigan attacked me last year, that you thought you knew who my parents were."

A long silence ensued and for a moment I wondered if I had asked the wrong question.

"Yes, I remember," Cade finally answered, his grip on me tightening again. "Unfortunately, I've been kept busy these past months, but I promise you Meghan, when I am entirely convinced of the truth, I will tell you."

I clenched my fists, fighting the odd desire to scream in irritation. It was perfectly clear he was withholding something from me, but frustrated as I may be, I didn't think I should press him. Taking a deep breath, I told myself to practice some patience and reminded myself that he *would* tell me. Some day.

We entered a small wood and I returned my thoughts to the present, contemplating what the Dagda might be like and wondering who else Cade wanted me to meet. What would *they* think of *me*? A Fae strayling, raised outside the Otherworld, without a clue as to how to behave or even function in Eilé. I was doomed.

Once we came clear of the trees, I spotted a massive dolmarehn at the top of a gently sloping hill. I gaped in trepidation, remembering the small ones on either side of the mortal world.

"It's huge!" I blurted.

Cade drew Speirling to a stop and nodded. "This one is meant to accommodate whole armies on the move."

I didn't like the sound of that, and I leaned closer to Cade as he led his horse between the massive stone columns. It seemed strange, not having blackness looming ahead, for I could see straight through the stone doorway and into the distance. On the other side I spotted more rolling land, barren of everything but mossy stones and grass.

The familiar sensation of passing through a dolmarehn tugged on my nerves, and before I took my next breath we were through. The scene looked almost the same, only the land rolled more smoothly and fewer trees grew here.

"By midday we'll reach the Dagda's house, if we can encourage Speirling to move at a brisker pace," Cade said.

I nodded, registering the uneasiness unfurling in my stomach again. I tightened my grasp on the stallion's mane as we galloped across the open plains, trying to ignore my anxiety.

A few hours later, our destination came into view. I had almost fallen asleep due to the boredom of being tossed around on a horse's back while staring at miles upon miles of empty landscape, but at least there had been great white patches of snow every now and again to break up the monotony of our journey. The sudden appearance of a family of steep hills, rising up out of the flatness like gopher mounds, caught my attention first. I blinked away my weariness, not sure if what I was seeing was an illusion. A thicket of trees curving off to the south and a plume of smoke rising from somewhere within those hills forced me to sit more upright on Speirling's back.

Ten minutes later we reached the base of the first hill. I assumed the smoke I'd seen came from a cabin, but if the Dagda lived here, wouldn't he have a much grander house than a cabin? I mean, he was one of the major deities of the Tuatha De Danaan, and the space between the hills seemed too narrow to accommodate a castle or a manor house. Maybe his abode was on the other side of the hills.

Meridian swooped down onto my shoulder and gave me a disconcerting glance.

Inside hill, she sent.

What?

Smoke. Inside hill.

I turned my gaze back to the hills, or rather, to the wide path meandering between them.

I looked up at Cade. "Meridian says the smoke is inside the hill."

He grinned in response, as if he knew some secret I didn't. Of course he did.

"The Dagda's home is actually within one of these hills."

I gave him my best expression of disbelief and he laughed, throwing up a hand in defense.

"If you'll allow me, I'll prove it to you."

I nodded and he moved Speirling forward.

We took the road between the hills and eventually it split, continuing in either direction around a huge mound

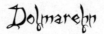

centered amongst them all. A wide ring of extra space surrounded this hill, as if the others had moved over to give the small mountain more breathing room. A heavy, carved wooden door stood slightly off center, built right into the hillside itself. And yes, several columns of smoke rose from narrow chimneys protruding from different places along the hill's sides.

Before I could ask any questions, Cade dismounted and walked up to the door, using the iron knocker to alert whoever might dwell inside of the presence of visitors. A minute passed, then another. Cade knocked again. I had been too busy gawking at the strange entrance and chimneys, that for a few heartbeats I forgot this was the Dagda's house and that I would soon meet one of the hero-gods of Celtic myth. When my moment of stupidity passed, my stomach took another plunge.

Finally, the door creaked open and a woman peered out, looking like she'd just crawled out of bed. She blinked wearily at Cade, and after taking in his entire form, her beautiful face broke into a wide grin.

"Caedehn! Oh sweetheart, what are you doing here?"

"Just dropping by for a visit, Alannah. Is my foster father in?"

Alannah huffed affectionately at him and cried, "Of course he is! Still in bed however, sleeping off a night of revelry, as usual!"

Cade smiled politely, then glanced in my direction.

Alannah followed his gaze and her clear green eyes grew wide with curiosity.

"Oh, now who might this be, young man?"

She had a light and teasing tone, but I tensed anyways. I didn't know her, and her raven-black hair reminded me of the Morrigan.

Cade lost his easy smile and he glanced over at me. "This is Meghan, the one I've told you about."

Alannah's eyes widened even further.

The one he'd told her about? I frowned in Cade's direction, but he wouldn't meet my eyes.

"Well, come in you two, we'll make breakfast!"

And with that, Cade stepped over and helped me off of Speirling's back as a young man emerged to lead the horse away. I watched as he guided the black horse around to the stables that were carved into the side of one of the smaller hills before following Cade and Alannah inside.

The interior of the Dagda's house was spacious, warm and in a rustic sort of way, cozy. Everything was wide open with several wooden beams and columns spread throughout. I found the brightness to be a welcome surprise, considering we were underground, but I grinned when I noticed a scattering of well-placed windows to help bring in sunlight. Smooth stone covered much of the floor and large rugs with intricate knot work designs helped add color. The place exuded luxury, but in a subtle way, reminding me of a mountain lodge in winter.

We hadn't moved beyond the main entrance hall when a powerful, boisterous voice filled the quiet atmosphere.

"Where is he? Where is that boy!"

Before I could so much as search for a proper hiding place, a huge man, dressed in a long embroidered robe worthy of a Renaissance Faire, came barreling down the hallway, followed by a retinue of women and wolfhounds.

I gaped, my eyes growing wide with surprise. The man stood even taller than Cade and had twice his bulk. No, not pudgy as I'd pictured him, but strong and solid, like a warrior recently retired from battle. His strawberry blond hair and beard contained a dusting of white, making me imagine he was in his mid-fifties. However, my knowledge of the Celtic legends suggested he was much, much older.

His pale blue eyes scanned the cavernous room until they fell upon Cade.

His slight frown changed immediately to a grin and those eyes, so full of intelligence and wisdom, brightened and almost turned gold.

"Caedehn! Why in all of Eilé has it taken you so long to come visit me?"

He flung open his arms and moved towards Cade, half tripping over his dogs on the way.

Panicking, I took a step back right before the Dagda wrapped Cade in a bear hug. If I wasn't so terrified of this overwhelming person I would have laughed at the whole scene.

The Dagda set Cade down and they started talking animatedly in that ancient language I didn't know. I had a strange inclination they discussed me, especially when the Dagda's eyebrows shot up and he cast me a curious glance. His eyes softened and he smiled once more. Now I understand why he had such a reputation for being a lady's man. I could almost feel the charisma pouring off of him.

"So, this is the Meghan you've written about."

He crossed his arms and examined me from head to toe. I stood still, too nervous to even breathe. He said something more to Cade, once again in their archaic language.

He nodded once and shifted his bright blue eyes on me while offering his hand. "I'm so very glad to meet you, young lady. Cade had nothing but wonderful things to say about you in his letters."

I took his hand warily and he gave me a firm handshake.

"Now," the Dagda stood up straight again, clapping his hands together, "anyone hungry for breakfast?"

In half an hour's time we were all seated in a roomy kitchen in which three of the walls consisted entirely of windows, giving us a view of the close hills on one side and a small lake in the distance on the other. I gazed around in wonder at all the pots and pans, wall hangings and herbs that decorated the space in a well-organized mess.

"Normally we eat in the dining room," the Dagda said with a roll of his eyes, "but since it is just family, the kitchen is more appropriate. Seems like the proper place to eat, in my opinion."

I glanced up only to find him smiling kindly at me. I darted my eyes towards Cade. He busied himself with studying his cup of tea. Family? Was I considered family? Because I was with Cade? Perhaps the Dagda had a different notion of the word, since Alannah and the other women had silently joined us as well.

At the end of breakfast, Cade asked his foster father about his cauldron.

"My Cauldron?" the Dagda replied in surprise.

"Yes, I hoped Meghan might get a chance to see it since she is just becoming familiar with her own magic."

The Dagda's eyebrows rose even further, then he grinned. "Of course! Come on, this way! Now mind you, I haven't used my dear Cauldron in centuries, so it may take some effort to coax the magic back to life."

I gave Cade a questioning look, but he merely grabbed my hand and grinned as he pulled me after the Dagda down a long hallway. At the end we took a set of stone stairs leading into a deep basement. We seemed to descend for miles before we came to an old door someone might find in a castle dungeon.

The Dagda grumbled as he fiddled with a set of keys, using five of them to unlock the door. The room we stepped into gave me the heebie-jeebies. Damp, stone walls surrounded us and a smell of dankness crept up my nose. Old torches, hanging in iron sconces, burst into flame as we passed, and I suspected magic was involved because the little pinprick near my heart flared with each flame burst.

Finally, we stopped in front of a huge kettle a little larger than a hot tub. Torches stood around the Dagda's prized possession as well, and as I got over the uncomfortable sensation of being in an underground dungeon, I took a moment to study it. The massive vessel appeared to be made of a dark bronze material, the sides decorated with several images I recognized from my books on Celtic lore.

"This is the Cauldron I used in the battle against the Fomorians so long ago." The Dagda patted a curved side affectionately, causing a low, chilling ring to shudder throughout the room. "So many lives restored because of its priceless power."

"Can I touch it?" I asked, surprised at my own bravado.

The Dagda smiled and nodded. "See if you can detect its magic."

Cauldron

Taking a deep breath I glanced at Cade. He nodded, his expression clear of any emotion. Tentatively, I reached out my hand and brushed my fingers over the cold metal. A flash of power shot up my arm and joined the speck of magic next to my heart. I hissed and drew my arm back, but the sensation hadn't hurt.

"Try again," the Dagda insisted, pressing his hand to the Cauldron and closing his eyes.

I did what he said, Cade as well. This time I pressed the flat of my palm against the metal and my mind became flooded with the images of the past. Epic battles and feasts had been supplied by this Cauldron. It had been used to bring the dead back to life and to cook a meal to feed thousands. The magic surging through the ancient vessel was exhilarating, and by the time I pulled my hand away, that power had a name: life. The Dagda's Cauldron contained the power of life.

I wobbled a little when I took a step back, Cade catching my arms so I wouldn't fall.

"Careful Meghan, the Cauldron can do that to you."

A smile lingered in his voice but I was too overwhelmed to respond, and the slight ache in the spot where my magic lay hidden was a bit distracting.

We left the dark basement several minutes later, all of us a bit humbled by what the Cauldron had revealed. Okay, maybe *I* was humbled, but my male companions were most likely just staying silent for my sake.

Alannah met us at the top of the staircase, her pretty face sporting a frown when she spotted me.

"What did you do to the girl?" she insisted as she pulled me away from Cade's supporting arms.

For a few moments, he didn't loosen his grip. Was Cade reluctant to let me go?

"She wanted to see my Cauldron!" The Dagda sounded defensive.

Alannah's eyes grew huge. "The Cauldron! Dagda, you know what kind of magic that toy of yours holds!"

The Dagda blustered, and I almost giggled.

"*Toy?* My Cauldron is *not* a toy!"

He sounded more insulted than angry, so I shook my head and pulled away from Alannah.

She protested, but I managed to find my voice. "No, I'm okay now, I promise."

We moved into the hall and Cade gazed towards the door. The Dagda, who had been grumbling about women and their fussing, recognized Cade's glances. His slight irritation melted away and his shoulders slumped.

"Don't tell me you have to be going already!"

Cade cringed a little. "I'm sorry, but Meghan still lives in the mortal world with her family. They'll notice if she's gone longer than a couple of days and I want to show her one more place before she returns to them."

Sighing hugely, the Dagda gestured in the direction of the entrance and called out, "Brennan! Come fetch my foster son's horse. He is leaving me and taking this wonderful girl with him."

A smile tugged at the corners of my mouth, despite the Dagda's woeful tone. I found comfort in knowing my presence would be missed.

All of the Dagda's . . . girlfriends? (I still wondered about their relationship with him) bid us a warm farewell. Alannah actually gave me a hug and I felt myself warming up to her.

The Dagda himself walked us out. He embraced his foster son, slapping him on the back with such force I thought he might have cracked a few ribs.

"Don't stay away for too long this next time around."

Cade promised to visit again soon and when the young man from earlier led Speirling around the hill, he jumped up onto his back and waited for me to join him.

I turned to the Dagda one last time.

"It was really nice to meet you." I extended my arm for another handshake. "And thank you for showing me your Cauldron, it was beautiful." *And so full of wonderful magic.*

Instead of shaking my hand, Cade's foster father scooped me up into one of his intense hugs. I didn't even have time to suppress my squawk of surprise. Fortunately, he didn't seem to mind.

"Promise to visit me again Meghan dear. And if that boy should ever mistreat you, you are more than welcome to come live here."

He set me down and held on to my shoulders so I wouldn't collapse. His smile was infectious and he said, "I've always wanted a foster daughter."

Tears gathered in the corner of my eyes. He meant every word.

"I-I promise," I managed, returning his smile before I joined Cade.

Dolmarehn

As we made our way through the hills and out across the plains again, Cade asked me quietly, "So, what did you think of the Dagda?"

I contemplated that for a minute, but I had formed my opinion the second I first saw him. "He's wonderful Cade. You were lucky to have him as a foster father."

Cade's laugh danced through the air, adding to the glorious happiness and sense of belonging that suffused me.

"Yes, but don't you go falling under his spell. He is far too charming for his own good."

I grinned. After all, he *did* have a point.

Eleven

Wildren

Darkness had fallen by the time we reached the castle and the sound of the waterfall greeted us when we entered the courtyard. Cade caught me as I half-fell, half-slid off of Speirling's back.

"Sorry," I mumbled, slightly embarrassed.

"It was a long ride, no apology needed."

Cade waited until I steadied myself before letting go of me.

"Think you can manage climbing a few flights of stairs?" he asked. "The only functional rooms are on the third floor."

I nodded sleepily. Tired or not, I could walk up stairs.

Cade inclined his head, then turned and whispered something to Speirling, slapping him lightly on the rump after removing the bags from his back.

"This way," Cade said, climbing the short staircase below the castle's entrance.

He pushed on an iron ring and the door swung open with a slight creek. Pitch blackness and a bone-deep chill greeted us inside. Cade picked up a torch, lit the top, and started leading me through the grand entrance hall and up the stairs to the upper stories.

Seeing clearly in the dark proved difficult, but as my eyes adjusted I noticed bare stone walls and beautiful architecture. I wondered what this place looked like when someone lived here; when the castle had been filled with furniture and tapestries. The pictures I built in my head made my skin tingle. How wonderful it must be to live in a castle.

By the time we reached the third floor, the chill had managed to seep into my bones. The rooms at the end of the hall appeared to be the most damaged and I caught a few glimpses of the white waterfall through a gaping hole in the back wall.

Cade stopped at the first door on the left. He opened it and then waited for me to walk in. Like the rest of the castle, the chamber was dark and cold, but I could make out a pile of wood next to a fireplace hidden in the shadows.

"This will be your room Meghan." His tone was somewhat careful.

I turned and arched an eyebrow at him. "You make it sound like this is your castle and your rooms to hand out."

I bit my cheek when I saw him flinch. Maybe I should have worded my thoughts in another way, but I found it strange that we were camping out in an abandoned castle. I mean, this place had to belong to someone, right?

Cade sighed and walked over to the fireplace. He added a few logs to the hearth and soon had a blaze going. I hadn't heard him strike a match, so I wondered if conjuring a flame might be another use for his glamour. Once the fire started blazing, the room became flooded with light and I gasped.

The apartment was gorgeous: two large, tall windows dominated the opposite wall and a carved, four poster bed took up the center of the room. A stuffed chair and a wardrobe occupied one corner and a thick carpet covered the floor. The colors were welcoming as well: pinks, greens and golds. Not overly feminine but soft enough to make the space pleasant.

"This is my castle, more or less," Cade said softly, still kneeling beside the fire.

I blinked away my admiration of the room and gaped at him in surprise.

"What do you mean, your castle?"

He took a breath and ran his fingers through his hair, standing up as if every joint in his body ached.

"It was left in my keeping."

I cleared my throat, then asked Cade the next obvious question, "Who left it to you?"

His gaze grew cold. "My mother, with the help of the Dagda."

Something about his tone warned me not to press further, so instead I asked him another question. "Why didn't you tell me this was your castle before? When we camped in the hills?"

He sighed and settled his hands loosely on his hips, dropping his gaze to the floor.

"I was a little embarrassed, to tell you the truth."

He glanced up and caught my surprised gaze. He gave a half grin. "I didn't want you to think less of me after coming to this place." His gesture was meant to include the whole castle, not just this room. "It's not exactly in pristine condition."

I simply stood and stared at him for a good thirty seconds. Was he serious? The slight reddening of his cheeks and the way he broke my gaze was answer enough. He *was* serious.

Swallowing back my own reluctance, I crossed the space between us and wrapped my arms around him and leaned my head against his chest. The hug was innocent, one I hoped showed my appreciation. Cade returned the embrace and seemed to relax.

"It's beautiful Cade, all of it," I said softly, breathing in his unique scent. I could so easily fall asleep leaning against him, and I almost did.

"That is why I took so long to contact you after . . ." he let his words trail off. I knew what he was referring to, but I didn't press him. Bringing up the awkwardness of what had happened when we had camped on the hillside would only ruin this moment.

He took a deep breath. "I wanted to make up for my behavior and ensure you had a decent place to stay when you came to visit Eilé. So I spent the last several weeks preparing this room for you."

I jerked my head up and pulled away from his embrace.

"Cade! You didn't have to do that!"

He nodded slowly. "Yes, I did."

A long silence spread between us and Cade got a strange look on his face again, the one that made my heart flutter and my stomach twist into knots. A log crashed in the fireplace and sent a flurry of sparks up the chimney, breaking the spell.

"I had better leave you then. I know you're very tired. If you need anything at all, I'll be in the chamber across the hall and two doors down. Your bag is in the bathroom through that door." Cade pointed to a door I hadn't observed earlier.

"Goodnight Meghan."

He moved silently through the room, pulling the door shut as he left.

"Goodnight Cade," I whispered to the emptiness.

I woke up to the sound of something scratching against the window. Grumbling, I rolled over in bed, luxuriating in the thick, warm sheets.

I ignored the noise until a single thought pierced through my mind: *OPEN!*

I bolted upright and blinked the sleep out of my eyes. Early morning light flooded the room and yesterday's memories came hurtling back. The Dagda, the Cauldron, Cade's castle . . .

OPEN!

I jerked my head towards one of the tall windows, barely making out the fluttering of white feathers through the frost-encrusted glass.

Meridian!

I threw the sheets back and scurried to the bay window, hissing when my bare feet left the carpet and hit the cold stone floor. I had to climb up onto a stone bench to get it open. I flipped the latch and pushed, and a very disgruntled Meridian tumbled in.

Ice, she sent. *Outside, all night.*

She flew over to the fireplace and fluffed her feathers.

Dolmarehn

A pang of guilt hit me. I'd been so distracted by the castle last evening that I'd forgotten to call her in. I walked over and stoked the embers, hoping they'd offer her some heat.

I'm sorry girl, I sent.

Her psychic voice grumbled but soon the tremors stopped.

While Meridian warmed herself by the fire, I returned to the window and gazed out. My mouth dropped open when I noticed the snow on the ground, not much, but enough to paint the landscape white. The view from this spot was wonderful: a slight glimpse of the rolling farmlands, grey forest and silver creek flowing below.

A soft knock at the door made me squeak and bolt away from the view outside.

"Meghan, may I come in?"

Cade, of course.

"Uh, just a moment!"

I quickly shut the window and threw a sweatshirt on over the camisole I'd worn to bed. I was just glad I had flannel pants on instead of something more revealing. I opened the door to find Cade, wearing his traveling clothes.

"Oh," I said, feeling somewhat foolish, "is it time to go?"

"I thought I'd get dressed first, and while you're getting ready I'll fix us something to eat."

"Okay, I can be ready in fifteen minutes."

I smiled and closed the door, rushing to get ready. I rummaged through my backpack and found my spare set of clothes. I brushed my hair and teeth in the bathroom Cade had pointed out the night before. To my delight, it appeared the

Otherworld, although lacking many of the technological advances of the mortal world, did have something akin to modern day plumbing.

After I was finished, I quickly made the bed and coaxed a much warmer Meridian onto my shoulder. The fire had nearly burned out, so I left it. Sighing, I peered around the room once more, secretly hoping one day I'd come back.

Cade met me the moment I stepped into the hallway and handed me a granola bar. Shrugging, I took a bite and soon realized I was ravenous. The bar was delicious.

Instead of heading back downstairs, Cade led me to the end of the hall. I followed him over a small stone wall, well, what used to be the back outer wall of the castle but had since caved in, and out onto a wide patio built up against the hillside.

I blinked at the morning sunlight and turned to glance at the waterfall, frothing white and misty in the near distance.

Before I had a chance to take in the sounds and colors of this marvelous place, Cade tugged me further along, heading for the edge of the terrace. A set of stone steps led down into the side of the canyon and to the mouth of a . . . cave?

I gave Cade one of my uncertain looks.

"We need to use one of the dolmarehn in the caves," he said.

"Oh, right. Uh, where are we going exactly?"

I hoped he didn't plan on dragging me to another dimension. He had said that some of them led to other realms besides the mortal and Otherworldly ones.

He grinned. "You'll see."

He let go of my hand and began walking down the stairs. Fergus, who I hadn't seen arrive, barked once and leapt after his master. Meridian's claws dug into my shoulder. Together, we followed Cade and Fergus. I stepped onto the small patio at the base of the steps and moved into the darkness of the cave. I reached out a hand to help guide my way and gasped when someone grabbed it and tugged me forward. I wanted to yell at Cade for scaring me half to death, but any words I might have spoken lodged themselves in my throat and I was sucked into the whirlwind of a dolmarehn's magic.

With Cade's help, I landed on my feet on the other side. I blinked and eyed my surroundings as Meridian took off, grumbling about the uncomfortable means of transportation. I found myself agreeing with her. That last trip had been rockier than the others.

I spun around, trying to become familiar with this new environment. Straight ahead of us a thick forest loomed, spreading far into the distance on either side of me. I glanced over my shoulder and my eyes grew wide. A huge lake, or the ocean maybe, stretched far across the land in the opposite direction of the forest. I couldn't tell where the shore ended on the other side and several small islands, bristling with pine trees, rose from the lake's surface like stepping stones. They, too, disappeared beyond my sight.

"Where are we?" I whispered in wide-eyed wonder.

Cade moved closer to me, and I sensed his warm presence at my back.

"We are on the edge of the Weald, and that is Lake Ohll, Eilé's largest lake."

"And where exactly are we going this time?" I asked, remembering Cade's mention of these places before.

Cade glanced over his shoulder at me, smiling. His eyes looked much greener here in this new place and I had to bite my lip to keep from sighing in appreciation. Why did he always have to look so beautiful?

"We are going to meet the Wildren."

Cade, oblivious to my inner turmoil, nodded towards the dark trees just in front of us as he took my hand once again and started leading me into the woods. I stumbled after him, his sure grip on my fingers the only thing keeping me from falling flat on my face.

"Really? The Wildren you told me about before?"

"Yes," he answered without turning around, "and one of them in particular."

Ah yes, the other person, besides the Dagda, he'd wanted me to meet. Who could it be?

"Um, is he as intimidating as the Dagda?" I pressed.

Cade turned around and grinned at me, not once breaking his stride.

"Oh, *she* is even more intimidating, I think. But I hope you'll like her."

I almost tripped. *She?* Why had his eyes glinted and why was he so eager for me to meet her? I gritted my teeth and continued after him, telling the jealous knot in the pit of my stomach to go away and mind its own business.

We walked for several more minutes, stepping over tree roots and around thick brush. I started picking up on the strange noises coming from places just beyond the trail, so I crept closer to Cade, clinging to his back. This seemed like the perfect place for unsavory faelah to lurk.

He turned and arched a brow.

"I thought I heard something," I hissed.

Cade smiled. "Most likely wood sprites and gnomes."

When he took in the expression of fear on my face, he added, "The docile kind."

I breathed a sigh of relief and banished the memory of the incident in the swamp with the non-docile kind from my mind.

We hiked for an hour, Fergus and Meridian scouting ahead and exploring on their own. The forest grew thicker the further in we went, and I began noticing the little creatures Cade had been talking about. Several were small, some only a few inches tall. Most of them resembled a gathering of twigs strung together in an oddly humanoid shape. They chattered to one another, but I got the impression the words they exchanged were pleasant ones. I liked them.

"Twigrins," Cade replied when I asked him what they were called.

I glanced up and spotted half a dozen of them peering at me from the side of a tree like wary squirrels, their round eyes large and curious. I smiled and they began chattering again, a sound which resembled rustling leaves and chirping birds. Their fingers were long and slender, for holding on to branches I assumed.

"In springtime," Cade murmured as we picked our way around the exposed roots of a huge fallen beech tree, "some of them will sprout flowers just like a fruit tree."

"You're kidding." I couldn't hide the delight in my voice. I hoped he spoke the truth. I'd like to see them that way someday.

He nodded his head, a smile gracing his face.

As he helped me over another large root clinging to the ground, the sound of a taut string being stretched to its limit cut through the almost silent air.

I froze when Cade's hand tightened on mine. Somehow, he managed to get himself between me and the base of the tree.

The hair on the back of my neck stood on end and I stopped breathing.

"Identify yourselves," someone said.

The voice was smooth and feminine, and I couldn't for the life of me decide where it had come from.

Cade stood up straight and said in a loud, clear voice, "Caedehn MacRoich of Eilé and Meghan Elam of the mortal world."

I held absolutely still, wondering if it would be enough to appease whoever had spoken.

A light rustling sound followed by a soft thud caused me to flinch. Only when Cade's tense stature melted away did I brave a look around him. There, fifty feet ahead of us on the trail, stood a tall young woman, a longbow clutched in her left hand. An arrow still rested against the string, but it sat easily upon her wrist. Her right hand was placed casually on her other hip and her weight was shifted to one leg. She looked like some forest bandit, what with her knee-high boots, leather pants, loose cotton shirt and thick leather jacket. A quiver of arrows strapped to her back completed the ensemble.

She stepped forward, a swagger to her walk, but her slow approach gave me a little time to finish studying her. The girl was beautiful with tanned skin and golden brown hair, curling away from her face like smoke. Her eyes were flickering between an intense pale grey and green. She smiled and the forest seemed to light up around her.

A few moments passed as Cade and this wild woman gazed at one another, and then, without warning, they both bolted forward and caught each other in a violent hug. The longbow clattered to the ground, temporarily forgotten. That's when I decided this must be the woman Cade had wanted me to meet.

Jealousy clawed at my heart again and I almost winced. What was wrong with me? I wasn't *that* girl, the one who drooled after a guy and treated any other female acquaintance like some evil enemy. That was Michaela and her gang. Not me.

I continued to watch their joyful reunion from the lower section of the trail in silence, the envious feeling in my stomach intensifying when I realized they were smiling and laughing with affection. *No! Stop it Meghan!* But I couldn't help it; apparently I no longer had any control over my emotions.

They eventually released each other and the girl punched Cade on the arm. Hard.

"Why haven't you come to visit, you great buffoon!"

I gaped, my burning resentment evaporating instantly. Huh?

Cade rubbed the spot on his arm where she'd hit him and grinned sheepishly. "I've been busy."

The girl wrinkled her nose in irritation and crossed her arms. "Too busy to visit your own sister?"

My gasp must have been pretty loud, because both of them forgot their reunion and turned to consider me.

"Forgive me," Cade said in that voice he reserved for only calm situations. "Meghan, I would like you to meet my sister, Enorah. Enorah, this is Meghan."

Enorah grinned brightly and cast Cade a prodding glance, then strolled over to me, thrusting out her hand. "Glad to meet you."

She had a strong handshake and her eyes danced with mirth, so I did my best to match her good humor, secretly chastising myself. *His sister you dork, just his sister. Besides, it's not like you had any claim on him anyways.* I set my jaw and kicked my conscience to the curb.

After introductions were over, Enorah guided us further into the forest. A half an hour later, the trees became even denser and darker and I couldn't hear or see the Twigrins anymore. I pulled my arms close to my body as the trail descended and hit a pocket of cold air. Cade reached out and placed a hand on my shoulder, reminding me of his presence and in his own way, telling me not to worry. He had insisted on walking behind me while Enorah led.

Meridian dove from the canopy above, a white streak of graceful wing beats, and came to rest on my shoulder. She chittered affectionately and nibbled my collar before fluffing her feathers and tucking her beak beneath a wing. Looks like I was forgiven for leaving her out in the snow all night.

We walked for what seemed like hours, Enorah leading us silently onward. I used the time to study her, noting that the only thing she appeared to have in common with Cade was his height and athletic build. But unlike Cade, who had a talent for going unnoticed if he wished, Enorah seemed to stand out like a beacon. Despite her quiet way of moving over thick tree roots or around massive boulders or through shallow streams, she stood out. Perhaps it was their magic, their glamour that set them apart. Maybe a Faelorehn's power was as unique as each individual and it radiated beyond them, unseen but obvious in how the world viewed them. I shook my head, not sure if my last thought even made sense.

"Almost there," Enorah said as she flashed a dazzling smile over her shoulder.

We'd been traveling in silence for so long I hadn't noticed that the trees had grown sparser, still huge but with room to run between them. The trail flattened out and stretched crossed a wide clearing, and in the middle of that clearing there stood several crudely built cabins. Smoke curled from stone chimneys and the laughter of children and the trickle of water somewhere in the distance reached my ears.

"Welcome to my home!"

Enorah clapped me on the shoulder with enthusiasm. I nearly staggered, but manage to keep my balance.

Several children, ranging in age from four to their late teens, came rushing out as Enorah let loose a harsh whistle.

I froze and felt Cade move in closer to me. I counted forty to fifty people in all, plus Enorah and about a dozen adults.

"Everyone, you remember my brother Caedehn?"

Enorah then turned and gestured to me. "This is his friend, Meghan. They've come to visit us for the day. Meghan, these are the Wildren, the wild children of Eilé."

Suddenly, several pairs of eyes were trained on me. I tried to hide behind Cade, but he drew me to his side and held me there. Eventually, I glanced at those who were watching me. No one smiled. Their faces were grim and dirty, and their changeable eyes seemed haunted. *Unwanted.* I frowned as I remembered what Cade had told me about the Wildren. My unease was immediately replaced with pity. These poor things.

One girl in particular stood out. She couldn't be any older than my own brother, Aiden. Her hair was the brilliant copper-red of autumn leaves and her huge eyes, a clear, pale hazel brown, flashed gold when I caught her gaze. She was holding an older girl's hand, and as soon as our gazes met, she whimpered and turned her face into her friend's skirts.

Enorah scooped up the little redhead and gave her a raspberry on the cheek. The girl seemed to forget her shyness and giggled, hugging Enorah around the neck.

"Now Tegan, I'm going to show our guests around, but you can join us later for the afternoon meal."

Enorah passed Tegan off to someone else and presented us with a guilty look. "I would offer you something to eat, but I'm afraid we are too late for the midday meal."

Cade assured her we'd brought our own food just in case.

The next few hours passed rather pleasantly as Enorah gave us a tour of their little community. Everyone had a task or chore, and she told us they managed quite well, considering they had no parents to care for them or guide them.

As we wandered from one place to the next, I took the time to study Cade's sister further. A sister. Why hadn't he told me? And why was she here and not at the castle with him? I tucked these thoughts away to ask him another day, when I had the courage.

After our tour, Enorah led us to the communal fire in the center of their small forest town. We sat down on logs and a few of the children came over, carrying pitchers and mugs. As they went skittering off, squealing in delight, she poured the liquid into the cups and passed them around. I took a sip of the cool, sweet drink and my eyebrows rose in surprise. It tasted like jasmine tea, but somehow better.

Enorah lifted her mug in a salute, grinning from ear to ear. Cade and I mimicked her.

"So, how long can the two of you stay?" Enorah asked after taking a drink from her cup.

Cade glanced at me and I said, "As long as I'm home before eleven tonight, my parents shouldn't worry."

He nodded before turning back to his sister. "We can stay for maybe an hour more."

She frowned in disappointment and set her cup down. I got the impression she wanted to ask me something, but all she did was lean back against her log and give Cade a long, meaningful examination. After a while, she grinned, inclined her head and took a deep breath. I wondered what silent conversation had passed between them, but Enorah started to speak, "Would you like to hear a story Meghan?"

"Uh, sure," I said, wondering where this new conversation might be headed.

"I was fourteen when Cade first came to us, did he tell you that?"

I shook my head, mildly surprised. There was a lot Cade hadn't told me, but I had no idea he had been with the Wildren before becoming the Dagda's foster son.

Enorah grinned and continued with her story. "There is an old hermit who lives on the edge of the woods in the hills, a retired Druid I believe, who is always bringing us news from outside the Weald. One foggy morning, I went out hunting along the fringes of the forest with a small group and the hermit stumbled upon us, holding a great big bundle of cloth in his arms."

"Not *that* big," Cade muttered into his mug in mock insult.

Enorah cast him a sharp glance, her eyes glittering in the firelight. "It was huge. In fact, I remember this clearly; I thought he had brought us a boar for our supper."

Cade snorted, but I ignored him, grinning at the sibling teasing going on between them.

"When I glanced down into the bundle, I saw the biggest pair of shimmery green eyes staring back at me."

The teasing vanished and affection colored her words. I smiled warmly.

"I knew he was my brother. It's those eyes, you know? Same as mine."

I squinted across the fire. Twilight hadn't fully descended on us yet, but I still found it difficult to see, what with the smoke from the fire obscuring everything. But she was right; something about her eyes did match Cade's.

"But why were you here," I asked, taking another drink from my cup, "and why was he brought to you? Wouldn't your parents want to keep you together?"

My question was met with silence. Enorah gave Cade a long, hard stare, revealing no emotion. Eventually, she picked up a log and fed it to the flames.

"We don't have the same parents. Well, we don't have the same mother," she answered as she curled her fingers around her mug, staring into the fire as if waiting to be sucked in.

"Oh," I said, feeling foolish and worried I had drudged up some past ghosts that wished to stay buried. "I'm sorry."

Enorah took a deep breath and sat up and glanced at Cade, then me. She smiled a little and I felt a bit better, but I expected story time was over.

"Don't worry about it. Now," she piped, downing the last drops of her drink before placing the mug firmly on the ground, "you have some rather interesting eyes yourself Meghan. How rapidly their color changes, especially when you are looking at my brother."

I had been taking a sip of the drink, trying to think of a way out of the awkward mood my question had put everyone in, but I'm sure I ended up inhaling most of it. I coughed a few times and Cade put his hand on my back. I could sense his tension through his touch, making my cheeks flame even worse. Thank the gods of the Celts the sky had finally grown darker. And that we sat close to the fire so I could blame my blush on the heat.

I glanced up at Enorah over the hand I held up to my mouth. She leaned further against her log, arms and ankles crossed in a casual warrior's repose, her eyes sparkling with mischief with one eyebrow quirked in amusement.

A knowing grin crept across her face and I clenched my teeth. Was I really so obvious? Did Cade know how I mooned over him? I suppressed a groan as my face grew hot again.

Before any of us was forced to come up with a face-saving comment to fill the silence, Tegan, the little red-headed girl from earlier, bounced up from out of the dark, squealing in fright.

Enorah's enjoyment of my predicament soon vanished as she scooped the little girl up into her arms.

"Hush now Tegan, what's amiss?"

Her voice, etched with concern, softened as she soothed the child. I soon forgot about my annoyance at her. She was genuinely concerned for the toddler. Enorah held the girl close, stroking her curly hair and crooning in her ear.

"Nigh'mare," Tegan mumbled wetly into Enorah's shoulder.

"Oh, those can't hurt you dear one! Especially not when my brother Caedehn is here, with his mighty spirit guide to keep watch over us."

Fergus, who had taken refuge next to his master, cropped one ear forward and lifted his head, panting as if agreeing with Enorah's claim. That seemed to comfort the small girl and soon her breathing deepened as she fell fast asleep in her guardian's arms.

Enorah glanced up at us, an expression of worry in her deep eyes.

"We found her, not far from here, wandering in the middle of the night a few months ago. She didn't have a stitch of clothing on her, and the look in her eyes . . ."

Enorah shivered and so did I. *I* had been found wandering and without clothes . . . Cade inched closer and I realized he'd never taken his hand off my back, but instead had moved it so his fingers rested just above my hip. I shuddered again.

"She had been sleep walking, and for days afterwards she wouldn't speak. She would only stare off into the distance with wild, haunted eyes. Finally, after the first week, she started to look at us and actually see us. She's had nightmares ever since."

"Perhaps we should take our leave. I'm afraid our presence might have stirred up too much excitement," Cade murmured softly.

Enorah cast him a sad gaze and nodded once, her lips drawn tightly together.

We all rose, Enorah still holding the girl close. She stepped forward, and with her free arm she gave her brother another fierce hug.

"Stay safe," she said harshly, tears forming in her eyes.

"Meghan," she turned to me and surprised me with a hug as well, "it was a pleasure to meet you."

Then she added, just loud enough for only me to hear her, "Keep an eye on my brother, huh?"

She winked and I blushed again.

"I'll do my best," I managed.

Enorah readjusted Tegan in her arms then said, "I'll assign you an escort to guide you to the edge of the forest. The day grows late and I can't promise the Morrigan's faelah won't be trying their luck tonight."

I gave Cade a horrified look, but when he nodded to Fergus I began to relax, but only a little. Fifteen minutes later the nighttime fires of the woodland village were no longer in sight and we were making our way through the thick undergrowth of the Weald. Full dark had set in by now, but the moon shone bright and those who guided us carried torches. Three young men, all about my age, and two older women made sure we didn't come to any harm along the way.

Once we reached the edge of the forest, we thanked our companions and slipped silently through the dolmarehn. The castle greeted us with cold darkness once again, but it had grown familiar to me. I grabbed my overnight bag as I slipped out, sweeping my eyes over the dark room one last time. Speirling met us on the other side of the drawbridge and I almost didn't notice his black shape against the twilight sky.

The ride back to the dolmarehn put my nerves on edge, and I half expected to be attacked by faelah along the way. I found it mildly amusing, however, that the Morrigan only seemed to send her minions after me in the mortal world and not here in Eilé. Perhaps she didn't know about my visits or thought I was weaker in the realm where I grew up.

I shuddered and forced those thoughts from my mind. Cade held me more closely, tucking the cloak he had lent me around my body.

"Almost home, Meghan," he whispered.

I grinned and allowed myself to drift off a little, thinking about the last two days and what I'd learned, both concerning myself and my new friends here in Eilé. *No Cade, you're wrong,* I thought as Speirling climbed the final hill before we reached the dolmarehn, *I think I'm already home . . .*

Twelve

Heritage

Before disappearing back into the dark forest behind my house, Cade told me he probably wouldn't be able to visit again for at least a month, but for some reason that didn't bother me. Perhaps it was because this most recent trip to the Otherworld had us parting on good terms. Or maybe it had something to do with the way he held on to my hand much longer than usual when saying goodbye before I took those last few steps into my backyard. I couldn't say for sure, but I liked the feeling that spread through me when I thought about Cade. I no longer suffered from a depressed, aching craving for him, but instead I anticipated seeing him again.

I wondered if school and my friends had an effect on my mood as well. We were facing down our final semester as seniors and Tully, Robyn, Will and Thomas were eager to take advantage of every opportunity to celebrate our dwindling high school days, including senior prom.

In the past, I would have shuddered at the prospect of going to prom, but Robyn, in her usual fashion, insisted we all go together as a group. I thought that was a great idea, until she turned to me and murmured, "Unless one of us has a special someone they want to bring along."

I shot her a bedraggled expression but all she did was waggle her eyebrows at me. Then again, why shouldn't I ask Cade to prom? We were friends, right? Would he even want to go to something so frivolous as a senior dance in the mortal world? At least I had several weeks to work up the courage to ask him.

I spent the month of February wondering about what my life would be like after high school. With everyone talking about graduation and their intended colleges, the subject was hard to avoid. I had no desire to discuss the future with my classmates because mine had already started heading down an entirely different path from theirs. They were planning for a life here on earth; I passed my days conjecturing whether the Morrigan wanted to kill me before or after I had a chance to graduate, and what opportunities awaited me if she didn't. And the more I thought about my future, the more it dawned upon me: I needed to be in the Otherworld with the other Faelorehn.

The idea of living in Eilé thrilled me and terrified me at the same time. I would be leaving my family, my friends, a world I'd grown comfortable with, a world that I understood. But I didn't belong here. I knew that for certain now, and telling them about my true identity and what my plans were . . . ? Such terrifying musings gave me a headache. At least I had until the end of May to figure it all out.

◎ ◎ ◎

During the second week of March, while still attempting to balance the needs of my friends with the conundrum of returning to the Otherworld after I graduated, I received a message from Cade. I woke up to find Fergus standing outside my sliding glass door so I followed him, hoping his master would be waiting for me. I tried to dampen the disappointment that arose when he stopped at the oak tree, but my hopes lifted when I read the note I found there.

Meghan,

I'm sorry I haven't been able to speak with you since January, but I was wondering if you would meet me after school today down in the swamp. I'll wait for you, but if you made other plans please leave me a note informing me when you can get a free moment. I have something rather important to tell you.

-Cade

My heart fluttered and a flush crept up my neck as I leaned against the tree. For some reason my legs refused to support me. All those wonderful moments from my last visit to Eilé went flashing through my mind: all the long, lingering glances, the times he held my hand a bit longer than necessary, the way his voice softened when he spoke to me . . . Could it be possible he felt the same way I did? Perhaps asking him to prom wouldn't be so hard after all.

Of course, trudging through the school day proved nothing short of agonizing. Tully thought something was wrong with me and Robyn kept pulling me aside, asking me if everything was alright with Cade. I practically ran the entire way to the swamp after my last class.

The object of my obsession, in his familiar, calm way, stood beside one of the tall eucalyptus trees, but something about his stance was off. He stood more rigid, more formal than usual. And his eyes . . . they seemed wrong somehow, and not just in a color-shifting, Faelorehn sense either.

"Meghan," he began, his voice clipped, "is there any way you could get away for more than two days?"

I had been expecting something completely different from him and this stiff, distant Cade reminded me too much of the time right before the Morrigan lured me into the Otherworld.

"Uh," I answered nervously, "I'm not sure, why?"

"Would you be interested in meeting your mother? Your Faelorehn mother?"

My heart stopped for a good minute. My Faelorehn mother? The woman who had sent me off to the mortal world, barely old enough to form memories? The one I'd wondered about, in the back of my mind, since learning where I'd come from? Did I want to meet her? No. Yes!

I must have stayed silent for too long. Either that or the look on my face was a daunting one, because Cade shifted into a defensive stance.

"Y-you found her?" I finally managed before blurting, "Yes, yes I would like to meet her."

A sudden, overwhelming thrill jolted through me, starting right beside my heart. I forgot about Cade's strange aura and focused on this new information. To finally learn about my heritage . . .

Despite my joy, however, I was also terrified. What if my mother had cast me aside after my birth because she had been appalled by me? I rubbed the spot where my glamour warmed me, frowning. Cade had told me I had a great deal of power and sometimes it took longer for such a sizeable amount of glamour to fully awaken. But what if he was wrong? What if she'd known this from the beginning? What if the reason she hadn't kept me had something to do with my lack of magic?

"There is a dolmarehn in a small town a few miles away from the castle that will cut the trip down to only an hour or so," Cade said, breaking into my thoughts, "but I thought you might want to spend some time with her."

"Sorry?" I said, still overwhelmed by his news.

He smiled, a cold, polite quirk of the lips. "I think three or four nights should suffice, don't you?"

"Oh, right, um . . ."

How was I going to disappear for three nights? A sudden thought popped into my head. Robyn's parents were going on a camping trip to Yosemite with their church group over spring break and Robyn planned on going with them. She had invited all of us: me, Tully, Thomas and Will, to go, but we had all declined for one reason or another.

I must have let my mind wander for a few minutes because Cade cleared his throat next to me.

"Sorry," I muttered, "I was thinking. Robyn invited me to go camping next week. Do you think it'll be enough time to inform my mother I'm coming to visit?"

It was so odd saying that word, *mother*, when not referring to my own mom. But I'd always known I'd been adopted, and I knew someday I would like to meet my birth parents. My skin prickled with goose bumps. Apparently that someday had finally arrived.

"That would be perfect," Cade said. "I'll meet you in front of the oak tree on the equestrian path next Monday morning?"

I started to nod my head before thinking everything through.

"No, wait," I blurted. "I need to talk to Robyn first, make sure she can cover for me since this is longer than usual. And then we'll have to make it look like I'm really going with her."

I grimaced. This would be tricky. Not only did I have to persuade Robyn to lie for me again, but I had to convince my parents I was going on a camping trip. I'd be packing a bag for my extended trip to Eilé, so perhaps that wouldn't be too much of a problem, but either my Dad had to drive me to Robyn's or Robyn would need to pick me up . . . And worst of all, if Robyn agreed to this, she'd insist on a heavier price than the last few times. I blanched again. She would definitely be wanting more than the juicy details.

I sighed and glanced back up at Cade. "I'll talk to Robyn at school tomorrow and leave a message in the oak."

He nodded and headed towards the dolmarehn. I let my mind wander as I walked home. My mother, my *real* mother. Cade had finally found her, and like he promised, he was going to make sure I would know her as well. Only when my happiness at the whole situation started to wear off did I remember there had been something very wrong with the way Cade had shared his news.

@ @ @

Dad dropped me, my duffle bag and my sleeping bag off at Robyn's while the sky was still dark.

"Alright Meggy." He leaned over and kissed me on the cheek. "Have a wonderful trip."

I grinned and climbed out of his truck, waving goodbye as his tail lights disappeared around the corner. Taking a deep breath, I crept up to the stoop and tapped on her door. Robyn, groggy-eyed and mumbling, cracked the door open and stepped out into the cold morning wearing an old pair of sweats and a bathrobe.

I eyed her dubiously. "Nice outfit," I said with a smirk.

"Watch it sister," she grumbled, "I didn't want to get up two hours before everyone else so that you could engage in some week-long tryst with a boy I'm beginning to think is imaginary."

I would have been annoyed at her, but one didn't often get to enjoy observing Robyn out of her element. She clearly wasn't a morning person. Besides, she was doing me a *huge* favor.

Our plan had been a brilliant one and, in my opinion, seemed to be working out beautifully so far. Dad had already driven off, so now I just had to wait for Cade to pick me up before any of the other campers arrived. My parents would think I was in Yosemite for most of the week, a place where cell phone reception sometimes didn't exist, and Robyn's mom and dad wouldn't even know we had made the plans. Since my parents and her parents never spoke to each other, I didn't have to worry about Mom or Dad asking them if I'd been polite during the trip, either. And Robyn's demanded payment, though a bit terrifying, was something within my reach.

"So where's this lover boy of yours? It's freezing!" Robyn said through a yawn as she pulled her robe tighter.

The deep rumble of a car engine broke the morning silence and I smiled as a familiar black Trans Am, almost blending in with the still dark sky, came rolling up the street. I glanced at Robyn, only to laugh at the expression on her face. Her eyes had widened and she stood absolutely rigid.

The sports car pulled up in front of her driveway and Cade killed the engine. With the supernatural grace I always expected of him, he climbed out of the car and shut the door. He wore what he normally did when in the mortal world: a pair of designer jeans and this time a hooded sweatshirt. On any other guy the look wouldn't be that flattering. On Cade MacRoich, however . . . And the quiet, strangled sound that left Robyn's throat only proved my theory correct.

I turned my head and glanced down at her. I almost burst out laughing. She was standing there like some mushy preteen girl who had just seen her favorite movie star or musician walk by. Robyn. Speechless. The world must have stopped turning. I smirked. I bet she was regretting her bed-head and shabby bath robe right about now.

Cade stepped up with his hands in his pockets, an easy smile on his face. Robyn's front porch light provided plenty of illumination to give her a full view.

"Hello," he said once he was in front of us. He turned his dark eyes to Robyn, pulling a hand out of his pocket and offering it to my friend. "I'm Cade, you must be Robyn. It's nice to meet you."

Robyn remained motionless a good twenty seconds before taking the hand suspended in front of her. I half expected her to fall down in a faint when Cade's fingers touched hers.

"Are these your bags Meghan?" Cade asked while Robyn continued her staring contest with Cade's chest.

"Yes," I answered. My face was beginning to hurt from all the smiling I was doing.

As soon as Cade walked away carrying my stuff, I felt Robyn's fingers grab on to my arm with a vice-like grip.

"Holy crap!" she hissed breathlessly. "Meghan! Where on earth did you find *him*?! He's so freaking hot!"

My grin only widened. Perhaps this had been a good way to pay Robyn for her cover after all.

I picked up my small backpack and turned to head over to the passenger side door, kindly being held open by Cade. Before I took a single step, however, I twisted around and gave Robyn an impish grin.

"Actually Robyn," I said with a burst of smugness, "he found *me*."

And with those final words, I slipped into my seat. As we turned the car around in the cul-de-sac and headed back towards the Mesa, I imagined Robyn standing on her front porch, staring off into the early morning darkness like a ghost stuck in some other dimension.

"Your friend isn't much of a conversationalist, is she?"

Despite the growl of the Trans Am's engine, I caught the slight humor in Cade's voice.

"Actually, that's the first time in my life I've ever seen her docile."

"Huh, I wonder why."

Oh, I know *why* . . . I thought while Cade downshifted as we pulled out onto the highway. Best to keep that little tidbit to myself, though.

The warm, fuzzy delight of basking in Robyn's shock soon faded when I gave my companion a sidelong glance. His voice had held a little more of his usual easy humor this morning, but something still seemed off about his stance; a slight dullness to his eyes and a hint of sadness to his smile. The anxiety tugged at my stomach like an angler's fishhook. What was wrong with him?

We drove until we reached the last road leading down into the swamp. Cade pulled off onto the wide, dirt shoulder and turned the key in the ignition. I took a deep, shuddering breath as he got out of the car and walked over to open my door. I had forgotten our purpose for visiting Eilé this time, what with Robyn's reaction and Cade's odd behavior taking up most of the space in my mind, but now it hit me: I was going to Eilé to meet my mother. I had so many questions for her, questions I needed to know the answers to, questions I considered too terrifying to ask. Why had she sent me to the mortal world so long ago? Was it because she didn't want me? Because I was flawed? Did she cast me aside in order to protect me? And if that was the case, why had she not tried to find me herself after all these years? Why was Cade the one to set this all up?

I almost twisted my ankle on my climb out of the car. Luckily Cade managed to catch me.

"Are you alright?" he asked as he lifted me up by the elbow.

"Yeah, sorry," I grumbled, "just thinking."

"A dangerous activity, apparently."

I glared at him, but his grin warmed me and some of the rigidness finally left him.

Nevertheless, I crossed my arms and scowled. "It is when your thoughts are focused on meeting your real mother for the first time in your life."

Cade's smile faded, his eyes returning to a distant place once again.

He sighed and said in a voice almost too low for me to hear, "At least you haven't had the time to learn your only value to her is that of a tool to be used and disposed of."

"What?" I asked, losing a bit of my chagrin.

Cade cast me an apologetic look. "I'm sorry Meghan, don't pay any attention to me."

I took a breath. "Your mother has disappointed you?"

Ah, so this explained his behavior. I had never truly asked him about his real parents because the one time they'd been brought up in the Weald, Cade and his sister had clammed up and I didn't want to pry. Now I wondered if I should have asked him about his real parents long ago. In fact, I suddenly felt pretty selfish. Despite his perpetual silence on the matter, perhaps what he really needed was someone to talk to.

Cade took a deep breath, then his eyes darkened and his face adopted a frightening expression. I took a small step back.

"Yes. My mother's disappointed me on many occasions."

I forgot the slight fear his sudden dark mood created in me and, gathering up my courage, reached out to take his hand. He didn't pull away, but he didn't look up either. Cade didn't want to talk about it, not yet at least, so I smiled and squeezed the hand I held. He squeezed back with less enthusiasm than usual. My questions could wait for another day.

Heritage

Cade released my hand and gave me a reassuring grin before he got my bags out of the trunk. We descended into the swamp, turning right when we found the wide dirt path leading to the dolmarehn. The sky gradually turned gray with dawn, but a thick blanket of fog kept everything relatively quiet.

As we approached the small crevasse, I sent a mental call out to Meridian. I had let her out earlier, before Dad took me to Robyn's. Fergus waited for us at the cave's entrance, panting contentedly and giving us his usual canine grin.

We waited for Meridian, and when she arrived we all stepped through the dolmarehn. I had one last thought before becoming swept up by the magic of the Otherworld: *What will I do if my mother is disappointed in me?*

@ @ @

Once in Eilé, we made our way to the castle to gather Speirling, and this time a brown mare for me, before we headed out. Cade led the way over the drawbridge, turning south on the road leading towards the ponds I had spied from the hills those few months ago. The land remained dormant, but the snow had gone and the weather seemed a bit warmer, as if spring was only waiting for the right signal before stepping forth.

"There is a dolmarehn in Kellston, a small town located on a lakeshore beyond these hills. It will take us almost directly to Erintara," he said.

"Erintara?" I asked as I nudged my mare forward. She had a sweet temperament and behaved rather well for a horse, thank goodness.

He nodded, not catching my eye. "The place where your mother lives."

"Oh, is it a town?"

That grin again, this time accompanied by a glint in his green eyes. "It's a town of sorts, I suppose."

I narrowed my eyes. "What do you mean?"

Cade turned his face towards me. "You will see."

With those final words, he kicked Speirling into a quicker pace.

Grumbling, I encouraged the mare to do the same. Why did everything have to be such a big secret with him?

About forty minutes later, Kellston came sprawling into view. The town's residents bustled about, finishing up morning chores and reminding me a little of the bees who visited the lavender in our front yard. I couldn't help but smile at the scene. The only other gathering of people I'd observed in Eilé had been the Wildren of the Weald.

We led the horses down the main road that parted the center of town, and as we passed I noticed several booths draped in colorful fabrics and ribbons.

Cade must have sensed my curiosity because he leaned over and whispered next to my ear, "They are preparing for their spring festival. The event usually takes place midway between Imbolg and Beltaine."

Thanks to Robyn's obsession and my spending half of last summer pouring over the information I'd found on the Celts, I had a decent knowledge of the four major Celtic holidays: Imbolg, Beltaine, Lughnasadh and of course, Samhain.

"The spring fair is a time for young men to show off their skills in order to impress the young ladies."

Cade grinned and pointed over towards the lakeshore where a group of boys competed in a contest: discovering who could throw giant rocks the furthest, from what I could tell. Several girls stood around watching, clapping and giggling as the young men either cheered on their friends or teased them for their lack of skill.

I smiled. Not too different from high school in the mortal world, apparently.

"It's also the time for lovers to take part in the bonding ceremony."

I glanced in the opposite direction now and spotted a young man and woman in their best clothes standing side by side, a ring of friends and family gathering around them and singing a pleasant song. The participants performed a simple, woven dance around the couple and little girls wearing garlands streaming with ribbons threw flower petals.

A bonding ceremony? Ah yes, a *wedding*. An Otherworldly wedding. I followed the ritual for a few moments longer, smiling at the happy participants and arching a brow in interest when the bride and groom exchanged what appeared to be decorative bracelets instead of rings.

"And," Cade continued, his voice growing amused and taking on a slightly deeper tone, "if a young man should have the luck of having a beautiful lady by his side, he is obligated to be a good sport."

I choked on a gasp of surprise as Cade laced his fingers with mine, loosening my grip on the mare's reins. He lifted my arm up for all the curious eyes to view and drew my hand to his lips. The crowd gave a boisterous cheer, waving colorful ribbons and banners and brilliant bouquets of flowers. After kissing my hand, Cade continued to hold it as the shouts and suggestive whistles continued to follow us down the road.

I was mortified. Thrilled and mortified. What had Cade been trying to prove to these people when he had kissed my hand? Was he simply being a good sport as he claimed, or might his actions mean something else entirely?

I bit my cheek to keep from grinning like an idiot. *Stop Meghan, he only wanted to show the townspeople his appreciation for the holiday.* Yet, I couldn't help but wonder: might I be more than just friend to him?

Before we broke free of the town a boy and a girl, both wearing crowns of flowers and ivy, skipped up to us and presented us with garlands of our own. Cade accepted them, smiling down at the children. First, he set the ivy crown on his own head, then reached across the space between our two horses and placed the floral garland on my own.

I sat still, knowing the townspeople continued to scrutinize us. Cade took his time to settle the wreath, pulling the ribbons free of my hair. Once all the leaves and ribbons were to his liking, he lowered his hand but allowed his fingers to rest against my cheek. I suddenly found the act of breathing to be a challenge, and the sounds of Kellston faded from my hearing.

His hand lingered for several moments more, and when I worked up the nerve to meet his eyes, what I discovered there astounded me. His irises had changed again, but this time some gray shone through the green, as well as something else, something far beyond color alone . . . Sadness? Desire? Regret? And then it dawned upon me, what emotion lingered in those haunted eyes.

I knew that look, had seen *and* felt that look before, long ago when I was young. Bradley, Logan and I had been playing in the backyard when the neighbor's cat came strolling over, a newly hatched baby bird in his mouth. We managed to get the bird away from him and spent the day cleaning it up. We made a nest in an old shoe box and quickly fell in love with the hatchling. When Dad got home he told us the baby bird belonged with its mother, so he helped us find the nest and got the ladder out. My brothers and I watched as he gently placed the bird back in the nest. All three of us had a sad glimmer in our eyes by the time he climbed back down. It was as if our hearts had been torn out.

Eventually, my surroundings became real again and I could hear the people of Kellston getting back to their preparations. The noise seemed louder, the smells stronger, and the colors brighter.

"Come on Meghan," Cade said softly, his voice stiff as he let his hand drift from my face. "Let's get you to your mother."

Almost the exact words my dad had spoken those many years ago. The irony was so cold I actually shivered.

🌀 🌀 🌀

The dolmarehn acting as the gateway to Erintara lay at the base of the foothills across the tip of the lake. The trip from Kellston to the dolmarehn had only taken thirty minutes, but it seemed like hours. Cade remained silent the entire time, his shoulders tight and his seat in the saddle stiff. I sucked my bottom lip between my teeth. I couldn't be that baby bird to him. Yet, if I was, why did it mean he had to give me up? Would my mother, whoever she might be, take me in and not let me go again? I never considered that to be a possible scenario, but the longer I reflected on it the more nervous I became. Or perhaps I was reading too much into everything.

The dolmarehn on the far end of the lake was big enough for the horses to pass through, but Cade waited for me to catch up nonetheless.

The cold silence grated at me, and finally I had to say something if only to shatter the strained atmosphere. "Cade, who is my mother?"

He turned and gave me a haunted look again, yet remained silent.

Speirling stepped closer to the dolmarehn.

"You could at least tell me her name!" I shouted, allowing my irritation to pour free. I was tired of being left in the dark. Exactly what game did he play? Lead the poor, ignorant Fae strayling on a wild goose chase like a donkey chasing after a dangling carrot?

Cade and his horse disappeared beneath the shadow of the stone gateway and I entertained the thought of riding my mare back to the mortal world where I could brood in my anger and fear. Only when I registered Cade's voice whispering back an answer to my demand did I change my mind.

"Danua," he said. "Your mother's name is, Danua. The high queen of Eilé."

Thirteen

Danua

No. He was lying. My birth mother couldn't be a queen, let alone a high queen.

I sat motionless while a heavy dose of shock numbed my nerves. The brown mare cropped grass as I continued to stare into the stone portal set into the hillside, just like the one linking Eilé to the mortal world. No! If my mother was a queen, like Cade claimed, she would've found a way to keep me, unless she honestly didn't want me.

Taking a deep, shuddering breath, I nudged the mare forward. I'd come this far, I might as well go the entire way and get the answers I wanted, despite my frustration with Cade.

I found Cade and Speirling on the other side of the dolmarehn, both of them standing still and grave, as if expecting the dead to rise up all around them and drag them into the afterlife.

A deep sigh left me as I wiped at my cheeks and turned to study our surroundings. Yes, I'd let my emotions get the better of me, and I needed a moment to recover. Too bad the beautiful scenery didn't help. A massive lake spanned the distance in front of us, and behind us were more small mountains. A broad road stretched along the shore in either direction and to the east I spied the edge of a sprawling city with a glorious castle standing atop a centrally-located hill. My mouth dropped open and I forgot my worry, my lingering shock and brewing fear.

"Erintara," Cade murmured beside me.

I flinched, not realizing he'd guided Speirling closer to my mare.

"And this is the other side of Lake Ohll."

A long silence ensued where neither one of us spoke a single word.

Finally, Cade drew in a deep breath and said, his voice tinged with sorrow, "I'm so sorry Meghan, I should have told you sooner. I had my suspicions, that Danua might be your mother. Only recently, though, did I become convinced of the truth."

I nodded, the tears still spilling out, but there was something I needed to ask him.

"Why does it seem like I've heard that name before?" I asked quietly, my throat tight. An old memory perhaps?

Cade remained quiet for several moments before answering. "Because you *have* heard it before, a variation of it at least. The Danube River and the Tuatha De Danaan, the tribe of Danu . . . They were named for Danua, only, the Celts of the mortal world called her Danu."

A hard punch to my stomach would have been more welcoming at the moment. So not an old memory after all, but the name Danu had come up a few times during my research.

Of course, I had been pretty preoccupied studying the Morrigan at the time and for good reason.

"And I'm her daughter," I said out loud, my voice sounding disembodied.

"Meghan, I should have investigated sooner. I might've been able to tell you this months ago, if only I'd put more effort into it. But I didn't. I knew if I'd been right, that if Danua truly was your mother, it would mean I-"

He cut himself short and raked his hands through his hair, fighting some internal battle I wasn't permitted to be a part of.

What Cade? It would mean what? I wanted to scream.

"Come on," he finally murmured, "she is expecting us."

We reached the city a half an hour later, and if I hadn't been so distracted by what I had just learned, then I might've appreciated the spotless, paved streets, the towering trees lining the paths or the quaint little restaurants and shops with their brightly painted signs. Thoughts of a well-manicured theme park, without the swarming tourists of course, came to mind, especially when the sound of light, cheery music met my ears and the faint scent of sweet spices filled the air around us.

The castle rose up above the city on a little hill surrounded by trees and open space. The paved road leading up to the castle's entrance proved to be an easy walk for the horses, and when we reached the outer gate the guards let us pass without too many questions. Cade spoke to them in the language of Eilé, his voice never betraying his emotions, whatever those emotions might be.

Several stable hands in crisp uniforms took our horses and we were escorted into the castle by more guards. The palace, like the rest of the charming metropolis, was beautiful, the tall spires and stained glass windows making me think of fairytales and princesses. I grimaced at the thought as we crossed the enormous marble entrance hall. According to Cade I was one of those princesses, though I didn't feel like I belonged in a fairytale. Well, not a happy one.

"Her majesty is just finishing up with her diplomats. You may see her shortly."

I swallowed hard and Cade took my hand.

Fifteen agonizing minutes later, the tall doors opened up and a flurry of finely dressed men and women poured out, all chatting animatedly to one another. To my immense relief, they didn't notice Cade and me standing to the side.

"Her majesty will see you now," the guard from before acknowledged only me. I would be meeting with the queen alone.

My stomach fell to the floor, my frightened gaze searching Cade's. His smile was grim, but he nodded, giving my hand one last squeeze before unlacing his fingers from mine. The tears had long since dried up, but my broiling emotions made me unsteady on my feet. The guard led me into the vast room, yet I barely had time to take in the high vaulted ceiling and the magnificent dais at the end of the hall before my eyes locked on the woman sitting languidly in the throne far ahead of me. I caught my breath. My mother. Danua, Queen of Eilé.

"So," she said, her voice strong and commanding, "you are my long lost daughter."

It was a statement, not a question. All of a sudden the hall seemed to grow larger.

"I-I don't know," I answered carefully, my throat growing dry.

"What name did the humans who raised you give to you?" she continued. "I should know what to call you."

I blanked out for a moment. Hadn't Cade told her my name when he arranged all of this?

I swallowed back my pain. "Meghan," I responded quietly, "Meghan Elam."

She arched a perfect eyebrow and rose from her throne, descending the steps of her dais with the grace of a dancer. Her movements were as fluid as water, the skirts of her scarlet dress spreading out behind her. She had the unmistakable presence that all the Faelorehn seemed to possess, but hers was all-encompassing. And she was stunningly beautiful.

I studied her as she paused in front of me, just as she scrutinized me. She stood tall and had dark, curly hair like mine. Her eyes, however, mimicked the color of the sea and sky, flickering between a variety of blues, greens and grays as she started circling me. I felt like a marble statue in a museum. Finally she stopped and looked me in the eye. I drew in a startled breath. Her Faelorehn power filled the room, a thick and almost tangible presence.

"May I?" She held out one of her delicate hands.

Nervously, I placed my palm over hers.

Her eyelids drifted shut and a cool sensation began crawling up my arm. When the odd prickling reached my chest and poked at the spot where my power resided, I flinched, pulling my hand back with a slight hiss.

Danua frowned and gazed at me. Her expression revealed a hint of sadness, yet I sensed disapproval more than anything else.

"You were not supposed to come here."

Her words brushed my ears, quiet and harsh.

I blanched, remembering those many months ago when the Morrigan lured me into the Otherworld in order to break the geis of protection my mother had placed on me.

"I know," I murmured, casting my eyes downward, "but I didn't realize it until after I had come to Eilé."

She sighed. "Well, you are here now so I suppose you want to hear all the details about how you came to exist and why you grew up in the mortal world."

Yes, I did want to learn as much as I could, but her words struck me like a well-placed slap. Boredom infused her tone, as if telling me about my father and why she had given me up proved to be as dull as repeating old gossip to her ladies in waiting.

I straightened my spine and followed after her as she gestured me back towards her throne. She invited me to pull up a chair as she took her seat on the dais. Without preamble, she jumped right into the story, so I sat and listened carefully, not wanting to miss a single detail.

"I have lived a long time Meghan, longer than most of the Faelorehn. For many of those years, I had a proper consort, but a century or so ago I lost him in one of the wars that tend to happen amongst our people. I ruled alone for decades, but one day a retinue from another land arrived with the hopes to establish trade and commerce between our two great realms.

"Among this group was a trained guard, some thirty soldiers strong, and one of these soldiers . . ."

She paused, her gaze growing distant, her harsh and serious mouth softening a little with the hint of a smile. Despite my unease at the whole situation, I bit back a grin. I understood what she meant. That must be how I appeared when I glanced at Cade.

She blinked and regained her composure, continuing her story as if an interruption hadn't occurred.

"He was young, handsome and his presence just filled the room whenever he entered my court. Not even half the year passed before we became lovers, but we were careful to keep our relationship secret."

She sighed and a sad look dominated her face once again. "Several months into our tryst he told me he was of Fomorian descent. I'm not aware of how much you understand concerning our history Meghan, but the Fomore have been our enemies for as long as I can remember."

I nodded. "I read about the battle. It's been written down as a legend in the mortal world."

She snorted, a very lady-like snort, and said with some sarcasm, "Yes, the Celts would have turned our dislike for one another into something of epic proportions. Only because our war spilled over into their world, something we never planned on happening. The Fomorians were retreating, trying to find a place to hide and recover; somewhere to escape the wrath of the Tuatha De. You see, the Faelorehn wanted to make sure our enemy never bothered us again."

I thought about her explanation for a few moments and it occurred to me that the Faelorehn meant to eliminate the

Fomorian race for good. The knowledge didn't sit well in my stomach. I didn't care how terrible a group of people may seem, genocide was not the answer.

"We made a mistake, on both our sides, to let our hatred build up so strongly to make us want to obliterate the other. I know better now not to allow others to sway me so easily."

She sneered and I wondered who those 'others' had been. Despite my horror at what she admitted, a sense of relief washed over me. My mother might be cold and distant, but cruelty seemed outside the limits of her tolerance.

I cleared my throat. "So, did you end your relationship with the Fomorian guard?"

Danua glanced down at me. "No, I didn't. But we practiced even more discretion as our affair continued. If the Faelorehn found out I had taken a Fomorian to my bed, the entire balance of our world would have been upset."

So theirs had been a forbidden love. Personally, I'd never been much of a fan of the classic stories concerning star-crossed lovers. Yet after hearing Danua's tale first hand, I felt nothing but sympathy for her.

"You couldn't end it?" I asked timidly.

She merely shook her head, revealing a heartrending, half-smile as she did so. "I was already in love with him."

A twinge of sympathy tugged at my heart. Falling for a guy, only to find out he was the enemy of your people, must have been tough. I realized this story wouldn't end well and I squirmed a little in my seat.

I swallowed and took a deep breath. "Where is he, my father, now?"

Danua laughed, soft and bitter. "So you've already concluded that my Fomorian soldier is your sire? You are rather perceptive, dear girl."

"Actually, Cade told me I was half Fomorian, so I just assumed."

Danua wrinkled her nose. "Yes, eventually my people found out and soon everyone, from the lowest born commoners, to the highest born lords, grew aware of my indiscretion. I became their hated queen, and they only remained loyal to me because they feared the considerable power I wield. As you can imagine, ruling the kingdom proved more difficult than before, but eventually they forgave me. At least enough for me to gain some control again."

"And this is why you sent me away, isn't it?"

I didn't need to include: *because I reminded you of my father.* The statement resonated amid the words I'd said aloud.

My mother detected the hidden statement and shook her head. "Yes. This is why I sent you away, so I could focus on ruling Eilé again, and so you would be safe."

My anger slammed itself against the lid I'd placed over it. I'd been so good about keeping it in check; about keeping all my emotions in check.

"You're a powerful queen of Eilé! How were you unable to protect your own daughter in the world where she belonged?"

My fingernails dug into the wooden armrests of my chair. I shot my hot gaze up at the Faelorehn queen. "How could you protect me when I was alone in another realm?"

I had hoped for a small flinch, or even for her face to take on a remorseful expression, but she betrayed no emotion.

Instead, a coldness glazed her features as she answered me, "That was the whole point, Meghan. By sending you away to a different world and by setting a geis of protection upon you, you were safer with your foster family than you would have been growing up here. You still would be, if you hadn't broken your geis and crossed over into Eilé."

I shot up out of the chair, my increasing anger overshadowing the caution I'd been so careful to show in front of royalty. "I had no idea a geis had been placed on me! I only found out after I entered the Otherworld; after learning I wasn't human! And when did you plan on telling me about my Faelorehn roots?"

Danua stood as well, her form seeming to take up the entire hall. My anger disappeared with a snap and a tingle of fear took its place. I sat down, suddenly remembering who I spoke to.

"You were never supposed to know you were Faelorehn!" she snarled. "You would've lived a happy life in the mortal world, never discovering what horrors existed here. You would have been safe there from the Morrigan and her faelah."

The room had grown darker, as if a storm brewed right below the ceiling far above us. In fact, I sensed the prickle of lightning getting ready to strike. I swallowed, more afraid than upset, but my emotions weren't fully subdued.

"You never answered my question. Where is my father?" I asked, my eyes burning with tears of fury.

A heavy sigh and the sound of skirts swishing told me my mother found her seat once again. I braved a glance at her and my anxiety eased a little.

Danua

She sat askew in her throne, not upright and alert like before. One arm she draped lazily over an armrest, the other she had crooked so her mouth pressed against her folded hand. She wasn't looking at me, but gazing out of one of the tall windows lining the hall. It was obvious by the way she held herself that her thoughts and her heart had drifted far away. The fine lines around her beautiful face seemed a bit more pronounced in that moment, as if her true age yearned to escape through the shell of immortality. I understood then that, wherever my birth father might be, she longed for him; still loved him.

She closed her eyes and rubbed her forehead with the hand she'd had pressed to her lips.

"He is no longer here Meghan. This is all you need to know. Now, if you don't mind, I'd like some peace."

I opened my mouth to say something: *I'm sorry. Do you want to talk? I'm your daughter, please let me comfort you.*

Before I got a chance to speak, however, a lady in waiting opened a side door and curtsied.

Danua spoke without glancing up. "Nettalie, please show my daughter to her room."

She waved a hand and Nettalie walked over and took my arm, leading me gently through the door. I cast a final glance over my shoulder and before the door snapped shut, Danua, the powerful goddess queen of the Faelorehn, bent over in her throne and covered her face with her hands.

◎ ◎ ◎

Nettalie led me down several hallways and up a few staircases before stopping in front of a large wooden door. The suite inside resembled the dream of any little girl wishing to be a princess, but such opulence would never shift my loyalties away from the room in Cade's castle.

"Dinner will be served in an hour, Miss. Someone will come fetch you." Nettalie curtsied again before closing the door gently behind her.

I fell onto the high bed, wondering where Cade had gone and hoping he hadn't left me here. Someone had placed my duffle bag on a chest at the foot of the bed and I noticed a small space serving as a bathroom off to the side.

I took a deep breath, releasing the air through my nose. So, I really was half Fomorian. And my mother was Danua. *Danu.* The River Danube had been named for her, and the Tuatha De Danaan called her their Mother. A queen who had ruled for centuries and wished for nothing more than to prove she remained strong and unbending, a pillar among the Faelorehn who would always be their most capable sovereign. Oh, but she was more than that; she was *my* mother, my flesh and blood mother, and she was heartbroken and wanted nothing to do with me. Everything made sense, what she'd said about her decision concerning me and what I'd concluded on my own, but it still hurt terribly.

I rolled over on the bed, seeking a plush pillow to hug. I wondered where my father might be. *No longer here . . .* What did that mean? Was he dead? Banished to some other kingdom or realm? And if so, could he be brought back to Eilé? Not just for my sake, but for my mother's as well. Couldn't the Faelorehn learn to accept him, in time? Would they ever learn to accept me if they found out who I truly was?

Too weary to get up, I simply shut my eyes and tried to take a nap. I felt confused, upset and angry. I had too many emotions trying to find space in my heart, so I just huffed a deep breath and let the day's shocks and revelations all wash over me.

I eventually fell asleep, my head resting on a pillow soaked with my tears.

Fourteen

Erintara

A soft tap on my door jerked me awake. I lay silent for several seconds, trying to remember where I was. The canopy of the bed I rested in wasn't familiar and my eyes were gritty and they ached. The tap came again, this time followed by a voice.

"Meghan?"

Cade. I sighed my relief and sat up, scrubbing my eyes with the heels of my hands.

"Hang on," I grumbled after sliding off the mattress.

As I made my way across the room, everything came crashing back to me. The beautiful castle in Erintara, my royal mother and what she'd told me about my father . . .

I pulled the door open and sucked in a breath. Cade no longer wore the simple clothes he donned while traveling through Eilé. Instead he had on a long, dark green coat that matched his eyes, fawn colored pants and knee-high black boots. He looked as if he'd stepped out of an eighteenth century ballroom. I merely stood and gaped as I counted the gold buttons running down the front of his coat.

"Meghan? Are you alright?"

"Uh, yeah, fine," I managed.

He eyed me warily, then stared at my hair.

My hands shot up and I groaned. It was probably a rat's nest. I bit the inside of my cheek and blushed, peering down at my rumpled clothes. Ugh, I must look like a hoyden.

"I came to tell you dinner will be served in half an hour and that one of your mother's ladies in waiting will be bringing you some proper attire," he said with a grin.

"Right, okay."

"And if you'll allow me, I'd like to escort you to the dining hall when you are ready."

He sketched a neat bow and I covered my urge to laugh with a small cough.

"Of course," I stated.

An older woman carrying a box appeared at the end of the hall, interrupting our friendly exchange. She studied Cade with a sneer, her eyes cold as she turned to me.

"Young lady, your mother wants you to wear this."

She pushed past me and set the box on the bed, curtsied, then crossed the room, giving Cade another nasty glare as she left.

I bit back my anger at her reaction to Cade. Leaving the door open, I walked over to the bed and pulled the lid off of the box. The dress inside was beautiful, a shimmery golden green color with tiny glass beads sewn along the seams.

I glanced over at Cade. He stood patiently outside my door and for a moment he reminded me of Fergus. I suppressed a grin and said, "If you don't mind waiting, it shouldn't take me too long to get ready."

He nodded and closed the door.

After washing my face in the bathroom and brushing my hair, I stripped off my clothes from earlier and stepped into the gown. The skirt was long and full and the bodice decorated with an embroidered floral pattern. The sleeves were quite short and when I tried to button up the back, I paused and a smidgeon of dread curdled in my stomach. I managed the first few buttons at the small of my back on my own, but I didn't get any further. A zipper would have been hard enough, but this was impossible.

I took a deep breath and stared at the door. Well, I had no other option. Holding the front of the bodice up, I scurried over to the door and pulled it open.

Cade wasn't right outside my room, but was standing further down the hall gazing out a window.

"Cade!" I hissed.

His head turned in my direction.

"I need your help."

When he stood only a few feet in front of me I pulled him inside and closed the door behind us.

"What's wrong?" he asked, eyeing the room as if he expected to find faelah hiding in the shadows.

"Um, I can't reach the buttons on the back of my dress, can you help?"

I let the question hang as I scraped my hair to the side with one hand while holding the dress up with the other. When I turned around Cade sucked in a breath. I wasn't sure if his gasp was a sound of delight or horror, but he readily complied and started buttoning. I felt every single golden button slip into place, and when he finished, he rested his hands on my shoulders.

A tall mirror stood across the room, one I hadn't noticed earlier when I first arrived. Now it reflected an image that warmed my heart and made my toes tingle: me in the beautiful dress, Cade in his fine court clothes with his hands on my shoulders. How I wanted the moment to last forever. Then I imagined him leaning down and kissing the spot where my neck and shoulder met . . .

"You look beautiful Meghan," he whispered behind me, breaking into my fantasy.

I grinned, unable to help myself, and watched my face redden in the mirror.

"Thank you. You look very good yourself," I answered after clearing my throat.

"But not beautiful, huh?"

I turned and glanced up at him, but he only smiled down at me, amusement painting his eyes a brilliant pale green.

"Now, shall we go down to this grand dinner?"

Cade offered me his arm and we descended to the first floor. I smiled sheepishly, glad his gloominess from before seemed all but gone. We met several people along the way, all dressed in their finest and eyeing us with curiosity. Some of them exuded hostility, like the woman who brought the dress to my room, but none of them spoke to us. As we drew closer to the dining hall, I clung to Cade even harder.

He lowered his head and whispered against my temple, "Relax."

Dolmarehn

I swallowed hard and tried to loosen my grip, especially when one of the noble women frowned in irritation as Cade and I passed her. The dining hall itself appeared as big as the throne room, and a huge rectangular table large enough to seat a hundred guests took up the room's center.

Dinner turned out to be a long, quiet event, and the formality of it nearly suffocated me. The young man seated to my right tried to make light conversation, but his explanation of how the first course had been prepared ended up being the most interesting thing he had to say. Everything else he spoke of had no meaning to me whatsoever: the fruitfulness of his land, the gossip of Danua's court, the general politics of Erintara. I found myself nodding and pretending to enjoy myself just to be polite.

Halfway through the second course I lifted my eyes and found Cade watching me. The men and women sitting around him were dressed well, but I had no doubt they were on the lower end of Danua's social ladder. Cade flashed an encouraging smile and lifted his goblet in a toast. I returned the gesture, feeling a little better, though I still longed to be at his end of the table. The members of Erintara's lower upper class were clearly a more cheerful bunch than those next to me.

Eventually, the grand meal came to an end and servants moved in to clear the tables. I expected dessert or tea to be served, but before anything else could happen, my mother raised a hand from her seat at the head of the table and everyone quieted down.

"As many of you know," she began in her clear, authoritative voice, "a guest arrived today."

My stomach fell to the bottom of my toes. What was she doing?

"This guest is a young woman, a young woman you might have seen poking around the castle earlier and who is currently sitting there to my right."

She gestured in my general direction in a bored fashion. Several pairs of eyes descended on me and it took every last shred of effort I possessed not to dive under the table.

"There is something you should also know about her. She has been living in the mortal world for the past sixteen years. She also happens to be half Faelorehn and half Fomorian."

The murmuring began as soon as Danua finished speaking. I shut my eyes for a moment, trying to will the anxiety away. *What was she doing!?* Hadn't she told me that they had scorned her for loving my father? Why would she point it out now, after they'd finally forgiven her?

"And," Danua raised her voice above the din of the dinner guests, "she is my illegitimate daughter."

The room exploded with noise; people talking with voices raised in order to hear their neighbors. The man sitting next to me gazed at me with wide eyes and a stricken expression, and I was certain that was the scrape of chair legs against the stone floor as he tried to move further away from me.

I took a deep breath and glanced up in Cade's direction. He sat stiffly, ignoring the chaos around him and gazing directly into my eyes, as if in doing so might pull me back from the abyss I was falling into.

"But since she is here," Danua boomed, the room growing darker, "I'll ask all of you to treat her as you would treat any noble of Eilé."

The murmuring stopped almost completely. Clearly, no one wanted to incite Danua's wrath.

Cade stood up abruptly, and even from where I sat I caught a glimpse of the fire in his eyes. "Your Majesty, legitimate or not, she is the daughter of a queen and deserves-"

"Do not take my hospitality so lightly that you think you can speak freely," she spat, the room cooling several degrees to match her growing anger. "It is because of you, Caedehn MacRoich, that my daughter broke her geis of protection in the first place."

Cade turned a sickly shade of white and sat back down.

"Yes," Eilé's high queen sneered, "I know all about the incident with the Morrigan and how it almost led to Meghan's death. So I recommend you watch your step young Caedehn, and take care not to forget your place."

I glared at my mother, all the emotions from earlier in the day churning up once again. Was she trying to humiliate me? And if so, why? What had I ever done to her to make her despise me so? If I'd been braver, and if images of being dragged back to this very room by armed soldiers hadn't invaded my mind, I would've stood up and stormed back to my own suite. Annoying one of the most powerful women in Eilé, however, didn't seem wise.

Dessert came a few minutes later and everyone ate in silence. No one seemed in the mood to chat anymore and I only stared at my pudding.

When the table was cleared, Danua invited her guests back to the ballroom to play cards and other games. She hadn't even looked at me since her upsetting declaration, so I took advantage of the shuffling crowd and started creeping away. The idea of playing games made me feel ill and I was sure that, despite what my mother had said about treating me as an equal, no one would want me there. I was half the enemy after all, and who knows what mischief I might cause.

The tears started coming when I reached the long hallway that would take me to my room. I dashed them away angrily. I was tired of crying, tired of being an emotional wreck. The sniveling, dramatic girl who had taken over my body needed to find a new host to torment.

Footsteps echoed behind me and I sped up. The last thing I wanted was for one of Danua's ladies in waiting or one of the nobles to find me in my current state.

"Meghan."

I took a shuddering breath. Cade.

"Meghan, wait."

I picked up my pace, almost running now. My room was only a few more doors away. I didn't even want Cade to see me. Unfortunately, he was faster than me. He caught up to me and wrapped his arms around me. I tried to fight him.

"Leave me alone!" I sobbed, attempting to punch him in the chest, but I was too tired and too upset to put any real power behind the attack.

"Shhh," he crooned as he pressed my head against his shoulder. "Shhh, now. Just let everything out Meghan, cry to your heart's content."

Dolmarehn

The dam gave way and I broke down. I hardly noticed when he led me to my room, picking me up and carrying me when I refused to walk. He opened and closed the door behind us and then strode over to the bed and sat down, me crying my eyes out and him rocking me in his arms and speaking softly in his ancient language.

His careful attention must have helped because the tears dried up and my sobs stopped. Cade placed me on the mattress and took a step back. I didn't even think about changing into something more comfortable, which was probably a good thing because I wanted Cade to stay. I rested my head on one of the many pillows, exhaustion finally taking over.

"I'm so sorry Meghan, I'm so sorry about everything," Cade whispered, his hand pushing my hair away from my face. "I never would have brought you here if I knew how Danua would treat you. We'll leave tomorrow, early in the morning before anyone else rises. We won't even give the queen a chance to stop us. I'll come and get you when it's time to go."

Something warm and soft pressed against my forehead and then several seconds later I heard the door close with a soft snap. I tried to tell Cade not to leave, but I no longer had the energy. I reached for my little well of magic, but the familiar warmth had gone cold in my chest. After only a few minutes, however, I managed to fall asleep and while I slept, I dreamed of the ruined castle with a pink and green room, and the soothing sound of a waterfall to chase away the nightmares.

Fifteen

Unworthy

Cade came early the next morning, as promised. I had slept in the gown, rumpling the fine fabric so badly that a little twinge of malicious joy cut through me. *Good,* I thought, *I hope that stuffy lady in waiting finds it first.*

I dressed in a clean set of clothes from my duffle bag as Cade waited outside my door. I relished being in my own clothes again. I glanced at the dress one more time and for some bizarre reason, I was reminded of the prom and how I planned to ask Cade to go with me. My stomach flipped over as I remembered the events of last night. He had taken care of me after my mother's grand announcement. If I asked him now, would he merely say yes out of pity? That's the last thing I wanted. I wanted him to go with me because he chose to, without sympathy driving his decision. I huffed in slight exasperation. There was no rush. I could wait a little longer to ask him.

Smiling like an idiot, I gathered all my personal things into my bag and stepped through the door to greet Cade. He gave me a curious look and arched his eyebrows. He too had returned to his customary jeans and t-shirt ensemble.

"A better morning I hope?" he asked tentatively.

I nodded, blushing from the memory of my melt-down the night before. We made our way down the stairs and got as far as the courtyard before we were caught.

"Meghan, a word."

Danua stepped out of the morning shadows, her imposing figure striking in a dark blue dress. The blood froze in my veins. Had she found out we planned to leave early? Had she been waiting for us?

I cringed as she moved towards a door to her left. She opened it then set her cold, ocean-blue eyes on me like a hawk eyeing a squirrel. I glanced at Cade and he released a breath I was certain he'd been holding for a good half minute.

"You'd better see what she wants," he murmured, "Danua's wrath can be worse than the Morrigan's if you push her too far."

I swallowed my irritation and nerves and crossed the flagstones, my footsteps echoing eerily off the tall walls of the bailey. The space we stepped into turned out to be a small outdoor sitting room. While the side facing the courtyard was a solid stone wall, the other side had a half wall and granite columns holding up the roof. A few benches and a matching granite table were scattered about and the spaces between the pillars gave a wonderful view of the city far below.

With a confidence I'd quickly become familiar with, my mother closed the door, crossed her arms and asked, "Where are you going?"

I returned her glare, trying hard not to start shaking. I crossed my own arms, mocking her stance.

"Home," I stated simply.

It didn't take a genius to realize 'home' meant the house and family waiting for me in the mortal world.

Danua didn't even bat an eyelash. "You won't be safe there."

"No," I countered, "but I'll be happy." *At least there I have a family who loves me.*

I turned and reached for the doorknob, only pausing when she spoke again.

"Live where you wish, but I will demand one thing of you."

I spun around in a flash, my teeth gritted and my eyes most likely flashing several different colors. "You will *demand* me? You didn't even want me, what gives you the right to demand anything of me?"

"The right a queen has over one of her subjects. And the right of a mother over her natural daughter. I do not want you associating with Caedehn MacRoich."

It felt like she'd slapped me. "I'm sorry?"

She sighed deeply and rolled her eyes to the vaulted ceiling. "I don't want you seeing that young man any longer."

"I'm not *seeing* Cade, he's my friend!"

"Oh please. I've noticed the way that boy looks at you."

For a moment I lost all of my bluster. Did he really? Look at me? I mean, look at me in the sense that he wanted to do more than just look at me? Ugh. My thoughts weren't making any sense. Sure, I had wondered about some of his glances, but who was I, so besotted with him I couldn't think straight half the time, to judge?

"He's not good enough for you," my mother continued.

"Oh really," I countered, forgetting my musings and instead rejoining the fight, "not good enough for the illegitimate, half-breed daughter you cast aside?"

"No, not even good enough for that."

That hurt. Not because she was so adamant about keeping me away from Cade, but because she hadn't argued with me when I'd described myself in such a base way.

"Besides, there are far better suitors for you, and all of them of acceptable birth."

"Suitors? Acceptable birth?" It was a harsh whisper, but she heard me. "I am not some piece of property you can marry off to one of your court nobles. I met them last night and I don't like a single one of them."

"Please, Meghan. You hardly spoke with them," she replied.

I bit back my anger. I took a calming breath, then said with all the confidence I could muster, "You gave up any right you had as a mother when you abandoned me as a toddler, and last night when you treated me like a burden."

"What do you want from me Meghan?" She turned on me, her eyes flashing and the air growing cold and hostile. "Didn't you want my acknowledgment? Isn't that why you came here? I claimed you last evening, in front of my entire court. Eventually the whole kingdom will learn about you. Isn't this what you wanted?"

She sighed and the room filled with a gust of frosty wind. "All I ask is for you to obey me in this one thing. Detach yourself from Caedehn MacRoich and perhaps we can start over."

I jerked my head up, my eyes filling with tears. She asked too much. I would never destroy my friendship with Cade to win her approval. He had done so much for me, and meant far more to me, than her. Mother or not, I didn't know her and so far I wasn't too impressed with what I'd learned.

With a raw voice I whispered harshly, "I will not stay away from Cade and you cannot make me."

I jerked open the door, slamming it behind me before she had a chance to say anything more.

Cade eyed me warily as I stepped out into the courtyard.

"Let's get out of here," I said, my voice shaking a little as I sped past him.

To my great relief, he quickly caught up to me without demanding to know why.

⊚ ⊚ ⊚

When we reached Kellston on the other side of the dolmarehn, most of the village was still asleep. I was grateful, for I didn't think myself capable of handling their optimism at the moment. Since the visit with my mother had been cut short, I still had a few days to fill before I needed to return home, so Cade invited me to stay in his castle. I didn't even have to think about my response. So for the next two days, Cade tried to help me coax my glamour out into the open.

"Your natural magic should be able to flow free from your skin, like this," Cade said, holding his palm flat and letting five golden flames dance from his fingertips.

I gasped and stared at him with wide eyes. He merely grinned.

"Most of the time I make the magic undetectable, but for educational purposes I took away that stricture."

I tried to follow his lead, listening carefully as he directed me on how to encourage my glamour to follow my instruction, but every time the exhilarating force would fill my arms only to stop at my fingertips.

"Why won't it work for me?" I cried, throwing my hands down as I plopped onto the ground.

Speirling, who cropped grass only a few feet away, eyed me with curiosity before getting back to his lunch. The lingering bad mood that had followed me from the visit to Erintara didn't help.

Cade only shook his head, joining me in the middle of the field. "It will, Meghan. Trust me. When your magic's ready, it will come fully awake and you won't even realize what hit you."

The next morning, Cade escorted me back to the mortal world. Meeting my real mother had been a disaster, and although I told her I wanted to go home to my family, I yearned to live in Eilé. I regretted our angry parting, and I hoped someday I'd be able to patch things up with her, but she would have to understand I wouldn't choose her over Cade.

Cade turned to leave, and in the next moment I remembered how I had been putting off asking him to prom. I hooked a loose curl of my hair behind an ear. I hadn't asked him the night my mother acknowledged me in front of her court because I feared he'd only feel sorry for me, and I'd come up with one excuse after another not to ask him during these past two days. Well, I was fresh out of excuses and to be honest, I was tired of being afraid; afraid of the Morrigan, afraid of my mother's disappointment and disregard, afraid to tell Cade how I felt about him . . .

"Um, Cade?"

He paused before stepping into the cave, then turned and waited for me to continue.

Ugh, I wasn't good at this, not good at this at all . . .

"Uh, well, this is my senior year in high school and prom is coming up, which is kind of a big deal. It's this dance everyone goes to and-"

"I know about prom," he cut in.

I chewed my lip again. Dang it. If he hadn't interrupted me I might have asked by now.

I took a deep breath and stared at the ground. "Well, I was wondering if you'd like to go with me. To prom."

There. I'd asked him. Now I just needed to wait for his response. My eyes weren't on him, so I felt Cade take my fingers in his before I saw him move. I started a little from the gentle touch.

"I would be honored to accompany you to prom, Meghan."

His voice was soft, and chicken that I was, I still couldn't look him in the eye. I cleared my throat and pulled my hand out of his so I could use my fingers to hook my hair behind my ear again.

"Great," I said, "it's on the first of May, a Saturday night."

Finally, I glanced at him. He stood back watching me, a small grin on his face. I grinned in return. No, I beamed. Cade said he'd go to prom with me!

"Are you sure about this Meghan?"

My smile vanished and a boulder the size of a house settled in my stomach.

Cade's tone took on a bitter note when he continued, "After all, you can do better than a Faelorehn bounty hunter with questionable parentage."

I merely stared at him, stunned. Had my mother spoken to him as well? Or had he heard our discussion? My cheeks turned pink, anger having a little to do with it.

"Did Danua talk to you?" I asked in a harsh whisper.

Cade flinched. "I accidentally overheard your conversation. I'm sorry Meghan. I didn't mean to, your voices carried through the door."

Oh no. What had I said? Had I mentioned anything about my own feelings towards Cade? Sure, I'd just been complaining to myself about being afraid to tell him what he meant to me, but I didn't want him to find out like this. *Oh crap!*

I decided to ignore the voice in my head and took a deep breath. "I don't care what Danua thinks of you."

I gazed up at him, met his eyes with my own, and crossed my arms. The boldness I sensed earlier started welling up again; the desire to banish all my fears. But unfortunately I wasn't brave enough to finally tell him the truth. That I loved him.

"She doesn't know you Cade, but I do."

His laugh was harsh and grating, enough to make me take a step back. He ran his hand through his hair and shook his head. He heaved a deep sigh and placed his hands on his hips, tilting his chin up to the treetops. The afternoon light got caught in his hair, turning the strands copper.

"Oh Meghan, if you only truly knew me, you wouldn't be so quick to defend me."

"What is that supposed to mean?"

I didn't intend to sound snippy, but my response came out that way. I had too much on my mind, that was my problem. I had just met my birth mother for the first time, a mother who had given me up years ago and was now trying to tell me how to live my life without even making a minor attempt to get to know me. Besides, even though I didn't want to admit it, what Cade said held some truth. I trusted him, was completely head over heels in love with him, but did I sincerely know him? Hadn't he kept things from me? Wasn't he *still* keeping things from me? So why did I jump so quickly to his defense? *Because he was the first one to tell you about who you are*, the little voice inside of me whispered, *and because he's the first boy to ever really care, isn't he?*

Cade must have detected my distress because when he lowered his head once again and caught sight of the expression on my face, he grimaced.

"I'm sorry Meghan. That was a stupid thing to say. Perhaps Danua's words got to me more than I'd like to admit."

His smile seemed genuine this time, but a lingering sadness tainted his voice once again.

He recaptured my hand and graced it with a kiss. "I look forward to prom, my lady."

Cade let go of my fingers and whistled for Fergus, and in the next moment the two of them were through the dolmarehn and on their way back to the Otherworld.

I think I stood outside the cave for a good five minutes before Meridian reminded me we should head home.

Yes, home, I thought. *Home, to a mother and father and brothers who love me.*

@ @ @

The rest of March and most of April flew by at warp speed. Everyone at school was obsessing over graduation, prom and the upcoming summer. I spent much of my time brooding over what I would do about Danua and how I was going to inform my family of my own plans. I'd turned it all over during the last several weeks and had come to a conclusion: on the day after graduation, I'd finally tell them I was Faelorehn and that I belonged in the Otherworld. I only hoped they would believe me and not try to cart me off to the psychiatric ward.

On Saturday, exactly one week before prom, I woke to find Fergus sitting at my glass door. Feeling a pang of delight jolt through me, I threw on a robe and my sandals and pulled the door open.

"Is Cade here?"

I hadn't seen him or heard from him since returning from Danua's court over a month ago. I had worried that she'd somehow gotten to him; convinced him to stay away from me or threatened him in some way. Hopefully, Fergus's presence could be counted as a good sign and not a bad one.

Clenching my teeth, I hurried after the wolfhound only to stop in front of the oak tree when he did. I furrowed my brow and reached around to the spot where Cade and I exchanged our letters. As I pulled the note free, Meridian swooped down from her perch, chittering happily as she playfully dive-bombed Fergus.

Unworthy

The parchment I held in my hand wasn't Cade's customary, plain white sheet of paper, but a heavier piece of stationary rolled into a tube, tied with a sheer gold ribbon and sealed with a fancy logo resembling the Greek letter omega.

I broke the seal, pausing only for a moment to admire it, and read the gilded letters, smiling by the time I reached the bottom. It was an invitation from the Dagda to join him and his fellow revelers this coming Friday for a Beltaine Eve celebration. And yes, Cade would be going as well. My birth mother may not have accepted me, but at least there were some people in the Otherworld who wished me well and enjoyed my company.

After returning to my room, I quickly penned a reply to the Dagda and wrote a separate note to Cade, to remind him he promised to attend prom with me, then brought them both back to Fergus.

After tying them securely to his collar, I patted him goodbye then showered and got dressed. Afterwards, I went upstairs to spend some time with my pesky brothers before Robyn and Tully came to get me so we could go shopping for prom dresses. It was looking like the beginning of a good day indeed.

❁ ❁ ❁

"I still can't believe Robyn's met him and I haven't," Tully pouted as she plucked at the taffeta skirt of a magenta gown hanging on the clothing rack in front of her.

Since Cade had agreed to go to prom with me, I finally caved and told all my friends about him, emphasizing that he was just a friend. Robyn had only snorted at me, but I ignored her.

"Oh, it was only because she happened to be in the right place at the right time," I answered Tully's question.

I grinned at Robyn and she returned the gesture. She had been a good friend, keeping my secret for so long.

"I can't wait to see what he looks like in a tux," Robyn sighed dreamily as she picked up a turquoise dress and held it up to herself. "What do you say, Meg? Think I'll be able to snag your boyfriend away from you if I wear this?"

She twirled around and Tully and I snorted with laughter.

"He's not my boyfriend," I insisted after I stopped giggling. "We're just friends."

"Sure he isn't, and sure you are," Robyn teased as she continued her dance.

Eventually we all found a dress, but I needed something for the Dagda's Beltaine party as well. I couldn't wear my prom dress since it was a bit too fancy, and I didn't really have anything at home, so we stopped in one more store before leaving the mall.

When I got back to my room I laid both garments out on my bed, admiring them each for different reasons. The prom dress was a teal green with a long skirt and spaghetti strap sleeves. The cocktail style dress I'd picked out for the Dagda's party was black and white with a shorter skirt that flared out at the waist. Sighing, I hung them both up in my closet and went out to check the oak tree for a response from Cade.

As I walked to the tree, I thought about my busy plans for the weekend. On Friday after school, I'd leave to go to Eilé, but my parents would think I was staying over at Robyn's. From what I calculated, I had plenty of time the next morning to return home from the Dagda's Beltaine party and get ready for my prom night.

I grinned. I would be exhausted and probably not in the mood to mingle with my fellow classmates, pretending I harbored regrets about high school coming to an end, accepting false apologies and claims of 'no hard feelings' from those who had never been kind to me. But I didn't care. Even if I knew the entire school had planned a prank to ridicule me, Meghan the weirdo, at my senior prom, I still wouldn't give a damn. They could laugh and offer their false smiles and fake comradeship all they wanted. It didn't matter because I would have Cade by my side. I smiled wistfully, imagining myself the inept heroine in some badly written stage musical. Once again, the very thought hardly fazed me.

The knothole in the oak was empty, but by the next day I had a response. Cade told me to pack what I needed for an overnight stay at the Dagda's and he would meet me Friday after school.

I clutched the note close, then headed back to the house. I decided to walk around the front this time since I heard Logan and Bradley playing basketball in the driveway. I grinned when I spotted Aiden watching them with keen interest.

I went and sat down on the retaining wall next to him, ruffling his dark hair with a free hand. He wiggled away with a smile, but made sure he didn't move too far away so that he could still touch me. I sighed. This was Aiden's method of finding comfort. He always had to be touching me. I didn't mind. Our special way of consoling one another comforted me, too.

Once Logan led Bradley by ten points, I stood up and went back inside, carrying Aiden with me. A twinge of sadness shot through my heart, making my well of magic flare a little. If I left to live in the Otherworld, who would take care of Aiden? I mean, I knew my parents would take care of him and love him, but we had a special bond. What would happen if I wasn't there to offer the comfort he always sought from me? I shook my head, telling myself to worry about the future later.

"Snow bird," Aiden murmured in my ear.

I glanced over my shoulder to see what had caught his attention, but didn't notice anything.

"What do you mean Aiden?" I asked.

He pointed. "White."

I looked again. Perched up in the eucalyptus, in her usual spot, sat Meridian, napping in the late afternoon sun, but I didn't see any other white birds.

I shrugged. "Probably a dove."

"Perty," he sighed as he clung tighter.

Once inside, I set him down on the couch with the twins and went to help Mom with dinner. She had a dish towel thrown over her shoulder, humming some nameless tune as she stirred what I suspected to be cake batter.

I leaned my elbows on the island and started flipping through a magazine. I often found it wise to wait and get instructions from her when it came to helping out with whatever culinary creation she was working on.

"So," she said, moving to the stove to check on dinner, "when do we get to meet this boy you're taking to the prom?"

I paused in my perusal of recipes and ads. I wondered when this conversation might come up. I took a deep breath and tried to sound casual.

"Saturday night. He's going to pick me up here after I come home from Robyn's."

Mom tasted the sauce for the chicken.

"Is he cute?"

I felt myself flush a little. "Yes." *Very cute.*

"What did you say his name was again?"

"Cade MacRoich."

Should I be nervous about this interrogation? These were the normal questions a mother might ask her daughter, right? I cringed at that. My birth mother wouldn't care, but Mom, well, she did care. She stepped away from the stove and wiped her hands on the towel.

"I don't think you ever told us how you met him Meghan."

Oh, good, I was ready for this one. I took a deep breath, closed the magazine, and rolled my eyes, trying to act annoyed at being burdened with so many questions.

"I met him in town one day when I was out with Tully and Robyn. We were at the bookstore and we both reached for the last copy of the same book, but he let me have it. We started talking and found out we had a lot in common."

There, that should suffice. I picked the magazine back up.

"So are you guys an item then?"

I blanched, rumpling the glossy pages between my fingers. "Uh, no, we're just friends." *Meg the broken record.*

Dolmarehn

My mom stopped her stirring, put her hands on her hips and arched an eyebrow at me.

"I thought you said he was cute?"

Yes, well, doesn't mean he returns the sentiment. I found it rather ironic that my mom should be thinking along the same lines as Danua. Perhaps they were picking up on some vibe I was oblivious to. Maybe Cade *did* want to be my boyfriend. My nerves prickled at the thought. But if he did, why hadn't he said anything? Why, when he kissed me that time he'd first taught me about my power, did he withdraw? Why hadn't he tried to kiss me again? I ground my teeth and forced all those stray thoughts away.

"Doesn't mean we're an item," I grumbled at Mom, answering her question.

She merely beamed at me. "Oh, I think it's only a matter of time honey."

I released a long breath as the magazine provided refuge once more. I hoped she was right.

Sixteen

Beltaine

O n Friday morning, I woke early and packed my duffle bag with my party dress, shoes and change of clothes for the journey home in the morning. I was supposed to be going over to Robyn's after school to stay the night, so I dragged it upstairs with my backpack.

Thomas pulled in the driveway fifteen minutes later and I called a goodbye over my shoulder as I left the house. I was tempted to skip school and leave early to meet Cade, but I knew we would have plenty of time to make it to the Dagda's party, and I didn't want to risk getting caught skipping class, not on the day before prom when I had the kind of parents who wouldn't think twice of banishing me to my room for the rest of the school year.

I found Cade waiting in the parking lot for me after school, just as his note had said. I made my way to his black Trans Am, throwing my backpack and duffle bag in the back seat before Tully or the boys got a chance to find me. I glanced at Cade and he smiled, his gaze lingering.

Dolmarehn

My heart skipped a beat as I recalled the conversation with my mom the night before. Talking so casually about being Cade's girlfriend was easy when he wasn't around. As soon as I caught him eyeing me like that however, I felt self-conscious once again.

"Ready?" he asked, shifting his car into first gear.

I took a deep breath and smiled. Time to have fun and forget about unrequited crushes, uncaring mothers and any trouble the Morrigan might be brewing up while I wasn't paying attention.

"Yup," I said.

Speirling greeted us when we stepped out onto the other side of the dolmarehn. Meridian, in her usual fashion, had joined me right before we left the mortal world and I watched as she fluttered off after Fergus to explore.

We took our time traveling to the Dagda's, since the party didn't start until later in the evening. Nevertheless, we managed to arrive before most of the guests. The Dagda was delighted to see us and his lady friends quickly took a hold of Cade and dragged him inside. I shot a glance over at them and laughed. I should be jealous about the way they fussed over him, but they acted more like proud aunts than anything else. Besides, I was distracted with our host. The Dagda stood dressed in his finest, his hair combed back and his beard trimmed. His rugged handsomeness didn't look a bit faded today yet I was certain his magnetic personality would only improve his appearance by the night's end.

The Dagda opened his arms wide and without a second thought I walked into them, accepting his bone-crushing hug.

"Hello little Meghan, I'm so pleased you accepted my invitation. Are you ready for a night of feasting and dancing and making merry?"

I laughed into his gold-trimmed tunic. How could I be so comfortable with a person I had met only once?

"I hope we don't party too hard. I need to look my best for my senior prom tomorrow night."

I smiled up at him, waiting for his confused expression, but he merely beamed and set me at arm's length. "Ahh, yes, this mortal world coming of age dance Cade has told me about."

That surprised me. Cade had told the Dagda about going to prom with me?

"Uh, yeah, that's right," I answered with an awkward grin.

The Dagda chuckled. "Well, as glorious as it may be, I'm certain that it won't hold a candle to my Beltaine Eve celebration."

He started to lead me inside, his entourage, still fussing over Cade, close behind.

"Now," Cade's foster father said in a lowered voice, "I am expecting many fine young men tonight, from all over Eilé, so I don't want you to think that Cade has exclusive rights to you my dear. It's high time you start getting to know more of us."

He winked, making me blush, and another thought surfaced in my mind. What if some of those young men were the same ones from Danua's court? I shuddered inwardly. If they were, I'd find a way to deal with it. Perhaps they had forgotten me by now. After all, it had been several weeks since I'd made my visit.

Eventually I was led to the room I'd be staying in. It was smaller than the one at Cade's castle or the suite in Erintara, but very cozy nonetheless. A cheery fireplace stood empty, waiting to be lit for the night, and a small, round window built right into the hillside offered a view of an enclosed garden. By the time my things were stored and I was in my black and white dress, Cade had arrived at my door.

I grinned when I spotted him, admiring the clothes he had picked for the Beltaine celebration. They weren't as fine as the ones at the high queen's court, but then again, those would've been too fancy for the Dagda's party. Instead he wore soft brown trousers, simple boots and a cream-colored tunic, all topped off with a deep blue vest embroidered with Celtic knot work.

When my eyes finally met his, I found him staring at me with the strangest expression on his face. I quickly glanced away, a wave of self-awareness making me fidgety.

I patted my hair. "Something wrong?" I asked.

Cade must've shaken himself out of whatever daze he was in because he took a breath and smiled, saying, "No, nothing's wrong at all."

He offered his arm so I gladly accepted it, a sense of nervousness flushing over me for some strange reason. *Calm down Meghan. This isn't Danua's court, but the Dagda's grand hall.*

Full dark had descended by the time we reached the common area. Someone had opened the huge door in the side of the hill, and several people came and went as they pleased, talking cheerily and laughing at one another's jokes. A roaring bonfire had been lit where the road forked to encircle the house, and someone's deep baritone voice rolled through the cold night air, retelling the epic story of the Celtic hero Cuchulainn. I paused at the door for a minute to listen as the man described the demigod's impressive strength and heroics, especially his ríastrad, the intense fury he would succumb to whenever in the heat of a great battle.

"Oh yes," Cade whispered cheerfully behind me, "no one could defeat Cuchulainn when his ríastrad took over."

I smiled up at him and we kept going, leaving the storytellers and captive audience behind.

As we moved through the hall, I realized the Dagda had been right; several young men, my age and maybe a little older, mixed and mingled within the crowd of revelers. And I noticed that a few of them were pretty cute, but none of them could hold a candle to Cade. Of course, I might be a little biased. I checked each of their faces and breathed a sigh of relief when I didn't recognize any of them. Good. Danua had claimed it wouldn't take long for all of Eilé to learn about her estranged daughter, but I hoped the news hadn't spread beyond her court. There came a certain kind of freedom with anonymity.

Cade went to go fetch us some drinks and I was left standing off to the side, my eyes darting about the crowd like a cornered rabbit. I shouldn't be nervous, but I couldn't help myself. I might be meeting some of my future friends tonight.

Cade returned with a plate of small sandwiches and two goblets filled with a pale golden liquid. I took one of the goblets and sniffed at the contents.

I arched a brow and blinked at him. "What's this?"

"You mean you've never had mead before?"

I gave him another puzzled glance and shook my head.

He smiled, his eyes crinkling. "Wine made from honey. Try it, you'll like it, but don't drink too fast."

I'd never had wine before. Well, Mom let me try champagne once at a New Year's Eve party, but only a sip.

Shrugging, I lifted the cup to my lips and took a small drink. My eyes must have grown huge because Cade burst out laughing. This stuff was delicious! Way better than champagne. Soon I finished my goblet and started asking Cade for more.

He laughed again. "Pace yourself Meghan. Mead's sweet but rather potent."

He took my empty goblet and set it aside.

"Care to dance?" he asked.

I took his offered hand timidly and soon we were skipping and stepping to a fast Celtic tune. The dance was meant for a large group, so I never found myself in Cade's company for too long and I felt less awkward since not everyone seemed to know the steps.

After the dance came to an end, we headed back to one of the several alcoves along the wall to observe the revelry for a while. For some reason I became overly aware of Cade's closeness and my heart, having rested after the lively dance, started beating faster once again. Looking at him would be too risky, so I kept my eyes lowered. We stood close together, in a dark corner of the room, with the music playing and the people shouting out joyously, but I heard nothing else besides my own heartbeat and Cade's as well.

"Meghan," he said in a low voice, too close to my ear to be considered innocent.

I took a slow, deliberate breath and glanced up. Something shone in his eyes, something intense and thrilling. I sucked in a sharp breath as his hand reached out to rest against my hip, the other hand moving towards my cheek. My heart hammered in my chest and I closed my eyes, but before I felt the brush of his fingers against my skin, a light, intrusive voice asked, "May I have this dance?"

Immediately Cade backed away and turned to face the young woman who had invaded our privacy. Well, semi-privacy. We were standing in the middle of a dance hall after all. She was shorter than me with long, golden-blond hair curling softly down her back. The blue dress she wore resembled the style I had worn at my mother's court and the design flattered her well-formed figure perfectly.

She stood in front of us grinning, waiting for Cade to either accept her offer or turn her down. She glanced at me for a half second, but it was long enough for me to see the change of color in her eyes and the quick expression that flashed across her face. I sucked in a sharp breath and retreated against the wall, a whole five inches away. I knew that look, oh did I know that look . . .

Cade glanced back at me, his face revealing disappointment and what I interpreted as an apology. I smiled and waved him on. He was far too polite to say no, and besides, it was just a dance.

He turned and heaved a great sigh, smiling easily and offering the blond a hand. "I would be honored."

She beamed and grabbed his hand, dragging him off to the middle of the floor where everyone had joined in another group dance. Before they pushed past the circle of people in front of us, however, she cast me one last scathing glare, her smile more malicious than pleasant.

I tried to recede further into the wall. *Stop it Meghan, this isn't high school, Cade's not your boyfriend, and all she did was ask him to dance.* But I knew better than that. After surviving four years of seeing that expression on other girls' faces, I understood what was going on. She wanted Cade all to herself, and she would go to any measure to get him. I hated how that made me feel. Not only was I helpless against such social battles, but she had every right to try and win Cade over. He'd made no promises to me.

After I managed to work myself up into a nice depressed sort of mood, I returned to the refreshment table and got some more mead, then came back to my spot on the wall to watch Cade and his new partner enjoy a slow dance.

I finished the goblet of mead faster than the last one. I was contemplating getting a third when one of the boys I had spotted earlier came strolling over. At first I thought he only meant to join a group of friends a few feet away, but he stepped between them and stopped in front of me instead. He grinned rakishly and crossed his arms over his chest. I eyed him warily, taking note of his high cheekbones and straight nose. He wasn't as attractive as Cade, but he would surely turn some heads at Black Lake High School.

"What's a pretty girl like you doing standing back here all alone without a dance partner?"

I actually peeked over my shoulder, almost bumping my nose into the stone wall.

"Me?" I said when I realized who he was talking to.

"No, the candelabra above you. Yes you." He smiled and held out his hand. "Care to dance, my lady?"

Oh, he was teasing me. Duh.

I cleared my throat and gestured towards the middle of the room. "Well, my friend-"

"Has abandoned you for another woman," he finished for me. "A rogue for sure. Let us put his memory behind you by taking part in the next dance."

Something about his manner, about the way he so arrogantly made presumptions, encouraged me not to trust him. However, a dance was just a dance, and perhaps it would help me forget that the blond girl had convinced Cade to be her partner for the last five songs.

"Sure," I said, smiling.

"Excellent!"

I offered him my hand and he took it, pulling me with more force than necessary onto the dance floor.

"What's your name?" he whispered close to my ear as we started in on a slower dance.

"M-Meghan," I managed, feeling a little flustered being suddenly so close to him.

He chuckled, his breath tickling my skin.

"Pleased to meet you Meghan, I'm Drustan."

Drustan and I danced for what seemed like hours. Every time one song ended, a new one began. I tried a few times to say I was tired, but he only ignored me and pulled me back into the next dance, often times pressing a little too close for comfort. After a while, I forgot about my misery, about going back to the alcove so I could find Cade, about the girl and her unspoken challenge.

I swirled and spun to the music, letting my partner lead me. I felt dizzy, carefree, alive. I was having a marvelous time, until I caught sight of Cade standing in the corner, smiling and talking with the pretty girl.

The mead in my stomach curdled into cold irritation. It wasn't because she talked to him, or that he seemed to be fully engaged in their conversation. It was the *way* she talked to him. Her hand rested on Cade's forearm and she leaned into him, a hair's width away from pressing her body against his. I gritted my teeth and focused entirely on them, stopping in the middle of the dance floor.

Drustan noticed my lack of movement and glanced in the direction I happened to be glaring. I'd always thought myself the sensible, non-jealous type. In fact, I prided myself on that. Apparently, I'd been wrong. I guess I never had a reason to be jealous before. Not until now, at least.

Drustan grabbed my arm in an attempt to lead me back into the dance, but paused when he followed my gaze again.

"Oh, there's another one," he chuckled.

Which only made my stomach burn more. So was this a habit of Cade's? Coming to the Dagda's parties and letting the girls fight over him? The memory of what he said to me the day I asked him to prom flared in my mind: *You don't really know me . . . Oh Meghan,* my inner voice whispered, *have you let Cade's charms blind you completely?*

"Come on Meghan, who cares about the young twit and Caedehn MacRoich. It's sad, really," he sighed.

For some reason, that caught my attention. I turned away from Cade and the girl flirting with him for the moment.

"Why is it sad?"

Drustan shrugged. "She's only showing an interest because no one's told her what he is yet."

A wicked gleam lit the boy's dark blue eyes. "The fun part is when someone finally does tell them. Maybe I can talk Niall into breaking the news so we can watch. Their reactions are always so comical. Meghan? Meghan, what's wrong?"

I forgot about my jealousy and a new anger grew in the pit of my stomach.

"And what exactly is he?" I demanded, crossing my arms and giving Drustan a hard glare.

"Oh come on! You must know. That's why I rescued you earlier!" He paused and shot me a befuddled expression. "Has no one told you?"

"No, no one's told me. But perhaps no one has told you who I am either," I countered.

What was I doing? Hadn't I been so thrilled earlier not to see any of Danua's nobles here tonight so I could be just Meghan and not the half-Fomore daughter of the high queen?

For a moment Drustan paled, but then he led us off the dance floor. We had caused enough of a scene by standing around while others tried to dance.

"Fine," he sniffed once we found another alcove, "Who are you then?"

I'd accepted Drustan's offer to dance only because I wanted to stop obsessing over Cade and the blond girl. I'd been selfish and wanted to make Cade jealous, too. I know my actions had been stupid and immature, but that hadn't kept me from following through. Now the young Faelorehn was annoying me, the way he spoke about Cade. His sneering comments made me think of my mother and how she also tried to convince me to stay away from him. And if I was being completely honest with myself, what Drustan said scared me to death. Cade had kept things from me, yes, and I had always assumed he did so in order to protect me or himself. Might this secret be worse than any of the others? Had I foolishly placed my trust in someone who had no qualms in lying to me? Was I merely another rube on Cade's list?

I sighed and peered back at Drustan. His eyes shone dark silver now and I wondered what color mine might be. I let my lip curl back and reveled in the numbing qualities of the mead that hadn't quite worn off before saying with a great deal of bravado, "I'm the long lost Fomorian bastard child of Danua."

Now *that* shocked him. He jerked his head back and his eyes grew wide and paled even further. Then they narrowed.

"You're as bad as him," he hissed, stabbing his finger in Cade's direction.

I stood my ground as Drustan continued, "There were rumors she'd taken a Fomorian to her bed, now I can see the rumors were true. And I let you touch me!"

Okay. I hadn't expected a reaction this bad, and after all I'd been through and after all my years of being made fun of, you'd think I'd be used to it.

Drustan turned violently and walked away, acting as if I had leprosy. I allowed myself to fall against the alcove in the wall. Taking a deep, shuddering breath, I tried to keep the tears from falling, but it was no use, especially when I glanced up to find Cade dancing with the stupid blond girl again.

I felt heart-broken and hopeless at the same time. I thought I was finally escaping a world that had shunned me. I imagined one day I'd be able to live in Eilé among my own people, to be normal for once in my life, but even in the Otherworld I wasn't to be normal.

A wash of hot anger flooded me and I slammed my fist against the wall. Wonderful, now my hand hurt and my tears fell faster. To my immense relief, the alcove was tucked further into the hall where darkness reigned and the noise of the dancing, laughter and music drowned out the sound of my sobs.

I pulled myself deeper into the recessed space and wrapped my arms around my legs, dropping my head onto my knees. I don't know how much time passed, but at one point someone touched my shoulder. I flinched and forgot about wanting to be left alone in my misery. I glanced up, my face contorted in rage and self-pity, ready to yell at whoever came to bother me.

A pair of bright blue eyes framed by a mane of pale orange hair stopped me short.

"What's the matter little Meghan?" the Dagda asked in a quiet voice.

Somehow, I heard his whispered words over the revelry in his dance hall. My bottom lip quivered. Despite my current mood, a sense of incredible happiness washed over me at the sight of him. I didn't know what it was about the Dagda that made me like him so much. He was a promiscuous, loud giant of a man, but he had a gentleness and understanding way about him. I guess this is what helped me trust him so easily.

I tried to open my mouth and tell him what had me so upset: Cade had found a new girl, my mother despised me, soon I'd be living in a strange world, separated from a family that actually loved me . . . But at the moment all my sorrow came flooding out in one overwhelming wave of emotion. I threw my arms around his neck and cried into his chest as he scooped me up.

"Hush now, little Faelorah, hush now," he crooned as he carried me over to another room.

Once there, he set me down on a spacious couch next to a roaring fire. The party still carried on in the other room, but the distant clamor didn't drown out the sound of the whispering flames.

"Now," the Dagda stated, picking up a pitcher and filling a small tankard with golden liquid, "you must tell me why the prettiest girl in my house is so upset on this, Beltaine Eve, of all nights."

I grinned at his attempt to cheer me, but my tears still fell.

"I'm sorry Dagda," I murmured, finally feeling a little ashamed of my behavior. "I think, I think it's just been so overwhelming. Discovering I'm Faelorehn, being hunted by the Morrigan, learning I'm the illegitimate daughter of Eilé's high queen."

I let out a deep sigh, wiping my eyes with the handkerchief the Dagda had given me.

"Yes, and I'm sure witnessing your young Caedehn receive so much attention while keeping you at arm's length isn't helping."

He grinned and I blushed.

"He isn't my Caedehn," I grumbled as I tucked a loose piece of hair behind my ear.

"No? Are you sure?" the Dagda said cheerily, as if speaking to a daft child who couldn't grasp the obvious.

I blinked at him again, this time with some surprise. His grin widened as he placed the tankard of mead in my hand. The honey wine cooled my throat but warmed my stomach and as I savored it, I thought about his question. No, I wasn't sure. That was the problem. Well, okay, I had no doubts on my end, but not Cade's. Sometimes I was wholly convinced he returned my affections, but then he would do or say something to prove otherwise. Like spending the whole evening with some other girl while I was left to dance with a cute boy who turned out to be a total ass.

I took a deep breath, then thought more about what Drustan had said to me.

"Drustan seemed to be appalled to learn I was the product of Danua's affair."

I stared the Dagda in the eye as the sadness welled up again. "Do you treat me kindly only because I am half Fomorian? Only because you feel sorry for me?"

The Dagda's blue eyes hardened into ice and he frowned. "Drustan o'Ceallaigh is an ignorant whelp. What exactly did he say to you Meghan?"

The anger in his voice surprised me.

"When I told him about being Danua's daughter, he went from being polite to acting as if I were something nasty he'd stepped in."

The fire sputtered and almost went out, and the room vibrated with violence. I set my mead down and cast the Dagda a worried glance. He was angry; cold and angry. Then the dark look passed.

"I'm sorry Meghan. His behavior sickens me."

I lifted a hand, glad to discover this god's irritation had dissipated.

"It's partly my fault. I told him who I was without even considering what the repercussions might be. I mean, I know my mother's nobles weren't too thrilled when she told them, but I didn't think he would have reacted so, um, negatively to the truth."

"And why did you tell him the truth?"

I frowned. Yes, why had I . . . ? Oh yeah, because he had made some comment about Cade.

"He said the younger girls didn't realize what Cade was and if they found out, they'd be horrified. It made me angry, so I got a little careless and told him I was Danua's daughter. I guess I did it to take his focus off of Cade." My own fear of what Drustan had insinuated, about Cade using me, I kept to myself.

The room grew cold again, the healthy fire nearly flickered out, and the cup of mead I held seemed to freeze in my hands. Fear prickled my senses, and when I worked up enough nerve to glance at the Dagda, his face was blank and distant and his eyes appeared as dark as night.

Finally, he spoke, his voice low and cold, "And did he tell you, Meghan? Did he tell you what Caedehn is?"

I set my icy tankard down with care and took a deep breath.

"No," I said carefully, "I was too angry at the time to ask him." And too afraid.

The sigh coming from the Dagda might've been winter's first icy breath.

I garnered my courage again. "What is he, Dagda?"

Beltaine

My voice was a whisper, so I expected silence or more anger. The sad hum that left the Dagda's throat sounded like defeat; weariness even. He ran his fingers through his hair, a motion that reminded me of his foster son, before letting his shoulders slump as he rested his chin on one hand.

"That, my dear girl, is Cade's story to tell. Don't get me wrong, you deserve to know, but Caedehn should be the one to tell you."

My own tension began to drain. Yes, deep down I wished to be told the entire truth. For a long time I'd suspected Cade was more than what he seemed, but I could never figure it out. I had always been too afraid to ask; terrified my terrible suspicions would prove true. Cade had never opened up to me. I think this is what hurt me the most, that he didn't trust me enough to talk to me when he needed to. And now I had people warning me to stay away from him. I wanted to understand why.

"Your trust means a great deal to him, Meghan. As secretive as he may seem, he would never betray it," the Dagda whispered.

I jerked back on the couch, my eyes wide. Had he read my mind?

"How'd you know that's what I was thinking about?" I croaked.

The Dagda grinned, his pale blue eyes sparkling once again. "It's written all over your face darling. For as long as I've lived, if I haven't learned anything else, I've learned how to read a woman's face."

He winked, which made me laugh.

He sobered up again and took a deep breath. "Promise me one thing Meghan, please?"

A hint of sorrow lingered in his words. I gave him my full attention.

"When you do find out, please try to understand. Please remember what he means to you and like you, he cannot help what he is."

I shuddered. That frightened me. Could Cade's secret really be so terrible? Could it make me forget I loved him?

I took a long, steadying breath and answered, "I promise. I would never betray his friendship."

The Dagda nodded, the sadness still burning in his eyes, then clapped his hands together before standing.

"Now, let's find something to help clean you up so we can return you to the festivities. Midnight draws near, and you'll not want to miss the show!"

I lifted my hands to my cheeks, wondering how awful I looked after blubbering half the night.

After washing my face and running my fingers through my hair, I rejoined the party. Several couples were lined up in the center of the hall, laughing and kicking up their heels to a lively song. I searched their faces and breathed a sigh of relief when I realized Cade wasn't among them.

I focused on finding him then. I felt pretty foolish about how I'd behaved earlier so I wanted to apologize if he had noticed. I hoped he hadn't seen how upset I'd been, but despite my embarrassment, I yearned to be with him for the rest of the night, especially after what Drustan had implied. Perhaps Cade and I could be outcasts together.

Beltaine

My search of the room proved to be fruitless. Just as I decided to give up and find a seat somewhere, I caught a glimpse of Drustan tucked away in another alcove, pressed up against the girl I'd seen Cade with earlier, whispering something in her ear. She seemed to be listening intently to what he said, the distance across the hall doing nothing to hide the expression of horrified shock now taking the place of confusion on her pretty face.

Drustan's grin revealed his malicious nature and the glint in his eye confirmed my suspicions.

I gritted my teeth. *The Morrigan isn't the only one capable of cruelty in this world,* I told myself.

Needing to cool my anger, I crossed the room, heading towards the entrance hall. One of the Dagda's guards eyed me with curiosity, but kindly stepped aside when I informed him I needed some air. The night hinted of frost, despite the fact it was spring, and only a few people remained standing around the dwindling bonfire.

I wrapped my arms around myself and threw my head back, gazing up at the stars twinkling through the branches high above me.

"They can be overwhelming if you haven't learned how to deal with them."

Cade's voice appearing out of the dark startled me a little. I turned to glance at him and frowned.

"I didn't display the best behavior in there myself," I mumbled.

Cold anger seemed to flash across his face and disappear just as quickly. "Drustan o'Ceallaigh had no right to treat you so callously. If word got back to Danua-"

"How did you know?" I cut him off, turning to gaze at him in the semi-dark with wide eyes.

Cade gave me a sad smile. "The Dagda told me."

"Oh." I dearly hoped the Dagda hadn't told him everything . . .

I sighed and cast my worry aside, focusing instead on what Cade had said about Danua.

"My mother wouldn't care," I grumbled as I turned to gaze back at the stars.

The gentle touch of Cade's hands on my shoulders informed me he had moved closer.

"She cares Meghan, believe me, even though she doesn't show it," he murmured. "In order to keep the balance of this world, she must not display emotion. Someday she'll be able to show you her true self. Until then, you'll just have to believe you have people here who," Cade paused, as if he were giving careful consideration to his choice of words. He released a tiny sigh and finished, "people who care for you."

My face warmed. A roughness tinged his voice, making my skin tingle, but I shook the sensation off. I hoped he was right, about having true friends here in the Otherworld. If, for some unforeseen reason things didn't work out with Cade and me, I had others to help me with my new life. The Dagda, for one, had made it clear I was welcome to stay with him, but I would worry about the details later. Time to change the subject.

I turned my head and peered up at Cade. He was watching me, making sure I didn't bolt.

"How can you stand those people talking behind your back and treating you with scorn?" I whispered, my tone harsh. "How do you tolerate their constant judgment and ridicule?"

"I learned to ignore them long ago."

"How long ago? How long does it take to get used to being an outsider?"

I really did want to know. If I was assured that someday the harsh and spiteful words and actions of others would cease to bother me, perhaps I could tough it out for now.

Cade only grinned, the light of the bonfire cutting a fierce shadow across his face.

"That all depends on the person. When you finally understand who you are, really understand, then their indifference won't seem so bad. Trust me."

I turned those words over in my head. Trust him. Despite my better judgment, I did trust him. Did he trust me, though? I was tempted to ask him why Drustan and the others shunned him, especially after what the Dagda had said, but I kept those questions at bay. Now didn't feel like the right time.

Cade took a deep breath and held out a hand. I stared at it for a moment.

"I suggest we head back inside, especially now that I've managed to extricate myself from the talons of that little blond harpy," he said, shuddering in what I liked to think was disgust.

I looked at him with wide eyes and he smiled back at me before continuing, "It's nearly midnight and we don't want to miss the spectacle my foster father has planned. Besides, don't you want to practice dancing for your prom tomorrow night?"

Forgetting my worry, I grinned back and took his hand. The moment we entered the loud hall, Cade pulled me into a fast jig and from that point on I forgot about my earlier jealousy, about Drustan's rude behavior, about what the Dagda had told me, about my worry over Danua. I was completely absorbed in the music and Cade's every word and lingering touch.

The Dagda's musicians played three more songs, one being slower than the rest, and Cade didn't give me up for any of them. All the awful events of the night seemed to melt away as he hugged me close and led me in a slow dance. I leaned my head against his chest, breathing in his unique scent and letting the smooth rhythm of a Celtic tune sweep me away. I felt, for the first time in weeks, as if this was exactly where I belonged.

Midnight rolled around and the Dagda had everyone clear away from the center of the room. He invited those who wished to display their talents to step up and give us their best. Cade and I watched in amazement and humor as several people tried to impress us with their juggling, acting or mimicking skills. We were encouraged by our host to boo the ones who failed at their task and cheer on anyone showing an unusual talent. By the end of the show, my face hurt from laughing so hard.

Partway through the performance, Cade left to get us some more refreshments. On his way back, one of the Dagda's guards entered from a side hallway and made a bee line towards him, intercepting him before he could reach me. The man gave a polite bow and handed Cade a rolled parchment sealed with wax. The guard returned to his post in silence as Cade studied the seal with a slight frown.

"What's the matter Cade?" I called out.

He didn't seem to hear me. He cracked the wax on the missive and started unrolling it. A sudden flourish of music pulled my attention back towards the dance floor and I laughed out loud when I saw the Dagda, his huge form, leaping from foot to foot, as limber and agile as a gymnast.

A light touch on my shoulder jerked my attention back towards Cade. He had moved closer to me, the piece of parchment held tightly in his hand. His face had turned grim and all the joyous light in his eyes had vanished.

I eyed the crumpled paper and spotted a small symbol on one corner. My heart stopped when I recognized the image. A black bird. A raven. I gestured towards his hand. "What does it say?"

Cade took a breath and ran his fingers through his hair, a sure sign something was distressing him.

"Cade!" I repeated, becoming frantic as I stood up and knocked the goblet I'd been drinking out of to the floor. The cup made a dull crack against the ground, spilling mead on the carpet as well as the stone.

Cade looked up at me, his eyes darkening as his anger rose. "A message from the Morrigan. She is on her way to the dolmarehn that leads into the swamp behind your house. She intends to enter the mortal world with the purpose of killing your family."

Seventeen

Disclosure

I didn't even pause to tell the Dagda I was leaving. The moment Cade told me what the message said, a roaring of some internal emotion flooded my senses. My fingers began to tingle and the little pit of magic next to my heart started glowing again.

I grabbed Cade's hand and tugged him down the great hall. He came easily with me, his own steps long to match my fast pace.

"If we push Speirling, we should arrive at the dolmarehn in half the time it usually takes. The missive said she was still several hours away from the castle, so with luck and speed, we'll reach the dolmarehn before she does."

I was glad Cade was talking, because I had lost the ability to speak. All my body knew at the moment was that we needed to race as fast as possible, back to my family before anything happened to them. If the Morrigan used her power against them, they wouldn't stand a chance. *No Meghan, don't think,* I told myself as the first sob broke free, *don't think about anything. Just get home.*

Cade realized my anguish and stopped abruptly, pulling me around by the hand he still held and locking me into a close embrace.

"We'll get back in time Meghan," he breathed against my hair, "we'll get there before she does."

I returned his embrace, wrapping my arms around him. His heartbeat matched my own, and I wanted nothing more than to lean into Cade; let his simple presence will away my fear and sorrow.

He held me for a few moments more, then just as briskly as he had scooped me up, he released me and pulled me through the huge door of the entrance hall of the Dagda's home. He darted back inside to grab a cloak, then threw the thick material over my shoulders and wrapped it tight in front of me.

A small group of boys loitering near the bonfire jumped at our sudden burst through the doors.

"My horse, please. The large black stallion," Cade said sternly.

One boy nodded and darted off. As we waited, I watched the flames of the fire dance and flicker in the breeze. The night would be cold and windy, and I sensed a storm blowing in. My whole body quivered and Cade pressed me close again, smoothing his hand over my hair and murmuring words in the ancient language of this world, none of which I understood.

The young boy returned, tugging Speirling behind him. Fergus trotted silently after him and I heard Meridian's distressed cries somewhere above us. Before I could so much as take a breath, Cade climbed on top of Speirling's back and pulled me up to sit in front of him.

"Tell the Dagda we give our apologies, but something urgent has come up," Cade called down to the startled boys.

He didn't wait for a reply, but dug his heels into his horse's sides and we went tearing across the ground, Speirling's hooves kicking up the dirt of the smooth road.

Cade kept one hand on the reins and one arm around my waist. His grip was protective, possessive even. If we were racing through the dark countryside for any other reason than to save my family from the Morrigan's wrath, I would have been tickled pink. Well, and a bit terrified of falling and being trampled. I took what little comfort I could in Cade's arms and tried not to let my mind descend into hysteria.

Unfortunately, my mind paid no attention to me. *Mom, Dad, the twins . . . Bradley and Logan. Aiden.* That's when I lost what remained of my feeble composure; thinking of Aiden. My baby brother, the one who looked most like me even though we weren't blood related. Aiden was the most helpless of them all. Not able to help myself any longer, I turned my head and buried it in Cade's shoulder and simply let the tears come. He started murmuring to me in those ancient words again as we sped through the night, but the agony in my heart just wouldn't go away.

Speirling ran the entire way, never seeming to tire. Thank goodness he was an Otherworldly horse or else he might have died from the effort.

Dawn's first light touched the horizon as we came up over a final rise in the rolling countryside, and the dolmarehn leading to Cade's castle towered into view. Cade gave his horse another nudge and we went flying down the hill, Fergus and Meridian, miraculously, still on our heels.

I must have dozed off during the night, despite the jarring ride and bite of the wind and rain that had finally caught up to us and despite the gnawing worry over my family. I felt stiff and groggy, and grit gathered at the corners of my eyes. Cade didn't slow Speirling as we entered the large dolmarehn. The familiar strangeness that always overcame me when crossing through these portals tugged at me, but the transition was quick and in the next breath we were thundering down the trail running alongside the stream behind Cade's home.

"Not long now Meghan. Only ten more miles or so and we'll be at the dolmarehn that will take us to your family."

I nodded, tightening my grip on the arm wrapped around my middle and trying to ignore the horrible dread coiling up in my stomach. What if we were too late? How could I live with myself if the Morrigan killed my family? I dashed those thoughts from my mind. They only fed my anxiety and I needed to be clear-headed right now.

The early morning sun bathed the countryside in golden light, doing its best to warm the land before the storm arrived. We had jumped ahead of the clouds by passing through the dolmarehn, but they would reach us soon. I hoped we'd be in the mortal world by then.

"Just beyond those hills Meghan, only a little further," Cade murmured, his voice no more than an inch above my ear.

We broke free of the woods and I spotted the castle below and to the left of us. I gazed out across the wide valley, remembering the first time I'd found myself in the Otherworld.

It seemed like ages ago, when I'd been foolish enough to fall into the Morrigan's trap and come so close to dying. I shook my head, forcing those awful thoughts away. I was with Cade now, and with any luck we wouldn't even see the Morrigan today.

My skin began to crawl. It had been a long time since she'd bothered to harass me, and even on the few occasions she sent her reminders (the demon bats and the strange pig), the resulting injuries barely left a mark. Okay, maybe the cut I got from the evil bat was bad, but in general, I managed to escape relatively unscathed. I should have realized she was preparing something far worse.

"Come on," Cade growled, kicking Speirling into a faster pace.

We descended the hill beside the castle and Cade's horse picked up his gait once we reached the fields, breathing heavily because of his efforts.

Speirling turned a final bend and when the trail leading up to the dolmarehn came into view, Cade released something between a horrified gasp and a curse, jerking on the stallion's reins in his state of shock. Speirling let loose a distressed whinny, rising up onto his hind legs and falling back to keep his balance. Fergus started barking and Meridian's fearful screeches rained down from above.

I clung to Cade and the saddle, trying to stay seated. I made an attempt to figure out what was going on, but the hood of the cloak obscured my view. Once the horse lowered his forelegs to the ground, I glanced up, drew the hood back, and trained my eyes ahead of us.

Disclosure

I nearly fell from Speirling's back as my face drained of all color. There, curling around the base of the hill like some menacing fog, stood an army of dark, terrifying faelah. But what drew my attention the most was the woman who blocked our path several hundred feet away. I was confused for a split-second. The message claimed she was on her way to kill my family, so why would she be standing here below the path to the dolmarehn, waiting with her minions? Why wasn't she climbing up the trail to pass into the mortal world?

Cade's arm tightened on me for a mere second, and in that moment I knew. Of *course* . . . My brain was worse for the wear right now, after spending the entire night playing freeze tag with my emotions while flying across the countryside on horseback, worried sick about my parents and my brothers. At least, that's the excuse I made for myself.

The Morrigan never planned to kill my family. She'd set this up, just like last time. She'd drawn me, and Cade as well, into her nice, neat little trap. She guessed I would come to save my family. She pieced together exactly what to say in order to draw me out into the open, far away from the Dagda, the one Faelorehn (besides my uncaring mother) who possessed the most magic to protect me. Now we were alone, terribly outnumbered and miles upon miles away from anyone who might help.

I gritted my teeth and kicked myself mentally. She'd done it again. She had tricked me *again*. And this time I couldn't even blame it on my own ignorance. I now understood what the Morrigan was capable of and I had a terrible feeling the price for my foolishness would be far greater than what I was willing to pay.

Dolmarehn

The soot-grey clouds that followed us from the Dagda's started gathering overhead and the rugged hills framing the valley seemed to cower in anticipation for what was to come. I tried to find solace in those hills; in the scattered trees growing on their peaks, but the small valley we now stood in brought to mind a bear trap, ready to snap shut and cripple me.

The faelah moved quickly and orderly, making a quarter mile wide semi-circle to enclose Cade and me, with the largest of them standing guard at our backs. Yes, the trap was set.

Neither Cade nor I said a word, nor did we look at each other. What could we say or recognize in one another's eyes that we didn't already know? The Morrigan had won. Her patience had finally paid off, and she'd won. I'd forgotten about Cade's hold on me, but then he loosened his grip and leaned forward.

"I'm going to get off the horse now," he whispered next to my ear, his voice revealing only a trace of the emotion he kept bottled up.

I nodded, not looking back at him. I thought it wise to keep my eye on the enemy, one that stood eerily still. The faelah were waiting for our next move, most likely. Cade slid off of Speirling's back, reaching up to lift me down. The horse danced nervously away, but not too far. I didn't like the way some of the Morrigan's monsters eyed him, as if they thought he'd be a quick and easy snack.

Something cold and wet pressed against my hand and my first instinct was to jerk it away. Fortunately, I didn't screech as well. I glanced down and sighed with relief when I realized it was only Fergus offering me comfort, and not some slimy creepy crawly thing of the Morrigan's.

Taking the wolfhound's cue, Meridian swooped down from the storm clouds and landed on my shoulder. Her feathers were ruffled from the wind and our break-neck journey, but other than that, she looked no worse for wear. I understood the spirit guides couldn't protect me from whatever the Morrigan had planned, she was just too powerful, but their presence comforted me nonetheless.

Something warm and reassuring laced with my fingers and I glanced down to find Cade's hand gripping my own. I squeezed back and took a deep, shuddering breath. We were in this together. This was my fault, the Morrigan wanted me, but Cade would not abandon me. And I knew why she was after me. She craved my raw magic, magic that was supposed to be far stronger than any other in Eilé, save for the natural power of the Faelorehn high lords and ladies themselves: the Celtic gods and goddesses. Too bad my glamour didn't seem to be working. *You've wasted your time!* I wanted to scream. *Turns out I can't even get it to leave my body.* Unfortunately, I didn't think she would believe me.

Taking a deep breath, Cade stepped forward, pulling me along with him. As we moved closer, I tried not to stare at the creatures standing on either side of the goddess. Many I recognized, both from their visits to the mortal world and from my first trip here. They were all dark in color and most of them resembled the rotting corpses of something long dead. They all stared at me, some without eyes, as if they were merely waiting for a single word or signal from their master to devour me. I blanched and Cade pulled me closer.

Dolmarehn

Ahead, the Morrigan waited, her dark cloak and skirts and black hair dancing in the wind. I didn't think I would ever get used to her imposing presence. I wouldn't be surprised if the storm held back its intense fury simply because she told it to.

Eventually we stopped walking and came to rest several feet in front of the Morrigan and the ten hellhounds standing by her side. I eyed them warily, their rotting flesh and glowing eyes still unsettling despite my many visits to the Otherworld.

"We wish to go to the dolmarehn," Cade said, his voice strong and clear.

The creatures growled, grunted and rattled in response to his statement, but they held their places.

"I do not see why you would," the Morrigan responded in a bored fashion. "There is nothing in the mortal world worth going back to."

My eyes grew wide and for a moment I thought I might pass out. Cade dropped my hand and put his arm around me instead.

"Meghan," he whispered, taking hold of my chin and lifting my eyes to meet his.

"No," I murmured as the tears began to form.

Cade whipped his head around and cast a hard glare at the Morrigan.

"You lie!" he hissed, and his constricting grasp on me only reflected my own thoughts. She very well might not be lying.

The goddess rolled her eyes. "I'm afraid you are right, dear Caedehn, much to my chagrin. Time constraints, you know. I'll simply wait and exterminate the mortal vermin after we are done here."

I almost passed out again, this time from the rush of relief coursing through me.

"And what, exactly, are we doing here?"

The strength in Cade's voice helped rally my spirits. Well, at least enough so that he didn't need to hold me up any longer.

"Isn't it obvious? You've been hiding this poor misguided creature for weeks, bringing her here to Eilé and secretly flaunting her before all sorts of Faelorehn, and I thought the time had come to remove her from your negative influence."

I stood up straight then, giving the woman a quizzical glare. *What?*

"Do explain yourself," Cade demanded through clenched teeth.

"I've drawn you out in order to claim fosterage of this lost Faelorehn girl."

"She doesn't need fostering," Cade snapped.

"Oh, but Caedehn! All Faelorehn are fostered! Do you want poor Meghan here to be an outcast when she makes Eilé her permanent home? In order to be accepted among the highest circles she must be fostered by one of the kings or queens of the Otherworld."

"She does not need to be fostered if she lives under Danua's roof. The high queen has plenty of subjects who might act as a foster parent, all of them worthy of moving in the highest circles. Your concern is unwarranted and unwanted."

Under Danua's roof? He must be buying time because I knew *that* was never going to happen. I was also pretty certain should Cade grow any tenser, he just might shatter from the effort of keeping still. But that wasn't my greatest concern. I listened carefully to what the Morrigan said, each passing word making my stomach knot with unease. Oh, she wanted to 'foster' me alright, but not because she felt concerned about my social status and reputation.

"Her own mother has shunned her, or so that's the word being passed around the Faelorehn courts," the Morrigan continued, her tone adamant, "and I've heard of no others who wish to accept her, so she's still a strayling. Therefore, I make first claim to her."

"No."

I gave Cade a surprised look. His negative response had been sharper than my own.

"I'll take responsibility for her," he continued.

In any other situation, my heart would've sung with happiness, but now was not the time for rejoicing.

The Morrigan smiled, though her expression held no humor. "You have no right, my dear boy. Not being one of the kings or queens yourself, you would need consent from a guardian or blood relation to take on such a responsibility and your guardian is not here, and I do not grant my permission."

It took a few moments for the Morrigan's words to register. After all, she was speaking of Otherworldly matters and class systems, things as foreign to me as Eilé itself. But what did she mean by Cade needing authorization from a guardian or blood relation? I assumed the guardian she mentioned could only be the Dagda, but he wasn't here. Or he could ask a blood relation for permission, and she wouldn't grant hers. Wait ... What?

I snapped my gaze up, taking in the goddess standing before me. Her eyes narrowed into something between suspicion and annoyance. I turned my head and blinked up at Cade. He wouldn't meet my eyes.

"What does she mean, she won't grant her permission?"

My question came out as a whisper, but from Cade's slight flinch I knew he'd heard me over the growing storm and the sickening chatter and growling coming from the army of faelah.

In the next moment, I realized the Morrigan had caught wind of my words as well. She laughed, a long, cruel, self-obsessive laugh, rumbling through the threatening air like thunder. I trembled, for I sensed her power building all around us like lightning charging the thick, heavy atmosphere.

"Oh my dear girl," she chuckled, wiping a tear from her eye, "are you telling me that my sweet little Caedehn hasn't disclosed the degree of our relationship yet?"

Cade remained absolutely still next to me, and my skin began to turn hot. I had a horrible suspicion I was about to learn something dreadful. The secret Cade had kept from me all this time, the thing everyone else seemed to be aware of, except me. The sting of tears prickled at my eyes and I fought them. Cade was supposed to be the one to tell me this, not my worst enemy.

The Morrigan grinned and locked eyes with Cade. The expression on her cruel, beautiful face conveying her barely retained glee.

"Why, he is my one and only son. And I am his dear mother."

I didn't mean to gasp, honestly, I didn't. It just kind of slipped out. In fact, I hardly registered the act because I was too busy being bludgeoned over the head with shock. *The Morrigan. Cade's mother!? Oh. My. God.* He was the son of a goddess? Oh, and now his disgust at my assumption the year before made perfect sense. No, not his girlfriend; his mother. Blood relation. Not an aunt or a cousin, but his *mother!*

"Not that I ever wanted a son, and Cade is proof as to why," she sneered, the look of enjoyment now replaced with annoyance and disgust. "He's been a severe disappointment since birth. A complete nuisance."

She turned her harsh glare on her son, the air all but crackling with dark red fire around her. I had pulled away from him but he still held on to me, tightly, as if afraid I would bolt like a rabbit.

The Morrigan continued, "All I asked of you, Caedehn, was for you to keep my Earth-happy minions in line and to rein in any lost Faelorehn that might be useful. And here you have the unwanted progeny of Danua and some Fomorian whelp, a combination you know is volatile and oh so full of magical potential, and you've kept her away from me all this time. Was that so much for a mother to ask of her son? To bring such treasures back to me? But no, you refused."

"You act as if I had a choice!" Cade retorted, finally releasing me and letting his anger show. I sensed it curling around him and he seemed to grow larger.

Far too much power brewed around me, what with the Morrigan and Cade's barely contained rage, the restlessness of all the faelah surrounding us and the angry storm above. I backed away slowly, afraid this gathering of power might somehow inadvertently destroy me.

I could just make out Speirling, skirting along the edge of the circle, only the unpleasant smell and chatter coming from the Morrigan's monsters keeping him in the valley. I had half a mind to run to him, leap onto his back, and force him to jump over the smaller creatures, but I would never leave Cade. He was the son of the Morrigan, but that hardly seemed to matter. Yes, I found it intimidating, but he was my friend, more than my friend. I loved him, and just like I'd promised the Dagda, I wouldn't leave him.

"You placed a geis on me, remember?"

Cade's hard voice snapped me back to the present. I best pay attention if we wanted to get out of this alive. Should survival even be an option at this point . . .

The Morrigan snorted. "A geis you broke."

"Please Mother," he countered in disgust, "our people have been breaking geasa since the beginning of time. What choice do we have?"

"It doesn't matter. Whether you had broken your geis or not, you still would've failed."

"Of course I would have," Cade said roughly. "No matter what I choose to do, you'll never be satisfied. You'll never stop taking your anger with my father out on me."

The Morrigan turned with frightening speed and her black skirts billowed around her, forming menacing clouds mirroring those hovering above us.

"Your father," she hissed, "took advantage of my good graces!"

Cade laughed out loud. "Your good graces? He tricked you, plain and simple, after *you* tried to beguile *him*. So really, you have only yourself to blame."

It seemed they had forgotten my presence, not a difficult feat considering I'd been practically struck dumb, and from where I stood, this conversation had been a long time coming. I arched an eyebrow when Cade glanced back at me. The look of guilt on his face suggested there was more unsettling information to come. Oh well. Nothing that was said or happened from this point on would change the way I felt about him and I was pretty sure I'd already learned the worst.

The Morrigan bared her teeth. "Cuchulainn was a fool, and he died a fool as well."

For the second time that night, my raw senses were doused with another helping of shock. So much for being prepared. Somehow between the roaring in my ears, the pounding of my heart, and the short-circuiting of my nerve endings, I found my voice, "*Cuchulainn* is your father?! And the Morrigan your mother?"

A cold numbness rushed to the tips of my fingers and toes. How ironic that the people at the Dagda's party had been telling stories of Cuchulainn only a few hours ago. But how could Cuchulainn, the Hound of Cullen, the seemingly invincible warrior hero of Celtic lore, be Cade's father? I couldn't recall ever reading or hearing about the Morrigan hooking up with Cuchulainn, but there was the time she'd tried to bait him in one of the epics I'd read.

"Wait," I glanced up at the Morrigan, ignoring the brewing hatred on her face, "you tried to seduce Cuchulainn, but he knew what you were up to." Or so the old legend had implied as much.

She crossed her arms and snorted. "Didn't keep him from pretending to take me up on my offer. He only used me and cast me aside when he was through."

"Just as you are trying to use and cast aside Cade?" I braved. Hey, we were cornered and most likely done for. Might as well get everything out in the open.

The Morrigan turned burning scarlet eyes on me. "Don't you *dare* judge me you pathetic fae strayling! I can't believe how you cling so pathetically to my son, knowing what he is and what he's capable of."

I ignored my blush and grumbled, "What are you talking about? I'm only now finding out about his parentage, and as surprising as it may be, none of it matters to me."

Cade stiffened next to me. I gulped. Had I given myself away; confessed what I'd been holding secret for so long? And, in the midst of all that was happening, did it matter anymore?

The Morrigan darted her eyes between us. For once, she seemed utterly befuddled. Then her composure melted into pure, malicious humor.

"What is this? Caedehn! Have you kept *everything* from the poor girl? No wonder she doesn't run from you in disgust, like all the rest."

I bristled. What did she mean, all the rest? I glanced up at Cade and, judging by his averted eyes, the anger must be clear on my face. It only lasted a few moments though. If he really was the son of Cuchulainn and the Morrigan, then he was very old, despite how young he appeared. Of course he'd had girlfriends before me. I couldn't hold it against him, but from what the Morrigan just said, there was more to it than that.

"So," the Morrigan continued, her voice sickly sweet, "you've never seen his ríastrad before, his battle fury?"

Cade blanched and I froze. *Ríastrad, battle fury* . . . A memory flashed through my mind, of me dying beside the dolmarehn and Cade contorting into something terrifying and grotesque. My face must have given me away because the Morrigan cackled with glee, her features momentarily faded into those of the crone she sometimes depicted. I shook in disgust.

"Oh, this is too much! Oh Cade, dearest, I think I shall prolong your girlfriend's death, so she can get a good last look at you; see what you truly are."

"No!" Cade shouted, cutting his hand through the air and stepping in front of me. "No, you won't hurt Meghan."

"But Cade, my pets are so lonely and they wish to play."

She lifted her arms and the earth on either side of her cracked and rumbled. Fear rushed through me like an icy poison in my blood. Apparently, negotiations were over.

The five hellhounds on opposite sides of her whined and started writhing as the goddess took up a chant, one that seemed to incite the magic of the earth and sky around us. I watched with revulsion as the Cúmorrig broke apart in front of me and grew into something far more terrifying than what they were. I clung to Cade's arm, peeking around him as the horror unfolded. The other faelah must have been nervous as well, for they began keening as they crawled over one another. I got the impression they desperately wanted to flee, but the Morrigan's spell held them in place.

Disclosure

The chanting deepened and the hounds grew in size. Their snouts elongated, the rotting skin stretching completely away to reveal bloody bone and long, wicked canine teeth beneath. Tangled, shaggy black hair sprouted behind their ears and down their necks, like a dark lion's mane. Their hind legs lengthened, pushing their new, massive size skyward, and their forelegs grew even longer as a set of long, curved claws replaced their hands.

When the transformation was complete, they stood around seven feet tall, their eyes glowing violet, their faces caught in a continuous snarl of hatred and agony. I glanced down and the reason for their cries of pain became apparent. Where their rib cages should have been were great, gaping holes dripping with blood, gore and what looked suspiciously like maggots.

I couldn't take it anymore. Still clinging to Cade, I turned my head and almost threw up. If by some miracle I survived this, I would need therapy for the rest of my life. Cade turned and kneeled down beside me, pushing the hair away from my face and speaking the calm, foreign words he always did when trying to comfort me. I felt foolish. Losing my cool wouldn't help in my attempts to prove to Cade I could handle the Faelorehn way of life.

"Come now Caedehn. I grow weary of this little game. Simply hand the girl over to me so you can get over your irrational little infatuation."

"Why, so you can steal her magic as well? Tell me Mother, how many had to die in order for you to complete that nasty trick?"

Cade inclined his head towards the new monsters, the ones that used to be the Cúmorrig.

I studied them through the curtain of hair Cade had failed to brush back with the rest.

"Unimportant creatures, all of them," she hissed, her fists balled at her sides.

"Your greed and disrespect for Eilé's bounty will one day come back to haunt you," Cade retorted.

"Maybe, but not before I get that delicious magic from your little half-breed. Now hand her over!"

Cade stood, pulling me up with him, then tugged me close and wrapped his arms around me, as if trying to make me a physical part of him. A heartbeat passed and the first drops of the storm's rain pelted the back of my neck. Not a good omen.

"No," Cade said, his voice rumbling through my core, making my dormant magic tingle to life. Oh, if only it would cooperate for me!

"No?" the Morrigan boomed. "You have no right to refuse me, a queen of the Faelorehn, goddess to the Celts. You don't stand a chance. I'll have my creatures fight you Cade, and ríastrad or no ríastrad, you are no match for them."

Cade relaxed a little and nodded his head.

"I know, but I'll not give her up."

Finally, Cade released me and put me at arm's length before turning to his mother. "I'll fight your faelah, and if I win you will forfeit your claim on Meghan."

The Morrigan snorted again.

"If they win, I offer you all of my glamour in exchange for her safety. After all, I too am the product of a volatile combination and my magic is rather potent as well."

"No!" I shouted.

The rain was coming down harder now, chilling my skin to match my emotions.

The Morrigan's eyes lit up. "Now that might be enough to tempt me. You do realize the price of your sacrifice, don't you my boy? There is only one way for me to get to your power."

Cade nodded again, his face unreadable.

"I know. I'll swear a blood oath to seal my offer if I must."

Several creatures hissed and the Morrigan gave a small scream of triumph. "Very well my dearest. Do give me your oath then."

I glanced between the two of them, fear and confusion fluttering around in my head. I heard the restless chatter of the faelah, the snort and rumble of Cade's horse behind me, the whine of Fergus and the screech of Meridian somewhere far above. The wind had lessened, but it still drove my hair into my face, and now I had the freezing rain to contend with. However, none of that was important.

"How will she get your magic Cade? What must happen? Can you fight ten of those things?"

I was babbling, but I had to have some answers.

Cade turned his face to me, and for the first time since stumbling into this hellhole I noticed just how dark his eyes had grown; how pale his skin had become.

"Cade?"

"Your safety is all that matters right now. My magic is only slightly stronger than yours at the moment. You are a greater source of power Meghan, but it's untried and unknown.

Let me do this before she discovers the potential of your own power; before she changes her mind."

That didn't answer my question and, in fact, only stirred up more of them. Cade released my shoulders and turned towards his mother.

"I'll fight your ten transformed Cúmorrig to the death. If I stand alive at the end, you will no longer hunt Meghan, nor will you harm her family. If I am defeated, you may take my power before it is returned to Eilé and leave Meghan alone."

I stood, rigid in shock. *No. No!*

"Cade! No! You will not sacrifice yourself for me!"

I yanked on his arm, trying to get him to look at me. He pulled away easily and drew his long dagger out of its sheath, dragging the blade across his left hand. I gaped in horror as blood welled up.

Cade held up his hand, the red slash running diagonally from the bottom of his index finger to his wrist, for all to see. "I fight this battle, and win or lose, you don't touch Meghan."

The Morrigan crossed her arms and sneered. "You are truly willing to risk your life for some worthless half-breed faeling?"

Her son said nothing, only glared at her with the same grim look on his face, his palm held up to the sky, the blood dripping down his arm to be washed away by the rain.

"If she is so worthless, then you wouldn't go to such trouble to have her. No, she is important, and I will forfeit my life to save hers if need be."

"Fool!" the goddess spat, moving aggressively forward. "You *utter* fool!"

Disclosure

She was now only a few feet away from him, and although he towered over her, her very presence made her larger than the rest of us. Reaching into her bodice, the Morrigan pulled out a long, thin knife and drew it across her own palm. She and Cade clasped hands, both looking as if they were trying to break each other's arms.

I could only stare and gape. How could this be happening? Even the mere thought of Cade dying, of not having him by my side, of no longer feeling his presence, made it close to impossible to breathe.

Cade stepped away from the Morrigan and moved closer to me. He placed his hands on either side of my face, pushing his fingers into my hair and letting his thumbs rest against my skin. My pulse quickened and the numbness suffusing my nerves began to fade away. I didn't even care that one of his palms was sliced open and probably leaving blood on my face.

"Meghan, there is something I need to tell you, in case this doesn't work out the way I hope," he said softly. "Something I should have told you a long time ago."

I held my breath, waiting for his words, but he simply gazed at me, his eyes so intense they were unable to settle on one single color.

What? I thought. *What do I need to know? Something about how to defend myself against these things you're about to fight, in case you fail? Some trick to get my pitiful magic to work so I can help you? Another shocking secret you've kept from me? What? Don't you dare tell me you are going to die!*

The moment stretched on forever, and I started to think of all the things I needed to tell *him*. Only problem was, all my words wanted to come flooding out at once and they got jammed up, like pebbles trying to pour from a bottleneck.

Finally Cade spoke, his voice calm, quiet, serious. "I love you."

Before my brain had a chance to register his declaration, it was thrown into a whirlwind of jumbled thoughts and emotions as he leaned down and kissed me as if the world were about to crumble to pieces all around us.

Eighteen
Riastrad

The kiss began as something gentle but soon deepened, and for a moment I forgot all about the chaos that was moments away from unfurling like a black cloud of death. Cade dug his fingers further into my hair, lowering one hand to my back as he pressed me closer. Of their own accord, my arms wrapped around him and I kissed him back with fervor. What had he said before all of this? Oh, yes. He loved me. That only made my stomach flip over again and I swore I sensed my stubborn magic burning fiercely through my blood.

Before I was ready, Cade broke the kiss and pulled away, leaving us both gasping for breath. He placed his right hand against my cheek and kissed me one more time, this one without all of the passion of the one before it. He let go of me, then turned and walked away, not bothering to glance back, as if he had already lost the battle and couldn't see me anymore.

A sob broke free from my throat, and only then did I realize how close to breaking I was. I hurried towards him, reaching my hands out, but some invisible barrier blocked me, knocking my hand aside. What the heck?

"Ah, ah, ah little faeling," the Morrigan crooned as she stepped away from her mutated Cúmorrig. "No interference from outside parties allowed."

The goddess reached up as if to caress my hair, but her fingers also met with the invisible shield, this one administering a slight shock. She hissed and drew her hand back, cursing in the language of Eilé. She sounded bitter and angry, but I was too intent on Cade to care what she said or thought. If she somehow managed to drag me off by the hair at that moment, I'm pretty sure I wouldn't even notice.

The circle of various faelah closed in around us, creating a dark ring of monsters. Speirling had finally found an opening and had trotted off, as far away from the battle as possible, and Fergus and Meridian were nowhere in sight. I didn't care. The only thing I cared about was Cade and the ten Cúmorrig he was about to fight. Cade was tall and strong, but the grotesque hellhounds were taller and appeared stronger.

"How are you going to defeat them Cade?" I whispered as the tears fell down my face.

The cold rain lashed at me and the wind chilled me even further. As the creatures circled around Cade, I began chewing at my fingernails. He didn't stand a chance. Suddenly a surge of anger hit me and the burning next to my heart heightened. I cried out in pain, wondering if the shock of everything that was happening would cause heart failure.

I glanced up to check if the monsters had attacked yet, only to fall back down on my rump in surprise. The beasts had made a circle around Cade, but he stood absolutely still, his arms held open at his sides, palms facing out, his head bowed in concentration. I could almost make out the rage and aggression pouring off of him, like heat waves rising off a road in the desert.

With sudden violence, one shoulder dislocated with a tremendous CRACK, then the other. His hair grew and formed into spikes and something that looked disturbingly like blood gathered at their points. The rain pelted down, making it run in crimson rivulets down his pale face. One of his eyes swelled to an unnatural size and I was sure it would burst out of his head. His clothing tore as he grew larger and more like one of the Morrigan's monsters.

There was one last crackling of joints and Cade stood transformed, slightly taller than the creatures surrounding him, but exuding a fury that terrified me. I gaped at him, my eyes gone wide, my tears long dried up. So this is what the Morrigan had been talking about. This transformation that had made Cade a pariah among his peers. This is what I'd witnessed when I nearly died a year ago.

I blinked up at the Morrigan, standing only a few feet away from me. She looked smug, eyeing me with condescending dislike.

"Who would want such a monster?" she crooned. "It's clear you've never seen my son overcome with his battle fury, this warp spasm. It's a shame he's sacrificing himself for you."

She sighed, having the nerve to sound like she cared. "If only I had convinced him to go into ríastrad before making the blood oath, it might have saved me so much trouble. You would've seen him in this form," she waved at her newly transformed son, now carefully eyeing the creatures that circled him, looking for a weak spot, "and like the others, you would have run away screaming. Eventually, he would have gotten over you and then I'd be free to seek you on my own, taking what I wanted. Now I'm going to lose a very useful tool."

My anger blossomed and spilled over. "I don't care about the ríastrad." I turned my eyes on her, my voice raw with emotion. "I love Cade. I would never leave him for something he has no control over. He cannot help who he is; who his parents are."

"Too bad," she snickered, nodding her head in Cade's direction, "because after tonight he will certainly be leaving *you*."

I shouldn't have looked because the battle had begun. I cried out when the long, clawed arm of one of the monsters swung out and made contact with Cade's own arm. But the move had been meant as a block and he quickly twisted the limb of the creature until it broke free of its body. The Cúmorrig howled in pain, and I swallowed back bile. Cade, in this horrible form, was brutal, fighting like a feral animal. His grotesque appearance almost made it hard to distinguish him from his adversaries.

The Morrigan yawned in a bored fashion as the battle raged on. A gust of wind and a sheet of rain slammed into us, driving me to the ground once more. I had long given up trying to keep my knees from getting muddy and the cloak I wore was already drenched.

"Such a shame, really," the Morrigan said above me. "He is far more useful to me alive than dead. Who is going to fetch back my dear little pets from the mortal world when he's gone?"

I swallowed, the lump in my throat proving to be an obstacle. No. Cade would not die. He *could* not.

"He won't die," I whispered, my head down.

I tried to ignore the sounds of the fight. The last time I glanced up, Cade had destroyed two of the monsters. I had no way of distinguishing between his shouts of outrage and their cries of pain. I guess I should try finding solace in knowing that if I could still hear them fighting, then the battle still continued. And if the battle still continued, Cade was still alive.

The Morrigan's laughter started out as a quiet chuckle, but soon rose to match the thunder overhead. "Oh, dear girl! He'll not survive this fight! Do you have any concept of the amount of magic I poured into my Cúmorrig?"

She leaned over me and willed me to meet her eyes. Reluctantly, I did. The irises were no longer deep red, but swirling with living flames. Her glamour at work. My stomach turned. I didn't want to know what amount of magic she poured into her diabolical creations. Nor did I want to know how many lives had been sacrificed to gain that power.

Minutes seemed to pass, hours maybe, and I sat there, helpless with nothing but the Morrigan's horrible commentary to shred apart my nerves. Eventually, Cade managed to kill a third monster, then a fourth and fifth. When two more died, I started to hope. Three left, only three more. I ignored the signs that Cade was tiring; convinced myself the bloodstains didn't belong to him. The storm raged on above us and the faelah surrounding the small valley kept up their disturbing chatter.

Another Cúmorrig down, then another. Only one left. My heart swelled with hope. Cade would defeat it, like he defeated all the others. But he appeared so weary, as if all of his magic had burned away, leaving nothing but a shell.

I watched, my lungs struggling to draw breath as the two of them circled one another. Cade struck at the monster, but the Cúmorrig deflected his swing. This last attack had taken too much energy from Cade. He staggered back, his head bowed as he caught his breath, and the remaining Cúmorrig reached back with its massive arm and plunged its long claws into Cade's abdomen.

"NO!" I screeched, running forward, tripping over the clumps of moss, grass and stones dotting the wide field as I tore through the magical barrier that had held me back all this time.

Crying, I pushed myself up, ignoring the sting in my left wrist, and gazed past my tears and the pelting rain to catch a glimpse of Cade again. Only fifty feet or so away, I spotted him. He was slumped over, the tips of the monster's claws protruding from his back. The ríastrad was leaving him. His battle fury was coming to an end and he was beginning to change back into the form I knew so well. With agonizing effort, he reached up, grabbed a hold of the monster's grizzled hair, and violently twisted its head, breaking its neck and killing it. Reaching down, Cade grasped the faelah's arm and slowly pulled the claws out of his stomach.

Another sob broke free, and I reached out my hand, though I was too far away. Cade dropped the arm and the creature crumpled to the ground. He stood for a few moments, turning as if he were intoxicated, until he found me. His eye had returned to its normal size and he was no longer as large as he'd been.

He gazed at me and I barely detected the last dregs of his battle fury blazing in his eyes. He smiled then, and for the first time ever, I noticed the beginning of tears in his eyes. He looked horrible. He was deathly pale and splattered with blood, despite the rain. I followed his left shoulder, down to where his hand covered the wound in his side. I should not have done that. Blood spilled freely from the holes left by the Cúmorrig's claws and it didn't seem likely to stop.

"No, Cade. We'll find someone to fix it." My voice hitched on another sob as I pathetically tried to comfort him.

He opened his mouth to say something to me, but a hacking cough took the place of words. He doubled over, a thin stream of blood spilling from the corner of his mouth. With one last gasp he collapsed to the ground.

"No!" I screamed again, crawling across the rain-soaked field, ignoring my injured wrist.

I blocked out the unmoving bodies of the mutilated Cúmorrig that lay scattered about. I only stopped after reaching Cade, and when I did, I nearly fell in anguish. He lay on his back, his hand still clutching his side, his eyes staring lifelessly up into the storm clouds above.

I refused to accept what I was seeing. I sat down, rolled his head into my lap, and began stroking his face. His hair was a mess and I smoothed it away from his forehead. He must have been tired after such a fight, so I closed his eyes for him, tears streaming down my cheeks as my heart shattered.

"No Cade, no," I murmured between sobs. "No, you aren't gone, you'll get better. You just need to rest."

But I knew. I'd known the moment the last monster impaled him. He'd been too overwhelmed by such a large number of foes, there had been just too many. I squeezed my eyes shut and let the despair flood over me.

"Why didn't you let me help you?" I whispered when my throat stopped aching long enough to allow words.

I scooped him up and let his head rest against my shoulder as I rocked him like a mother rocking her infant to sleep, and all around me the storm raged on. The faelah that had been surrounding us all this time, watching and barely reining in their desire to join the fray, started their complaints again.

"Such a pity," I heard above me. But the voice held no pity at all.

"Such a waste of useful talent. Really, so foolish. I should have refused his blood oath, but oh, the boy has always been headstrong."

I was too distraught to respond, to even think of how I should respond. I simply sat on the wet ground, holding Cade close and denying that he was gone.

"Well, I am a very busy goddess and I'll ask you to please move out of the way. I'm owed quite a large amount of magic, and when someone is so freshly sacrificed as Caedehn is now, their power is even more potent."

I didn't move. My mind had started to buzz, and a strange, warm tingling began to bloom in my chest once again. Another reminder of my useless, pathetic, worthless magic. Why must it be so weak! Why did my glamour refuse to work for me! Why didn't it help me save Cade?!

"Move strayling! Once I take the power owed to me, I'll break through the barrier created by his oath and take yours as well! Drop that corpse and obey me, or I'll make your death far more hellish than his!"

Something burst in me then, something next to my heart, and for a few seconds I thought one of my major arteries had ruptured, spilling blood into the gaping hole in my chest. I didn't collapse, though, nor did I begin to convulse. In fact, I felt light and full of energy. I took a deep breath and rose to my feet. Funny, if I didn't know any better, I'd say I was floating. I stepped away from Cade, but not so far away that the Morrigan could get to him without pushing past me.

And that's when I realized the overwhelming awareness flooding my senses reminded me of my magic, only this time it was ten times more powerful than before. A rush of warm and cool sensations coursed through me like waves crashing against the shore, and a delicious realization pierced my mind: my glamour was finally fully awake and ready to do my bidding. My fear of the Morrigan had vanished, and for the moment I cast my grief aside.

"Cade might have sworn a blood oath with you, but I didn't!"

And then I let my raw power free, willing the swirling essence to take full control and forcing it to the tips of my fingers, exactly as Cade had taught me. This time, my glamour didn't stop there. The new experience was the most exhilarating thing in the world, like a pure rush of adrenalin but far more intoxicating. The magic left my fingertips in a bright flash and sprung forth from my hair. I imagined I looked like some terrifying angel of vengeance, standing in my ruined Beltaine party dress with Cade's lifeless body at my feet, my arms spread wide, my head thrown back with my hair flaring out all around like a dark halo.

The earth trembled beneath my feet and the wind and rain stopped. I dared to open my eyes. The clouds above had parted, creating a column of sunlight shining down upon me. I lowered my head and gazed at the carnage scattered over the field and gaped. All of the faelah, every last one of them from the huge, bear-like creatures down to the ones that were no bigger than mice, lay strewn across the valley floor, charred black.

I shot my glance up at the Morrigan and saw on her face something I never thought to witness in my life: fear. She had paled and her ever-present confidence seemed to vanish. Despite my torn heart, I grinned with malicious vengeance because I sensed my own power surging once again. I lifted my arms, admiring the beautiful blue lightning crackling between my fingers, and summoned all the magic I had left. With a cry of anguish and loathing, I threw my arms forward, channeling all of my power directly at the Morrigan. I doubted I'd be able to kill her, but I was pretty sure I could do a good deal of damage.

The goddess' eyes went wide with shock, but before I got the chance to so much as singe her perfect hair, she clapped her palms together above her head, spoke an ancient word of power, and transformed into a huge raven. My blue lightning missed her by inches, and as she squawked and let the winds of the fading storm carry her away, I collapsed onto the ground next to Cade.

My body was drained, both mentally and physically. And magically if I was being completely honest. I now understood what Cade had been talking about with regards to magic. Too bad he wasn't here to enjoy it with me.

The thunder rolled in the distance and the rain had long since diminished. The sun was well above the eastern horizon, but still a good distance from its midday location. The soggy ground pressed against my cheek and when I curled my fingers into a fist, I found Cade's damp shirt gathering between them. I lifted my head and winced from the pain pounding away at my skull. I blinked the remaining tears from my eyes and glanced around. If I hadn't just lived through hell, I would have appreciated the beauty surrounding me. The clouds above were still dark, but below them the golden rays of the morning sun lit the raindrops, making the small valley resemble a field of glittering gems. That same sunlight splayed upon my face, warming my skin for the first time in over a day. I closed my eyes and tried to find some consolation in the welcome radiance, but since my hands still clasped Cade's shirt, I couldn't bring myself to feel any relief.

You're alive, Meghan. You were sure the Morrigan would kill you, but you survived! I sighed. *Oh, but Cade didn't, did he? What will you do now that he is gone?*

It was too much. A painful cry tore free of my throat and I clasped his ruined shirt even tighter, burying my face into his chest. I had never experienced despair like this and I was certain I would never recover. I don't know how long I lay across Cade's cold form, but at some point in time a shadow passed over me and something tugged at my sleeve.

"Go away," I rasped.

I knew it must be one of the Morrigan's minions, one that had somehow survived my wrath. But I didn't care. In fact, I secretly hoped the creature would attack and kill me, then the pain would be over.

The faelah nudged me again. I blindly swiped out an arm and screamed, "Go away!"

My fingers brushed something warm and the sound of hooves and a surprised whicker jolted me away from my misery. I glanced up and saw a black horse standing a few feet away, eyeing at me as if I were crazy. Well, he did have a point.

"Speirling," I managed softly, biting my lip to keep it from trembling. "Oh Speirling, he's gone!"

The horse only whickered again, tossing his head and dragging his hoof against the ground. Despite my sorrow, I was glad the faelah hadn't harmed him. He moved closer when he realized I wasn't going to lash out at him again. I didn't shoo him away this time, either. I could really use his comforting at the moment.

Speirling nudged me once more, so I placed a hand against his nose to let him know I appreciated his presence. I stroked his cheek, but he pulled away and turned towards the east. I stared at him, a bit hurt by his actions. He didn't seem distressed by the fact that Cade lay in the mud, broken and destroyed by the faelah. No, he seemed alert, impatient even, as if he was eager for us to leave and head back to the castle.

Eventually he came back over to me and lowered his head. I fought my desire to simply lay there and wallow in my misery. Instead, I reluctantly reached for his bridle, using it to pull myself upright. Luckily, the stallion stayed beside me or else I would have collapsed back onto the ground.

I turned back to gaze at Cade's prone form and a deep pain rose up and threatened to choke me. *No, you're not dead*

Cade. This is only a terrible dream and I'm going to wake up at any moment . . .

A wave of dizziness caused me to fall against Speirling's flank. He turned and nudged me with his nose, as if trying to keep me on my feet. And then he swung his head to the east again, released an irritated whinny, and started walking away.

"No Speirling, no! We can't leave Cade."

He stopped, but refused to turn his head from where he stared. I clenched my teeth and tightened my hands on his bridle, focusing on the knot work pattern etched in the leather as I willed the nausea and impending panic to pass. The design seemed vaguely familiar, like several small horseshoes interlacing and repeating. In my haze of hysteria and despair, I thought they looked a little like the seal on the invitation the Dagda had sent me. Little omegas laced together.

I snorted. What a stupid thought to have at such a time. Then my brain froze and I sucked in a sharp breath. No, not omegas. And that hadn't been an omega on the Dagda's seal either. I had been holding the image upside down. It had been the crude representation of a cauldron.

I stood up straighter, a sudden rush of realization passing through me and giving me new strength. *The Cauldron . . .*

"This is the Cauldron I used in the battle against the Fomorians so long ago," the Dagda said as he patted it affectionately. "So many lives restored because of its priceless power."

The memory faded away and I was left standing, dumbstruck, in the middle of a meadow littered with the gruesome aftermath of a great battle.

"Speirling!" I hissed.

Suddenly, my legs were no longer numb and my heart was beating once again.

"Speirling! The Dagda's Cauldron!"

Tears formed in my eyes, but this time they weren't the result of sorrow. "There's still a chance to save him!"

I wanted to jump up and cheer, but I was still very weak from my outpouring of magic. A whistling sound above me drew my attention to the sky. I glanced up and spotted Meridian, a white blot against the dark grey.

"Meridian! Quickly! We have to get Cade onto Speirling's back. Where's Fergus?" I sniffed and wiped at my face with the edge of the sodden cloak.

Asleep, Meridian pressed against my mind as she came to rest on my shoulder.

"How can he be sleeping at a time like this?"

Then I remembered something Cade had once told me. Spirit guides lived as long as their masters did.

"Oh no, where is he?"

Forest.

I glanced behind me into the thick trees scattered all over the hillside.

"He could be anywhere," I said to myself.

I didn't have time to go searching for him. I wanted Cade alive as soon as possible, in case there was some grace period between death and regeneration when using the Cauldron.

"We have to leave him for now Meridian, but as soon as Cade is better, he'll find us." I hoped.

Kiasfrad

I turned to the black horse standing beside me. "Speirling, you are a smart boy, and I need your help if you want to save your master."

He gazed at me with dark brown eyes, his way of showing compliance.

"Now, I need you to get as low as you can . . ."

I tugged on his bridle to let him know what I wanted, and he lowered himself to his knees.

"Good!"

Using what little strength I had, I pulled Cade's lifeless body up and over his horse's back. He was heavy, so by the time I had him where I thought he might not fall off, I needed to sit for several minutes to gain my breath.

Before I persuaded Speirling to rise, I climbed up behind Cade, holding on to him so he wouldn't crash to the ground.

"I'm sorry," I whispered into his ear as we set off, "I'm sure this won't make you feel any better when you are conscious again, but it's the best I can do."

With one last glance behind me, I urged the huge black horse up onto all fours. I wrapped my arm around Cade's middle, letting his head roll back on my shoulder as I dug my heels into Speirling. With a snort of alarm, he took off across the rocky valley floor and made his way east, towards the dolmarehn that would take us to the Dagda's Cauldron.

Nineteen

Miracle

All I could think about as we tore over the rain-soaked earth was that we must move faster. Speirling was already running as swiftly as possible, his snorting breath and heaving chest signs that he was close to his limit. I was surprised that I managed to keep Cade, and myself, on Speirling's back, but I imagined my magic had a lot to do with it. I sensed the power flowing from my skin, warming me and making the ride seem less jarring.

Speirling slowed before entering the dolmarehn that would take us to the Dagda, and Meridian's needle-sharp claws dug into me as we braced ourselves for the transport to the other side. Once there, Speirling picked up his pace again and I groaned when the first icy drops of rain pelted my hot face.

"Meridian, see if you can fly ahead and warn the Dagda of what has happened."

Yes. Swift, she answered.

And with that, she was gone from my shoulder and lost in the chaos of the storm. I wondered why the rain still fell on this side of the dolmarehn since the clouds had been moving west, but when Speirling stumbled, the idea of rain and storms was quickly driven from my mind.

"It's okay, you didn't fall," I managed, patting him with affection.

His breathing was labored and his steps faulty, but he had to reach the Dagda's house. When he stumbled again an hour later I eased him back a little. A slower pace would cost us time, but there would be no hope for Cade if Speirling collapsed while we were still several miles from our destination.

I gritted my teeth against my worry as the stallion's gait slowed. I had tried to distract my mind as we moved ever eastward, but every chance it got, my brain kept dredging up the horrible image of Cade in the final minutes of his fight with the Cúmorrig. I envisioned him standing there, the last vestiges of his battle fury, his ríastrad, leaving his body wrought with tremors. The monster, taking advantage of a slight moment of distraction, plunging its dagger-like claws into Cade's abdomen. The look in Cade's eyes as he gazed at me one last time before collapsing . . .

I squeezed my eyes shut as the tears burned them again.

"Speirling, keep moving, please. Go at whatever pace you can, just don't stop," I rasped as I leaned over and rested my head against Cade's back.

A tired whicker, a distant roll of thunder, and the icy lash of rain against my bared neck accompanied me as the black horse carried us across the open fields of Eilé. Before I let unconsciousness finally claim me, I pressed my lips to the icy skin at the nape of Cade's neck and whispered for his sake only, "I love you."

I woke when the force of my body hitting the ground knocked me back to my senses. A few moments passed before I caught my breath, and another minute dragged on as I realized the horrible scenes flashing in my mind were not the remnants of a nightmare, but the memories of the horror I had recently lived through.

I blinked up at the great horse standing before me. He looked absolutely exhausted and was even now lowering to his knees as if he might collapse. Just before he rolled over on his side, I recognized the still form on his back as Cade. My Cade, who had died protecting me. Crying out in anguish, I rushed over and pulled him clear just as Speirling fell over.

"Oh, no Speirling."

I placed a hand on his side, hoping he was only extremely tired and not on the verge of death. I had pushed him too hard, and now Cade had no chance of recovery. I wanted to cry, to sleep, to just roll over and let my soul depart my own body.

Turning my face to the sky, I let out a massive sigh. The sky was dark with clouds and my eyes blurred with tears, yet I managed to make out the silhouettes of huge, dark shapes surrounding me. But not just any dark shapes: hills. I turned my head to the right and spotted a familiar door, two lit torches standing guard on either side of it. The Dagda's house.

Crying out in pure joy, I rushed over to Speirling and gave him a hug, though he was too fatigued to notice.

"We made it!"

Without thinking, I grabbed Cade's shoulders and began dragging him towards our sanctuary. He was so heavy, and I really should have left him and run for help, but I couldn't bring myself to leave his side.

It took ages to drag him to the door, even though it stood no more than fifty feet away. The bonfire from last night's Beltaine party still burned off to the left, nothing more than coals now, hissing and spitting in the rain. Finally, reaching my destination, I collapsed. Icy rain pelted me and ran down my neck and under the collar of my cloak. I was getting tired of the feeling, but I knew soon I would be warm and dry.

I trembled and strained against my own weight as I pulled myself up so I could pound on the door. Although the rest of my body was damp and freezing, my eyes and cheeks burned as tears of desperation broke free once more.

I must have hammered the wood with my fists for a good ten minutes, because by the time someone arrived, my hands stung and bled. One of the Dagda's female companions stared down at me, not Alannah, but one with blond hair and wide blue eyes.

"Oh! My dear, what in the name of the Morrigan happened to you?"

I gritted my teeth. If only I had the strength to tell her.

"Please," I rasped, my throat raw and my emotions nearly run dry. "Please, Dagda. Cauldron."

I slumped to the ground beside Cade's still form, leaking cold rain and mud all over the earthen tiles and beautiful rugs of the Dagda's abode. I was half conscious when I heard a commotion behind the blond woman and soon many voices were barking out urgent orders.

Someone lifted me. "Cade," I breathed, barely a whisper. "Cauldron."

Dolmarehn

"Hush now darling, hush," the Dagda said, for once his voice raw with anguish.

He carried me through the cavernous halls of his home. I thought I detected the warmth of a fire in the great room, the scent of food wafting in from the kitchen, the laughter and music and general joy that surrounded this god-king of the Faelorehn. Sleep tried to claim me as he hurried me along, but I fought it. Eventually he placed me on a dry, soft mattress.

"No," I tried to say; tried to fight. "Cade."

A huge paw of a hand rested on my forehead. My mind floated in a warm and blissful sea, and I no longer fought the sleepiness creeping up on me.

"Rest, dear heart, and let me do what I can for Caedehn."

I sighed, and smiled. The last thought I had before everything went blank was the memory of Cade's passionate kiss before he sacrificed his life to save mine.

☗ ☗ ☗

I woke up with a vague recollection of what had happened before I fell asleep, or passed out. The warm buzz of happiness that seemed to permeate throughout the Dagda's mansion clung to the edge of my awareness, but the memories of the fight with the Morrigan kept dive-bombing my brain like angry wasps defending their nest: the horrible monsters with the scent of death clinging to them, the Morrigan's threats and the battle that ensued, Cade telling me that he loved me. Cade dying . . .

I gasped out a sob and covered my mouth with my hands. *No . . .*

Miracle

A light chittering sound drew my attention to one of the posts of my bed. Meridian sat perched on top, looking morose.

Sorrow, her mind said to mine.

Yes, I replied in the same way as tears tracked down my cheeks, *sorrow.*

The door to my room cracked open, letting in a draft that danced with the fire in the corner fireplace. The Dagda himself stepped through the entrance, his huge frame appearing weary, his face looking bleak. That only made the tears flow more freely.

"I was too late," I whispered, my throat closing up with pain.

My heart clenched and I convinced myself it wouldn't be long before it shriveled up and died. Cade had given his life for me. Because he loved me. I suddenly grew angry. Why had he done such a thing? Didn't he know how much *I* loved *him?* How was I going to go on without his smile, his encouragement, his touch? I was alone in this strange place once again.

The Dagda moved closer, never saying a word. He sat down at the foot of the bed, making the mattress dip and creak dangerously.

"Meghan," he said.

I couldn't look at him. I could only cry into my pillow and let my anguish take over me as I pushed away all of his overwhelming, cheerful, happy-go-lucky charm. I didn't care if the Celts viewed him as a god. I didn't care if I had grown to like him. I didn't care about his stupid, magical cauldron . . .

"Meghan, Caedehn is going to be fine. He was very far gone when you brought him here, but as soon as I put you to bed, we placed him in my Cauldron and began the revival rights. He'll need several weeks to recover fully, but he is alive."

All I heard was his last words.

"Alive?" I breathed, daring to glance up from my pillow.

The Dagda merely nodded, his usually twinkling eyes looking slightly dull with worry.

"Yes, very much so," he murmured quietly, putting a hand upon my forehead as if I were a troubled child recovering from a nightmare. "You were right in bringing him here."

I released another wave of tears and caught my trembling lip with my teeth while trying to take a few deep breaths. I had never been so relieved in my life.

The Dagda stayed with me for several minutes and I did my best to relate to him the details of the night. He listened quietly the whole time, even when I paused several times to let a fit of crying pass. His face was grim by the time I finished.

"So your glamour has finally revealed itself, and the Morrigan is aware of it." He sighed and stood up, gazing down on me with those ancient eyes of his. "She should be rather indisposed for a while Meghan, but I think you ought to seriously consider. making the Otherworld your permanent home. Now that your power is free, you'll only grow stronger and learn to wield it better. You'll also need Eilé's own magic to replenish yours if you want to remain strong enough to continue thwarting the Morrigan."

I nodded as I shut my swollen eyes. "I know. I've been thinking the same thing for a long time, coming to live in Eilé."

"Well, I think we can give it at least a month or so before any permanent decisions must be made. I'll let you rest now. You experienced a terrible ordeal tonight."

He started to leave, his massive size taking up most of the doorway. He stopped before entering the hall and turned to glance at me, a mischievous glint in his eye. "I believe you've gone and disrupted our quiet, comfortable lives, Miss Meghan."

"I know. I'm sorry."

He sighed, still smiling. "You and Caedehn have started something huge, there is no doubt about that. Though, such a conflict was bound to occur sooner or later. Besides, a half-Fae and half-Fomore cannot exist without bringing some sort of turmoil into the world. Your strong magic is now the bone of contention, Meghan, but you mustn't take on all the blame yourself. After all, you can't help who you are."

"The Morrigan won't stop until she gets what she wants, will she?" I asked, the sudden realization sending a new bolt of terror through me.

The Dagda sighed and leaned against the door frame. "Every powerful Faelorehn king or queen will want to take advantage of your power. Don't worry Meghan, Caedehn will help guide you when he is recovered, and if you're willing to trust me, I'll help you as well."

He stepped away from the door, moving closer to my bed once again. He placed a gentle hand on my shoulder and tilted my chin up with the other one. "But Meghan, the choice is yours. You cannot let the Morrigan or any of the other Faelorehn make you think that you must serve their side. You must choose what's right for you; you must decide who and what is worth fighting for."

I relaxed back into the soft pillows, but something still worried away at my conscience. Taking a shaking breath I said, "That's why they shun him, isn't it?"

I glanced up at the Dagda with shimmering eyes. He shot me a quizzical look, but remained silent.

"Cade. Why Drustan and his friends don't like him. Why Danua doesn't want me around him. Because he is the Morrigan's son."

The drawing of a deep breath, followed by a terse, "Yes," gave me the Dagda's answer.

On top of everything else, I felt sick to my stomach. Sadness wasn't the cause, however. No, only deep anger had the ability to make me so ill.

"Why?" I hissed. "Cade can't help who his parents are, and he isn't evil like her."

"Unfortunately," the Dagda answered, "he suffers from guilt by association. The Morrigan has done unthinkable things in order to increase her power and keep her hold over the faelah. And because of the geis she placed on Cade, he was forced to help her."

I sucked in a breath, horrified. What had she made Cade do?

The Dagda quickly shook his head as he held up a hand. "Do not fret Meghan. Cade was able to resist most of what his mother insisted. He never took part in anything too appalling, and most people know this."

I pulled my knees to my chest and rested my cheek on them. Still staring across the room, I whispered, "Then why do they still treat him like a criminal? He isn't his mother."

The Dagda gave a jaded smile. "Is there no one back in the mortal world who judges you by what they perceive to be the truth?"

Miracle

I opened my mouth to argue, but stopped. He was right. People in my world were constantly judging others based on their actions and what their peers said about them. And they were ready to accept just about anything as truth. The popularity of tabloid magazines was testimony to that. I looked up and found Cade's foster father grinning at me, his kind eyes twinkling.

"So you see," he continued, "our nature encourages us to formulate our own version of the truth. It is much harder to convince others of your merits once they've convinced themselves of your faults. But do not worry, Meghan. As long as Cade can count on you and his other friends to care about him, it won't matter if most of the others do not."

He smiled at me again and for the first time in several minutes, I was comforted.

"Now," the Dagda stated, standing up once more and clasping his hands together, "you get some rest and on the morrow, I'll assign a guard to escort you back to your more familiar realm."

I shot my eyes up to meet his as a realization burst through me. "My family! I was supposed to be home last night, to get ready for prom!"

I groaned and dropped my face into my hands. How on earth had I forgotten about my life in the mortal world? Oh, yeah, extreme trauma can do that to a person. What were they going to think? What were they thinking right now? Did they think I was lying in a ditch somewhere, murdered? Had Robyn told them about my lies? I groaned again and felt the panic rising, my newborn magic trying to rise up as well. Suddenly, it seemed as if someone had opened a window and the storm outside was flooding into the room.

"Meghan! Meghan, you need to calm down," the Dagda exclaimed as he rushed to my side, wrapping his arms around me. "Your magic is newly unleashed and you might hurt yourself and destroy my house."

I forced myself to relax and blinked up at him with teary eyes. "Why did my power have to awaken now? Why didn't it help me before Cade fought with the Morrigan's Cúmorrig?"

The Dagda rocked me, comforting me the way Cade once had.

"I think your magic has been awake Meghan, but it had no reason to become furious. Something powerful had to happen in order to get your glamour to stir."

I sighed and nodded against his chest. That made sense.

"Now," he said, pulling away from me so he could look me in the eye, "you might be rested enough to ride home. I'll insist on sending most of my guard with you, however."

I released a pent up breath and the small storm my wild magic had been creating vanished. Later, when Cade was healed and I recovered from this whole ordeal, I would learn how to control my magic and put it to good use. I held my closed fist up to my mouth, hiding a sudden grin. Perhaps Danua would think differently of me now.

"When will the guard be ready to escort me?" I asked, anxious to return home and assure my family I was still alive.

The Dagda stood up again and chuckled. "I'll instruct them to saddle their horses." Then his humor dimmed a little and he asked in a more careful tone, "Would you like to visit Cade before you leave?"

Miracle

"Yes," I said instantly, "yes I would."

Alannah brought me a change of clothes, something more fitting to the Otherworld, but I was glad to get out of my black and white dress. It had been ruined and now served as a reminder of the atrocities of the previous night. When I finished getting ready, the Dagda led me down another hall. Despite what he had said, terror gripped me at the thought of visiting Cade, to see him so injured and defenseless.

He came to a stop in front of a door and released a massive sigh. "Now, he looks bad Meghan, but he will mend, I promise. He won't gain consciousness for at least another week or so. Those creatures of the Morrigan took a lot out of him."

He paused and lifted my chin with one of his large, calloused fingers. I forced myself to meet his eyes, their bright blue turning a deeper color.

"He must love you very much to have done what he did and you must return that love just as fiercely, to have brought him back here. For those reasons alone, my care for him will not falter. I'll make sure to return him to you as he was before."

I nodded, comforted by the Dagda's words.

The room we stepped into was large and resembled all the others I'd seen. A fire roared in the fireplace set in one wall and I glimpsed the storm still pummeling the earth with rain through a large diamond paned window. The huge, four poster bed however, caught and held my attention more than anything else.

Crying out, I ran forward, coming to the bed's edge and just barely stopping myself from leaping onto the mattress. Cade rested there, his bare arms and chest exposed, the rest of him tucked snugly under the comforter. One arm lay stretched out beside him, while the other was draped across his abdomen. His head rested against a pillow with his face tilted towards the fireplace.

"Careful Meghan," the Dagda murmured behind me.

I heeded his warning, but my hands crumpled the bedspread anyway and I heard the thunder grow louder and the rain fall harder outside. I had been warned, but seeing him like this still tore at my heart. His face was the palest I'd ever seen, at least the parts that weren't bruised and swollen. His entire chest was covered in more contusions and cuts, the worst being the slices through his side where the mutated Cúmorrig had stabbed him.

"Do not fret, my dear girl. He is healing; alive. And he'll keep healing, just give it time."

The Dagda's soft voice and kind touch helped ease my distress, but only a little.

A new thought came bursting forth to the front of my mind and I nearly choked, partly in shame for forgetting and partly because it had appeared so suddenly.

"Fergus!" I blurted. "We had to leave him behind, because when Cade fell, well you know . . . Meridian said-Meridian!"

I whipped my head around and the Dagda lifted his hands. "She's hunkered down in the stables, resting with Speirling. What about Fergus? Where did he fall?"

"She said he was in the forest, near the site where the battle took place. Near the dolmarehn leading to the mortal world."

Miracle

The Dagda sighed. "My guard will find him and bring him back after they accompany you to the mortal realm. Don't worry, he'll heal as Caedehn will."

I released a breath of relief and turned back towards the bed. I watched Cade's slow breathing for several minutes and only when I was certain the rise and fall of his chest wouldn't stop, did I let my relief break free. The storm immediately let up and the rain slowed to a gentle patter.

The Dagda placed his huge hands on my shoulders.

"Time to say goodbye. I'll send word when he is improved, but it may be a while."

I nodded then glanced up at Cade's foster father with tears in my eyes. He grinned, somehow understanding what I asked, and stepped out of the room, taking one of the servants with him.

I let go of my breath and moved closer to Cade, gently lacing my fingers with the hand resting beside him. He was as cold as ice, but I tried not to let it upset me.

"Cade," I breathed, not sure what to say. "I'm going to go back to the mortal world soon, but when you are better, and after I graduate, I'm coming back here to be with you."

Now that I knew how he felt about me, my fears seemed to have vanished. I was thrilled and frightened at the same time, thinking about living in the Otherworld, among my own kind, with Cade . . .

Taking one more deep breath I leaned forward, touching my lips to his. He didn't return the kiss, of course, but it didn't matter. I pulled my face away from his and moved in closer so that my mouth came to rest right below his ear.

Dolmarehn

"I love you too, Cade," I whispered, remembering the look in his eyes just before he'd kissed me, "I love you too."

I sighed, squeezed his hand once more, and stood to leave. When I reached the door, I glanced over my shoulder. It was probably my imagination, but I could have sworn his color had improved. Smiling, I left the room and joined the Dagda. He led me to the entrance of his home and outside I found his entire guard, mounted on horses, waiting for me.

I gasped, then spun around and gaped at the Dagda. "This is too much!"

I turned back and counted thirty men and women, armed to the teeth with weapons and armor. He had said half his guard, not all of them!

The Dagda took my hands and turned me to face him.

"No it isn't. You almost died last night, along with Caedehn. He gave his life for you, and are you to think I'd let you go wandering off, unprotected while the Morrigan may be plotting revenge at this very moment? I think not! They are honored to see you to the dolmarehn."

Before I had a chance to protest any further, he whistled and someone came trotting around the hill, leading a beautiful bay mare with one arm and carrying a white bird on the other.

"Meridian!" I cried.

She chittered and flew off of the young man's arm, landing on my shoulder and nibbling affectionately at my hair.

"Now, I will bid you farewell my lady. Worry not about your Caedehn, he will be safe in my abode."

The Dagda grinned and his characteristic merriment returned. His kindness overwhelmed me and before I could stop myself, I threw my arms around his shoulders and gave him a fierce hug.

He returned the hug just as enthusiastically, chuckling as he did so.

"That will be enough my dear," he declared in his mischievous way, setting me back down on the ground. "I do not want to face Cade's ríastrad once he heals and finds out I've been accepting your affections."

I blushed, but smiled anyway, warmed by his gentle teasing.

Taking one last look around, I walked over to the mare and with a little help from Cade's foster father, I managed to climb into the saddle. I waved goodbye once more and we started out on our journey. The soldiers made me travel in the middle of the group and the large number of them slowed our progress. To my immense relief, we encountered no nasty faelah the entire way and the weather, though not sunny and warm, didn't get any worse.

By the time we reached the small dolmarehn that would take me back to the mortal world, back to my family, a late afternoon sun shone down on us. I slipped off my horse, sore but grateful my feet were on solid ground. I thanked the Dagda's soldiers and told them I would be fine on my own once I stepped through the dolmarehn.

With one last glance around at the scattered stone pillars and crooked trees, I sighed and approached the cave. Meridian swooped down to sit on my shoulder, and as I moved further into the gateway, I tried not to think of what would be waiting for me on the other side.

Twenty

Confession

When I took my next breath, I was already through the portal. I only knew this because the air smelled different here, like eucalyptus and dust. The strange thing was, I never sensed the uncomfortable pull of magic that usually accompanied a trip through one of the stone gateways. Come to think of it, I hadn't felt anything when we had passed through the other dolmarehn either.

Sighing, I climbed free of the small cavern and stepped out into the woods. I merely stood still for several minutes, trying to get a hold of my wits while I let the late afternoon light warm my chilled skin.

I had been gone for two whole days. I hadn't come home Saturday morning and I had missed prom. My friends and family were going to kill me. Where the Morrigan had failed once again, they would most definitely succeed. All of my worry had been used up on Cade, but now that I knew he was safe and healing, a new anxiety pierced my heart.

Confession

I took a deep breath and stumbled up the trail. I was beyond sore and my emotions were still raw from the events of the day before.

When I reached the house, I noticed it was uncommonly quiet. I paused before continuing. All I wanted to do was sneak into my room, collapse on my bed and pretend this was all a dream. But it wasn't a dream.

I put off entering the house for as long as possible before making my way around to the front porch. I tried the door, cringing when I discovered it was unlocked. What I found when I stepped into the living room made my heart sink. Dad sat on the couch, his arms around Mom. Clearly she'd been crying. My two oldest brothers rested on the floor, staring at the carpet as if a favorite pet had died. The twins were too young to understand why everyone was upset, so all they did was tug on my mom's shirt, trying to figure out what was wrong.

Aiden noticed me first. He stood apart from everyone, watching the door as if he sensed I'd be returning home soon. How odd, especially since, between all of them, he had the weakest grasp on reality. Perhaps that is why he didn't seem worried. "Meggy!" he cried in his young voice.

He darted across the floor, his arms pumping, and flung himself around my legs.

My parents darted up off the couch, their worried faces melting in surprise before contorting with fury.

"Where on *earth* have you been?! We called Robyn's parents and we had to practically strangle that girl to get her to tell us you'd run off with some boy. Meghan! What were you thinking!?"

My mom. Never, ever, had I seen her so angry, or so upset. Just last night I witnessed the death of the boy I loved and somehow managed to deflect the ire of a powerful goddess. I'd survived a close brush with an unpleasant death at the hands of the Morrigan, but the rage and pain rolling off of my mom almost brought me to my knees.

I didn't cry. I should have, for the guilt churning in my stomach ate at me, but I needed to do something first, something that would require bravery, patience and an enormous deal of self control. I couldn't wait for graduation, and now was, in its own perverse way, the perfect time.

"Mom, Dad," I looked them both in the eye, noting how my dad flinched when he took in my haggard appearance and strange clothes, "Logan, Bradley, Jack, Joey."

I glanced down at Aiden. He gazed up at me with his pale, blue-green eyes and I sensed his love tugging at my heartstrings.

I took a deep breath and lifted my gaze once again.

Courage, Meghan. You faced down the Morrigan. You can do this . . .

"I have to tell you something. Something you need to know about me, about where I came from . . ."

So I told them everything. Well, maybe not everything, but as much as I thought they should know. I explained to them how I met Cade two years ago, how he'd told me, and showed me, who I was. How I could see creatures from the Otherworld and how I had visited Eilé several times. I told them I was Faelorehn, the daughter of Danua and a Fomorian soldier. And I told them that after I graduated from · high school I would return to the world where I belonged. I didn't have a future in this world, among the mortals. What happened between me and the Morrigan I kept mostly to myself, only giving them the basic picture without all the gory details. I didn't want them to worry more than necessary.

When I finished talking, I bent down and picked up Aiden. He was getting so big, but I could still hold him, still needed to hold him, especially now. He comforted me in his own quiet way as I waited for the accusations to start.

"Have you been doing drugs?" I expected to hear from my dad.

"Perhaps we should find another psychiatrist." I waited for Mom to say.

Only silence followed, a long, terrifying silence. So I decided to prove it to them. I wasn't sure if my newfound magic would work so soon after being violently unleashed, but I had to try. I set Aiden down and focused on the little pinprick of glamour and willed my power to rise. The magic grew and spread throughout my body, pleasantly warm and thrillingly cold at the same time. My eyes were closed but a soft brush of wind tangled with my hair. When the rustling of paper and the surprised exclamations of my family members met my ears, I knew I had done enough to prove I was telling the truth.

I called my magic back and opened my eyes. The expressions on their faces broke my heart. Fear. Pure fear.

The tears swimming behind my eyes broke loose. I began to shake, reaching out for the back of Dad's recliner because I didn't think I'd be able to stand much longer. Everything I'd been holding in and trying to avoid since the Morrigan lured me and Cade into her trap was finally breaking free.

Before my hand met the recliner, I felt myself being pulled into a fierce hug.

"Oh Meghan!"

Mom . . .

Soon Dad wrapped the both of us in his arms. I cried, letting everything out, all the lies, all the fear, all the anxiety. We probably stood together like that a good fifteen minutes, however long it took me to purge myself of everything that had been holding me back. Eventually, Dad loosened his grip and stood back and Mom did the same. They held me at arm's length and looked me in the eye.

"I find it very hard to believe what you just told us," Dad said, his voice raw with emotion, "but I've always wondered about those visions of yours, and your eyes. And whatever you did just now to bring a small tornado into the living room wasn't anything earthly."

He gave me a sad smile. I tried to swallow the lump in my throat.

"Will, will you at least come visit us?" Mom said, sniffing back her own tears. "And if you are to run off with some young man, at least have the decency to introduce him to us."

I nearly collapsed. Had I misjudged the fear in their eyes? Then it dawned upon me: they weren't afraid *of* me, they were afraid *for* me.

A choked sound escaped my throat, both a sob and a laugh. I grabbed them both into a hug once again.

"I'm so glad you finally know!" I cried.

I felt my dad sigh and my mom sniffle again. "Oh Meghan, after everything we put you through when you were younger . . ."

Mom trailed off, averting her eyes.

I shook my head and glanced between both of them. "No, you didn't know Mom, Dad. It's not your fault."

A few moments passed where we all simply stood around gazing at one another. Logan and Bradley remained uncharacteristically quiet, the twins kept babbling about making the room windy again and Aiden was giving me the strangest look.

"So, where is this Cade you've told us about?" Mom asked in a lighter tone, breaking the subdued moment. "I'm assuming he is the same boy who was supposed to escort you to your senior prom last night."

My face must have drained of color, because she lost the little bit of cheer that glowed in her eyes and frowned. "Meg?"

"He's extremely sick Mom. He had to stay in Eilé to recover. When he's better I'll bring him back here so you can meet him."

She seemed worried, but I gave a faltering smile and said, "He's in good hands."

Things settled down a little after that. Mom got to work making dinner while Dad called the police department to tell them I had just been delayed and my cell phone battery had died.

The hot prickle of threatening tears gathered in the corners of my eyes as guilt washed over me again. I dashed them away, reminding myself if I'd been capable of coherent thought the night before, I would have sent a message.

The next day I stayed home from school; Mom insisted I rest. Apparently I resembled someone who'd been lost in the forest for weeks, living on nothing but pinecones and the condensation collected off of leaves. Gee, I looked that great, huh?

I slept in, relieved when I woke up and remembered no nightmares. The scratching at my door reminded me Meridian had been left out all night. She flew in, scolding me as she landed on her perch in the corner.

I spent the rest of the day tidying my room and finishing the homework I had planned to do on Sunday after I got back from the Otherworld. I shook my head, banishing those memories to the back of my mind. Homework seemed futile at this point, but the work helped to distract me. At least for a little while.

After an hour of fighting with my history book, I tossed it on my bed and stood up. I desperately wanted to go back to Eilé and make the journey to the Dagda's house to check on Cade. Despite the fact that my parents now knew who and what I was and that I could come and go from the Otherworld, I didn't think they'd let me leave. Not until I regained my health and they came to terms with my little revelation from the night before. I frowned and forced myself to try a different section of homework.

Later that afternoon I got a call from Tully, followed by one from Will and Thomas. They were all happy to learn I was okay and couldn't wait to see me at school tomorrow. Another dose of guilt hit me when they told me how they spent their prom night trying to help my parents and the police figure out where I might be.

After finishing with them, I took the initiative to call Robyn. I wasn't sure what threats and punishments she had received from her strict parents on my account, but I had to make amends. My lies had gotten her into trouble, after all. Her father answered the phone, and only after he gave me a long moral lecture on what was proper behavior between a young man and a young woman, did he let me talk with Robyn, but only to apologize since Robyn was grounded for a month.

To my immense relief, Robyn sounded happier to hear my voice than angry. I told her at least a dozen times how sorry I was. She brushed it all off, saying she was only concerned when I didn't show up the next day and when my parents called the police. She said all would be forgiven if I gave her every last detail of my time spent with Cade. I blew a strand of dark, curly hair out of my face. Looks like I'd be spending the rest of the day fabricating a believable story with enough juicy tidbits to satisfy my inquisitive friend. Or maybe, like with my family, I could just tell my friends the truth. Okay, perhaps not tomorrow, but it might be a good idea to consider doing so in the future. It would make my life a whole lot easier and would help when it came time for me to leave for Eilé.

Tully picked me up the next day and after giving me a bone-crushing hug, we headed to school. To my great chagrin, I discovered a whole new truckload of colorful rumors had been spread throughout the school about my being MIA. Not only did I get plenty of knowing glances from my fellow classmates, but a few of them took the liberty of telling me exactly what they thought.

"Word on the street is you're shacking up with some homeless guy, Meghan. I had no idea you were so desperate."

Michaela West. Surprise, surprise. She had managed to stay out of my hair all year, but I guess she had some last-minute insults to throw in my direction before we parted ways for good.

Tully tensed next to me and Robyn opened her mouth to provide some of her own acidic comments, but before they could do anything, I conjured up some of my power and concentrated very hard on Michaela's perfect ponytail. I grinned and released my glamour in what I hoped was one, precise burst.

The scream that met my ears as we continued walking past Michaela and her stuck-up friends was like a balm to my heart.

"My *hair*!" she screeched.

Tully gasped and Robyn snorted. I couldn't help it. I turned to see what sort of damage I'd done and laughed out loud. Michaela had dropped her books and her hands were now frantically trying to tame her wild hair. The ponytail had vanished and every perfectly ironed strand stood on end. Oh, I was going to love this new magic of mine, I could already tell.

🌀 🌀 🌀

The final weeks of my senior year passed by in a haze of graduation preparations, final exams and parties. I put on a good face for my friends, acting as if I felt sorry to be done so soon and that I'd miss them when we all went off to college. And I would miss them and I did feel a bit sad, but not to the same degree as the rest of them and not for the same reasons.

I still hadn't conjured up the gumption to tell them what I had told my family: that I wasn't human and I'd be moving to the Otherworld to hopefully patch things up with my birth mother and figure out how I was going to thwart the Morrigan when she decided to come after me again. Because she would be coming after me, one of these days.

None of it seemed real to me yet, so on the day of my graduation, as I stood on the bleachers with the rest of my class, I let my mind wander a little. Two years ago the thought of graduating high school terrified me. Me, out in the real world, attending college, getting a job and trying to balance tough classes all at the same time. Yes, I had been afraid of moving on with my life the way a normal human being my age might.

I chuckled harshly as our valedictorian finished her speech and everyone cheered. I wouldn't be going to college, or getting a job or facing down difficult exams. Oh no. I'd be going to the Otherworld, to Eilé, where I'd start my new life. The life I should have had from the beginning. Instead of finding employment at the student bookstore or a campus café, I'd be fighting off dangerous and terrifying monsters, *and* a vindictive goddess. No college homework for me. Nope, I'd be studying my long lost heritage, trying to fit into the society of the Otherworld and figuring out what I had to do to get my mother to see me as the daughter she wanted. Yes, it was daunting, but I would have Cade by my side.

A shiver of wonderful anticipation, strong enough to drown my fears for the time being, washed through me as we got ready to throw our caps. Caedehn MacRoich loved me. I didn't care that one of his parents was a notorious hero of old and the other a spiteful goddess (a goddess who had my demise checked off as the top priority on her to-do list). I didn't care that he transformed into a grotesque monster when he needed to fight for his life, or for the life of someone he cared about. I didn't care because I loved him back, every part of him, and it meant I would not have to face the unknown alone.

My turquoise cap flew into the air with everyone else's, the tassels dangling from the ends like fluttering birds' wings.

Here's to my future life in Eilé, I told myself. Was I afraid of what it entailed? Nah, I wasn't scared. I was *petrified.*

Acknowledgments

As always, I want to extend my thanks to my family and friends, for encouraging this passion of mine and for understanding the time and effort it demands of me. I'd also like to once again acknowledge P.A. Vannucci, for the *Faelorehn* font he designed for this book. Many thanks for your artistic input and for developing a typeface that captures the essence and magic of the Otherworld. Finally, I want to express my appreciation and unending gratitude towards all of my readers. Without your dedication to my writing (and gentle prodding every now and again), my Muse might very well lounge around all day and do absolutely nothing.

About The Author

Jenna Elizabeth Johnson grew up and still resides on the Central Coast of California, the very location that has become the setting of her *Otherworld Trilogy*, and the inspiration for her other series, *The Legend of Oescienne*.

Miss Johnson has a degree in Art Practice with an emphasis in Celtic Studies from the University of California at Berkeley. She now draws much of her insight from the myths and legends of ancient Ireland to help set the theme for her books.

Besides writing and drawing, Miss Johnson enjoys reading, gardening, camping and hiking. In her free time (the time not dedicated to writing), she also practices the art of long sword combat and traditional archery.

For contact information, visit the author's website at:

www.jennaelizabethjohnson.com

Connect with Me Online:

Twitter: @JEJOescienne

Facebook: https://www.facebook.com/pages/Jenna-Elizabeth-Johnson/202816013120106

Goodreads: http://www.goodreads.com/jejoescienne

Other books by this author:

Otherworld Trilogy
Faelorehn (Book One)
Dolmarehn (Book Two)

The Legend of Oescienne Series
The Finding (Book One)
The Beginning (Book Two)
The Awakening (Book Three)
Tales of Oescienne – A Short Story Collection

For contact information, visit the author's website at:
www.jennaelizabethjohnson.com

A sneak peek at the third book in the Otherworld Trilogy, Luathara:

One

Purpose

The creature was utterly disgusting, whatever it was. Faelah, yes, but I didn't have a name for this unfamiliar beast. Not yet, at least. So, what to call this one . . . I'd have to come up with something creative, some new word to describe the half-dead creature resembling a possum, coyote and rabbit all rolled into one. Perhaps I could combine the first two letters of the names for each of the animals: po-co-ra. Huh, *pocora.* It even sounded like an Otherworldly term.

The thing, the pocora, jerked its head up from whatever poor creature it feasted on, bony jaws dripping with gore. My stomach turned, and not just because of the brutal scene. The faelah was eating one of Mrs. Dollard's cats, the chubby one that obviously hadn't been able to outrun this particular enemy.

I gritted my teeth. I wasn't attached to my neighbor's cats, despite the fact I once spent a summer caring for them, but the poor thing hadn't deserved to die at the mercy of an Otherworldly monster.

I took a deep breath, pulling an arrow free of the quiver slung across my back and deftly positioned it in my bow. I'd become quite good at this in the past several weeks; arming my longbow with an arrow quickly and without making a sound. I stretched the bowstring back and aimed the arrow's tip at the creature, steadying my arms while trying to concentrate. With a twang, I released the string and fixed my face with an expression of satisfaction as the arrow pierced the mummified hide of the pocora. The creature squealed like a pig and fell to the ground, kicking and clawing and attempting to remove the hawthorn arrow. If I had used any other wood, the faelah might've stood a chance, but even as I watched the small monstrosity struggling to regain its feet, smoke lifted from where the hawthorn shaft burned through nonliving flesh. I crinkled my nose at the acrid smell and turned away. Generally, I didn't like killing anything, but the faelah of Eilé were an entirely different matter. And they weren't technically alive, either.

The creature's screams ceased and it went still. I waited a few more moments before moving close enough to pull the arrow free. I always kept the arrows from my hunts. It wasn't like I could go down to the local sporting goods store and ask for arrows made with hawthorn wood. I wiped it on a nearby patch of grass out of habit. Whatever remained of the faelah would already be gone, however, burned off by magic. I glanced back over my shoulder as I left the small clearing behind, but the pocora had already disintegrated into ash, its glamour no longer keeping it alive and whole in the mortal world. I sighed and turned my eyes to what was left of Matilda Dollard's cat. I would pay her a visit later and tell her I'd found her pet's remains in the swamp. Another poor victim of a coyote attack.

Clear, a bright thought said in my mind, forcing my thoughts away from the gruesome scene.

I shaded my eyes and glanced up into the eucalyptus leaves only to catch the brilliant white flash of a small bird of prey darting through them. She had been scanning the forest for more faelah. I grinned.

Did you catch anything? I sent to my spirit guide.

Meridian chittered and sent back a joyous, *Tasty.*

That would be a yes.

I heaved a deep breath and pulled my quiver back onto my shoulders. Mid-morning had become late afternoon and I knew Mom would be worried if I didn't get back soon. After having confessed to my family I was Faelorehn, an immortal being from Eilé, the Otherworld, and that a vindictive goddess was out to get me, she had been a little more protective of late. I guess I couldn't blame her.

Meridian finished up with whatever she had caught and then set her focus on accompanying me back to the house. The walk home took a good fifteen minutes, but I didn't mind taking my time this afternoon. I had a lot on my mind, after all. Actually, there had been a lot on my mind since my junior year in high school when all of this stuff concerning the Otherworld got dumped on me like a ton of bricks, but for the past month I had even more to worry about.

I made my way back to the main trail leading out of the swamp and thought about what had transpired just before graduation. It sometimes made me sick with anxiety, but I couldn't help that. The Morrigan had tricked me, once again to my chagrin, into thinking she meant to go after my family. A few years ago, she would have been happy just to kill me. Now that she knew I possessed more glamour than the average Faelorehn, she was intent on using me as her own personal supply of endless magic. She probably would have succeeded if Cade hadn't stepped in. Cade . . .

A pang of regret cut through me and when I reached the spot in the trail where a fallen tree blocked my way, I leaned heavily against the rough trunk and pulled a well-worn note out of my pocket. The message wasn't from Cade, but from his foster father, the Dagda. I unfolded the edges and began reading.

Meghan,

Cade is improving every day, yet he is still very weak. I know you wish to see him soon, but please give him a little more time and don't cross into the Otherworld. The Morrigan has been lying low; no one has seen her lately, but that doesn't mean she isn't lurking in the shadows, waiting to cast her net. For now, you are safer where you are. Cade will come and get you as soon as he is recovered.

-Dagda

The note should have made me happy, and it did when I first received it a week and a half ago, but I longed to visit Cade so badly I ached. I needed to know he was safe and I needed to witness with my own eyes that he was healing.

I folded the worn paper into a perfect square and returned the note to my pocket, then climbed over the log and kept on walking. Last May I'd been all set to go to prom with the guy of my dreams, Cade MacRoich, the gorgeous Faelorehn boy from Eilé who appeared one day like some guardian angel to save me from the Morrigan's faelah and to tell me all about my strange heritage. Unfortunately, on the day of the prom, we both got tricked into running headlong into the evil goddess's trap. Only, Cade wouldn't let her have me, and right before he took on almost a dozen of her monsters, he told me he loved me. And then he died.

I stopped for a moment and craned my head back and leaned on my longbow, soaking in the filtered sunlight trickling down between the leaves above. I shut my eyes and tried to tell the knot of worry in my stomach to go away. Cade had died, he died defending me and the trauma of such a terrible experience forced my power to surge forth, scaring the Morrigan away, at least for the time being. The sudden rush of my glamour had soon faded and the reality of what had happened slammed into me like a train. I was convinced my heart would tear itself asunder, for Cade had sacrificed too much.

Only after recovering from my hysterics did I remember Cade's foster father, the Dagda, an ancient Celtic god-king, happened to own a magical cauldron with a reputation for reviving the dead. A frantic horse ride against a driving storm later and I dropped like a fly at the Dagda's door, a lifeless Cade in my arms. I'd arrived just in time; Cade would recover. But he never got to hear me tell him I loved him, too.

I had returned to the mortal world, an emotional and physical wreck, only to finally confess the truth to my family: I was an immortal from the Otherworld, the daughter of a Celtic goddess and the high queen of Eilé, and one day I'd be going back to the world of my origins. Let's just say after such an ordeal, I needed something to keep me distracted, to give me purpose so I wouldn't lose my mind completely. Thus, I had taken up hunting for the faelah on my own. Heck, before the Morrigan's attack, Cade constantly pestered me about practicing my archery and this way I could kill two, maybe three, birds with one stone. I was getting some much-needed practice in, I was keeping the swamp clear of dangerous faelah, and I was keeping my mind occupied. Yup, three birds.

I fingered the note in my pocket once more as I stepped onto the equestrian trail leading to my home. I hoped the Dagda was right; that Cade was recovering. I so desperately wanted to turn around and head for the dolmarehn in the heart of these woods, to travel back to the Dagda's home and see Cade, but like the Dagda said, I'd be an easy target in the Otherworld. And I agreed with the other thing he'd mentioned as well. I had no doubt the Morrigan would be looking for me.

Gritting my teeth, I turned my mind away from those dark thoughts and picked up my pace. By the time I reached the end of the path, I welcomed thoughts of a shower and a sit down with a good book and some hot chocolate. Summer was in full swing, yes, but the coastal fog was already creeping in and the early evening would turn chilly. I planned on crossing our backyard and slipping in through my sliding glass door, but a barrage of young boys accosted me before I could even step foot on the lawn. Apparently my brothers had been waiting for my return.

"Meghan!" Logan whined as he rushed forward. "We wanted to go with you this time!"

He crossed his arms, and yes, actually stomped his foot.

Purpose

I blinked at him and my other brothers as they gathered around me, a small army of Elams.

"Huh?" Despite my claims that my hunting ventures helped purge my mind of everything Otherworldly except the faelah themselves, my wandering thoughts still found ways to wrestle free of the bonds I'd placed on them. I didn't have a clue what he was talking about. I'd been too busy reminiscing.

"We want to help you hunt!" Bradley offered, thrusting out a fist which happened to be clutching a small bow.

Oh. *That.* I cleared my throat and took a breath. When would they realize no meant no? I was still getting used to the fact that my parents and brothers knew about my Faelorehn blood. After keeping my identity a secret for so long, I found it easy to forget I had told them (and shown them) what my Otherworldly power could do.

I squatted down so I would appear less imposing to them. Hah, *me*, imposing . . .

"I'm sorry guys," I said, feeling only slightly guilty. "But you can't go faelah hunting with me. It isn't safe for you."

"You go," Bradley put in.

I rolled my eyes. "I'm Faelorehn Bradley. I have magic, remember?"

Not that it would make any difference. Whatever power I managed to store up in Eilé during my last visit had most likely burned out after my battle with the Morrigan. I was running on empty and it would take another extended stay in the Otherworld to get me back up to a level where I could do some real damage. But they didn't need to know that.

"And I'm glad you didn't come with me," I continued. "I encountered something really creepy today."

And just like that, their scowls were replaced with wide eyes. "What?" Jack and Joey, the twins, whispered together.

I grinned, despite the fact that the encounter had been more ghastly than usual.

"Well, I'm calling the faelah I killed a pocora, but I'm not sure what it's called in the Otherworld."

They remained silent, waiting for me to continue. "It looked like a cross between a rabbit, a possum and a coyote, and I think it might have been mummified."

I had explained early on, right after telling my family the truth, that anything concerning Eilé would have to be kept top secret. I made all my brothers double swear, spit and shake on it (tantamount to a blood oath, or in the Otherworldly sense, a geis). They were not to repeat a single thing they saw or heard to their friends or classmates. Having to keep this promise, and not being able to go on my hunting adventures with me, was practically killing them. So, whenever I came back from one of my faelah target practices, I distracted their disappointment with a detailed description of whatever I happened to kill. Worked every time.

"Did you shoot anything else?" Logan piped in, forgetting his previous irritation at being left behind while I got to have all the fun.

"No," I said.

Their shoulders slumped, so I thought the conversation was over. I started to stand back up and nearly fell over when Bradley blindsided me with a completely different question.

"So, when do we get to meet your boyfriend?"

After regaining my balance, I blinked down at him. "What?"

Purpose

"Your *boyfriend*," he crooned, "the guy in the Otherworld you always talk about. When do we get to meet him? Or is he imaginary?"

I blushed and gritted my teeth. I did *not* always talk about Cade. Always thought about, yes, but I only ever talked about him with Mom, long after my brothers' bedtime. *Little, eavesdropping cretins.*

"He's not my boyfriend," I grumbled, glaring at Bradley.

Then I paused. Or was he? Before the Cúmorrig had overtaken him, Cade had told me he loved me, but the last several weeks had given me plenty of time to think about it. Did he really mean it, or had he only said so because he realized he wouldn't survive the fight? Did it mean he might have acted rashly? Of course, it didn't change the fact that *I* loved *him* . . .

"Sure he isn't," Bradley snickered.

"I bet you let *him* go hunting with you," Logan muttered.

I scowled at him again. I'd have to try and analyze my scattered thoughts later. "He's my friend, and he'll meet you guys when he's better. He's very sick right now."

That's right, because being brought back to life and recovering from what had killed you in the first place could be considered a sickness . . . sure.

To my immense relief, my younger brothers decided not to hound me about Cade anymore. We all headed back up towards the front of the house, but before we even got clear of the backyard, Meridian dropped from her perch in the eucalyptus trees above and came to rest on my shoulder.

The boys all started arguing and crowded in again, forcing me to stop so I wouldn't trip over them. They absolutely adored Meridian. She used to use her powerful glamour to keep herself hidden from them, but now she understood it was safe to be seen and she no longer bothered with the disappearing act. Besides, I think she was rather infatuated with my little brothers as well, and I often wondered if she thought of them as her own little merlin chicks.

Chase game! Meridian sent as she chittered excitedly, leaping off my shoulder and darting around the backyard as my crazy brothers ran after her. She loved playing this game with them. Even Aiden, all too often happy with simply watching from the sidelines, joined in. My heart warmed at seeing him play like a normal boy, but a painful lump rose in my throat again. This was all temporary. I couldn't stay with my mortal family forever.

Feeling rather morose, I reached into my pocket again and brushed my fingers against the thick paper of the Dagda's note.

Be safe Cade and come back to me soon, I thought.

I turned to sneak back into the house, but the sudden presence I detected near my leg made me pause and glance down. Aiden. Apparently he was done playing chase. Yes, I would be leaving the family who took me in and raised me so I could live in Eilé, where I belonged. In Aiden's own quiet way, he was telling me how we all felt about it: none of us wanted to let go. I wasn't human, though; I needed the safety the Otherworld and its magic would grant me, especially now that my power had shown itself. Moving to Eilé would be hard, and I think I would miss Aiden the most, but I had to be brave.

Fighting the well of pain in my chest, I removed Aiden's hand from my shirt and curled my own fingers around his. He looked up at me, his blue-green eyes trying to tell me something, but like always, his autism kept him from saying what he needed to say. Luckily, I'd become rather good at reading his face.

Taking a deep breath, I stood with him as my other brothers kept at their game with my spirit guide. I set my quiver down and leaned my bow against the house, then bent over and pulled Aiden into a rib-crushing hug.

"I know buddy, I know," I whispered as he wrapped himself around me. I managed to hold on a little longer before a tear escaped. "I'll miss you too."